The
Burning
Boy

The
Burning
Boy

NICOLA
WHITE

First published in this edition in Great Britain in 2022 by
VIPER, part of Serpent's Tail,
an imprint of Profile Books Ltd
29 Cloth Fair
London
ECIA 7JQ
www.serpentstail.com

1 3 5 7 9 10 8 6 4 2

Typeset in Sabon by MacGuru Ltd

Printed and bound in Great Britain
by Clays Ltd, Elcograf S.p.A.

The moral right of the author has been asserted.

A CIP catalogue record for this book is available from the British Library.

ISBN 978 1 78816 414 6
eISBN 978 1 78283 645 2

MIX
Paper from
responsible sources
FSC® C018072
FSC
www.fsc.org

for Denise

I burn but I am not consumed.

1

Dublin, 1986

The night is balmy, for once, and a couple stop in the middle of Temple Lane to kiss, not noticing that I'm standing above their heads. I hope they won't be long.

I do love a dare, as Jess well knows. We'd been staying in the warehouse for days before we noticed the locked room. When she said I'd never manage to break into it, I had to prove her wrong. I went out one window, and now I'm waiting on the sill to go in at the other. I look over my shoulder and there's Jess's worried face on the other side of the glass. I want to throw her our bravado line – *I trained in Paris, you know* – but that would give the game away.

After some unattractive slurping and fumbling, the boy and girl move on. There's a short iron bar sticking out of the wall between me and the window I'm aiming for – some kind of underpinning of the rickety warehouse. I grab, swing and reach. The trick is not to think about it. I punch the pane that is only cardboard, and hang on to the metal frame, catch a breath there. Put in my arm and lift the latch.

Jess pops her head out of the other window to check I've made it.

'I'm in!'

I pull open the window and manoeuvre myself inside. When I turn back to pull my other leg in, I notice a man down in the shadows, looking up. Shit. But it's only the guy who often hangs out near the gay centre. Baggy denim jacket, hair in a greased quiff, grey moustache. He's forty if he's a day. Mr Brylcreem, Jess calls him.

One day we'll march him in there ourselves. Liberate him from himself. I'll make sure he pays for the drinks.

The room is a labyrinth of boxes. Video players, televisions, Walkmans. Or should that be *Walkmen*? All very shiny, very sellable. But I'm looking for the fags – that's what Jess is antsy for, she said there's bound to be cartons of fags in any dodgy treasure trove. There's a crate of alarm clocks packed in a satisfying grid of boxes. You wouldn't think alarm clocks would be so popular. I open one of the little boxes. But there's no clock in there under the packing, there's something else.

Then the sound of someone on the other side of the door, handling the padlock, removing it from its hasp. There's no time to get out of the window, no way down if I did. I close the crate of clocks and hide behind a tower of boxes.

'Mottie?'

'Jess! I could bloody kill you!'

'The key was under one of the tiles all the time. Oooh!' Her eyes glimmer in the dark at the sight of such plenty.

'Careful what you touch. These are serious people.'

I'm not going to show her the drugs. It's best we ignore the drugs. But she's already opened an old travel chest that she's found under the window, and the street light pours in on some rolled-up things that look like maps. Everything else is shiny new, but these are old, like junk.

She takes one out and uncurls an edge. There are painted trees on it and the lovely edge of a long-ago lake. My blood sets up a hum.

'We could put one up on our wall. Make it more like home.'

I tell her it would be unwise to take anything. I sound like some kind of schoolteacher and it's not a role I'm attracted to. I'm a bohemian to my toes, fellas, but there are risks I decide to take and risks that are just not worth it.

Jess takes out rolled canvases of various sizes. At the bottom of the trunk there is a small panel wrapped in a piece of curtain. Jess pulls off the wrapping and, although the light is dim, I can see that the painting is exquisite. Colours that remind me of cocktail cigarettes and sugared almonds. I move closer to take it from her hands and glance out the window as I do. Mr Brylcreem is no longer looking at the gay centre. He's looking up at us.

2

'I didn't notice him following me. He was very light-footed.'

'Where did you say this was?'

The pub was filling up. Gina Considine leaned over the little table to hear Fintan better.

'Down along the quays,' said Fintan, 'towards the docks. It was after closing time, and I didn't want to go on clubbing with the others, so I thought I'd *take the air*. A little detour, a little circulatory perambulation.'

'There's nothing down there, no proper lighting even.'

'Well, quite … but the moon was full, and so was I. So I was strolling along, feeling very poetic and yearning, when I notice there's another shadow sliding up beside mine. I looked round with what you might call a *questing* smile – and he had a little knife in his hand.'

Fintan laughed shakily, losing some of his archness.

'What did he look like? What did he say to you?'

'Stand down, Detective, I'm not asking you to investigate.'

'And I'm not buying you another drink until you tell me.'

They had known each other since college, her first Dublin friend. His gentleness had attracted her, and his innocent face, which hid an inner steeliness and ambition.

'*Give us your money, faggot*, I believe it was. By this

stage I was backed into a doorway. I said it was in my trouser pocket and he could get it himself. You should have seen his face. A picture of beautiful confusion.'

'Jesus, Fintan!'

'I think he almost ran away.' Fintan tipped his glass to his mouth, only a couple of melting ice cubes left in it.

'Did he hurt you?'

'No! I gave him the wallet – course I did. That's why you're buying the drinks.'

'If you give me a description, I'd be happy to see what I can do.'

'He was not unhandsome. A little disarrayed around the teeth, but good cheekbones. Diamond ear-stud – *ugh*. Wiry. I guess you have to be fit to be a mugger. I don't want it reported. I told my bank I thought the wallet had slipped out of my pocket. It's going to be a week before I get a new card, though.'

'Why do you even tell me these things?'

'To spice up your life, my darling. Another vodka and tonic for me.'

'You'll get yourself killed one day.'

'Remember Gerry and Frank – Frank with the bow ties? Did I ever tell you how they met? One night Frank was walking home along Merrion Square and a man started following him. Frank says he never looked behind until he got to his front gate. Thought he was going to be jumped by some thug, but it was just little Gerry standing there, puppy-dog eyes, waiting to be asked in. They've been together five years now. True love can be found in the strangest places. You should know.'

'Fuck off. Was that what you were looking for down the docks – true love?'

Fintan shrugged, lengthened it to a shudder.

The noise in the pub was rising by the minute. Two incoming girls joined a merry table beside them, and Gina was forced to squeeze up on the bench, moving her coat and bag close to her body. She was still in her office clothes, as was Fintan. This was supposed to be a quick drink after work, but they were already three down.

'Let's go round to the Moonlit Gate,' said Fintan, grabbing her wrist. 'There'll be more space, and better talent.'

Considine didn't want a long night and had no intention of going somewhere like the Moonlit Gate, but she finished her drink and followed him through the crowd and out onto the pavement.

'Are you absolutely sure you don't want me to do something about your mugger?'

'Always the rescuer, aren't you?' To dramatise his point, Fintan flung himself across the street into the path of an oncoming car, which was forced to swerve. He careened onto the opposite pavement as the car beeped furiously and wiped his brow with an exaggerated flourish.

Considine cursed and nipped across to join him. Perhaps he'd been drinking before they met.

'What is it with you?'

He threw a casual arm around her shoulder to propel her towards the pub. 'I like a little frisson, a little added charge. Preferable to sitting on the monogamy sofa, watching game shows.'

That was a dig at her. Fintan inevitably got spiky as

the blood alcohol rose. They turned the corner and the Moonlit Gate came into view, one of the few Dublin pubs reliably patronised by gay men and, sometimes, a smattering of lesbians. Although he was in the Civil Service, Fintan had no fear of being spotted in a pub like that. Sometimes it seemed that Dublin really was loosening up. Even if the Gardaí weren't.

'Do you have any money at all?' she asked.

'I've got an emergency tenner.'

'That'll do you. I need to slope home.'

'What? Oh, c'mon.'

Considine stood her ground. 'Terry's expecting me.'

'Bollocks to Terry! Don't you get tired of domestic bliss? Don't you want to let rip, like in the old days?'

'You're mistaking me for someone else. The only thing I ever ripped was a crisp packet.'

As they argued, two young men stepped out of the pub. One was tall and dark-haired, broad about the shoulders and conventionally clean-cut, in a bomber jacket and jeans. He stood looking in a friendly way at Considine and Fintan. His companion was slight, eccentric-looking, with long, feathered blond hair and kohl around his eyes. He was wearing some kind of furry jacket and seemed eager to get away, even plucking at the tall guy's sleeve. Considine wished the man would stop staring. She glared at him and, in the moment she met his eyes properly, she realised they had met before.

The boy with the make-up yanked his companion into a stumble. 'Come *on*,' he insisted, linking his furred sleeve with the taller man's arm and pulling him away with surprising strength. Considine struggled to remember who he was, even as they hurried away down the street.

Fintan stared after them, a hand pressed to his chest in mock longing. 'I would kidnap that too.'

'Don't you get tired of it, all this panto?'

'Well, you're in a shitty little mood tonight. I always say you were a lot more fun before you joined the *filth*. But, you know, I can hardly recall it now – *so* long ago.'

The bickering made Considine feel more weary than angry. She had fallen for the line that the friends you make in college are the friends you have for life. They had both been more fun in college, perhaps. It was a mistake to hold on to someone for the sake of the past.

Fintan hated that she was with the Gardaí, thought it was in bad taste or low-class. Working in Leinster House, at the centre of government, made him feel above the fray, though all he did was write boring reports about exports, as far as she could tell. It did make him an excellent gossip on a good day. Tonight wasn't a good day.

'You just want me to come in with you as a prop until you find someone you fancy,' she said. 'I've got better things to do.'

'Does watching television with Terry really count as better?'

Considine didn't tell him that she couldn't risk going into the Moonlit Gate any more, not since Superintendent Martin had called her into his office for a 'chat' to talk about unfortunate rumours that he trusted were untrue. She had been so deep in shocked denial that she hadn't been able to adequately assess what evidence – if any – he had on her.

'You're a mean drunk, Fintan.'

She took off in the same direction as the two young men had, down towards Dame Street, half waiting for Fintan to call her back or throw another sarcastic grenade. But when she glanced behind her, he'd already gone inside. He was possibly as tired of her as she was of him.

The taller of the young men, the clean-cut one, was loitering at the end of the street. She wondered whether to cross and avoid him, but he looked at her with an expression of such open friendliness that it drew her on.

When she got close, he addressed her by rank.

'Detective Sergeant,' he said, and she immediately had a flash of him on some day training course she'd done in Templemore, neat and attentive in his uniform.

He gestured towards the lights of the bar.

'When I saw you—'

She cut him off. 'I'd never say anything to anyone about where you were.'

He shook his head. 'That's not what I meant.'

A piercing note ripped through the street, a whistle in the dark. Considine squinted. At the mouth of a lane she could make out the glamorous boy. He gestured the young Guard to him, a light beam flickering in his hand.

'I've been asked to go and look at something ... by my friend there. An extraordinary thing, he says, and when I saw you I thought: who better to have along with us?'

God only knows what nonsense he was about to get himself involved in, Considine thought.

'Is it a body?'

He laughed. 'I certainly hope not.'

'Sorry, I only do bodies.'

Another whistle from the alley. The young guy looking highly pissed off.

'You're funny. I like that. Thanks for your help anyway.' He reached out a hand to shake hers.

'I've been no help to you,' she said, stepping back. There was something altogether too eager about him. 'And I'd appreciate it if you don't mention where we met.'

He lifted his rejected hand, regarded it and turned it into a cheerful wave as he went to join his pal, off to some adventure in the warm night. She had no need of anyone else's secrets.

3

'You're sure you want to go ahead?'

The vet's syringe was loaded with pale-blue liquid. *How could she even be asking that question?* Vincent Swan thought, when he was already holding his old cat steady on the black rubber tabletop, hands cupped around furry shoulders.

'My wife gave me the impression it was *you* who said it was necessary. That there was no point in him suffering.'

'I wanted to make it clear that it's still your choice.' The vet had cherub curls and a maddeningly young face.

'Thanks a bunch.'

She startled at his tone. The syringe dribbled. Benny started to purr, a buzz against Swan's palms. Oh, this was awful. A pulsing pain started up on one side of his skull, the point where most of his headaches began.

'I'm sorry,' he said.

'It's just that I've been dealing with Mrs Swan.'

Yeh, well, Mrs Swan couldn't hack it, he thought, but he said, 'I understand, please do … do proceed.'

The needle slid gently into the shaved patch of leg and Swan felt his cat loosen, slipping from his grip. Benny hadn't been eating properly for weeks now, mere skin and bone. Swan laid the cat on his side and stroked him as he grew still.

'That's him gone now,' said the vet. Swan ran his hand over Benny one last time. 'Do you want to take him home with you or leave him with us for disposal?'

'I'll leave him with you.' If it was up to Swan, he would have buried him in the garden, but the garden was all Elizabeth's territory now, and she didn't want a little grave in it.

All the chairs in the tiny reception area were occupied when he emerged from the examination room with his empty cat carrier. A woman with a Labrador by her knees gave him a look of great pity. A candle burned on the reception desk, the one with the sign beside it saying: *When the candle is lit, someone is saying goodbye to a dear friend. Please show respect.* He'd scoffed at it in the past. So why were his eyes filling now? *Dear friend, dear friend.*

He paid his bill, though he hadn't really caught what the amount was, just stuffed a couple of tenners at the receptionist and it seemed to do.

'Can I use your phone?'

She looked like she wanted to refuse him, but he was in a strong position.

He rang the office and asked to be put through to Detective Considine. The phone rang out at the other end, although the wall clock told him it was past ten o'clock. When the operator came back on, he asked to be put through to Detective Sergeant Barrett instead. The receptionist was starting to look a little impatient. Swan held up a finger to stall her.

The vet stuck her head out of the examination room. 'Snuggles McGlynn!' she called, and a young woman with a caged rabbit rose eagerly.

'Declan Barrett here,' said a voice from the receiver.

'Thank God someone's there. It's Swan.'

'I've been on early shift for a fortnight. I'm never *not* here.'

'Well, I've been held up. Can you tell Considine I'm on my way?'

He and Gina Considine were due to review some case files together. Swan didn't want her thinking he'd left her to it, though he did have one more thing to do.

'She's not here right now. There's a bit of excitement over in the park, and I spotted her chasing after the ambulance on her bicycle.'

'What kind of excitement?'

'Don't know, boss. There's two squad cars and an ambulance attending. I saw them blaze in, but now they're hidden by the trees. Wellington Monument direction.'

'Two cars sounds serious, Barrett.'

'I don't know anything about it.'

'A bit of curiosity never hurts in this game.'

'Thanks for the wisdom.'

Swan hung up.

Barrett was a constant irritant, alternately over-cool and over-ambitious. But there had been a general slump among the whole team of late; it had been a quiet year for the murder squad. Not that Dublin had turned into Eden; there were all too many heroin deaths, suicides, punishment beatings by crime gangs or paramilitaries. But not much had fallen within their particular rubric, and the rumours of cuts – or even the disbandment of the unit – ran wilder than usual in the corridors of Garda HQ. Their new superintendent would be wanting to make changes too, if only to show he had arrived.

He thanked the vet's receptionist and stepped out into the sunshine, fully intending to return the wicker carrier to his wife right away. He had thought Elizabeth didn't need him for anything any more, and it had satisfied his vanity that she'd wanted him for this sad task. Perhaps he'd be invited in for a cup of tea and he could reassure her that the procedure had gone well, that there had been no suffering.

By the time he got back to where he had parked his car, the nauseous pulse in his head and the relative lightness of the empty cat basket hanging from his hand had drained him. When he opened the driver's door, a nasty heat wafted from the interior.

He swung the carrier into the boot of his car. He decided he'd talk to Elizabeth later, on the phone, not put himself through standing like a travelling salesman on his own doorstep. When they had first lived together she only tolerated the presence of Benny because he was Swan's cat, but she had learned to love him over time. Swan had travelled in the opposite direction in her affections. He'd had to give up his home in the separation, but Benny got to stay on, the dribbling old bugger.

Swan rolled down the car windows and sat behind the wheel without turning the ignition. His throbbing head was looking for something, some spark of interest that would light the way out of this gloom. Otherwise he might well sit until the dark came down.

Then he remembered Considine, racing off on her

bicycle after the sirens. What had she found when she got there? He turned the engine on. Ah, the old curiosity. It wasn't much, but it was enough to get him into work.

4

The Phoenix Park is not a dainty park. It fans out from a point west of the city centre and north of the Liffey, a stretch of grass and trees that is not as neat as a city park, but not as wild as countryside, either. It has roads running through it and an odd selection of buildings and institutions lodged in its green acres. There are landmarks like the Papal Cross and the obelisk of the Wellington Monument, and in between all these things run herds of deer, perhaps the descendants of those hunted by viceroys and dukes in the bad old past. On its north-eastern side are ranged the low barracks-style buildings that make up the main headquarters of the Garda Síochána, to which Considine was headed before her detour.

She found the two empty patrol cars parked up on a verge not far inside the main entrance. The ambulance was there too, and the ambulance men were moving about inside it, with the door open. There was no patient. She looked towards the nearby copse of trees, shading her eyes, and saw some movement there. As she lifted her bike over the railings, a uniformed Guard emerged from the trees and shouted in her direction, holding up his hand to tell her not to approach. Considine felt in her pocket for her ID and lowered her bike down onto the grass. The Guard was no one she recognised. He had a narrow, aerodynamic face.

'I've come from the depot – the Investigation Unit,' she explained, holding out her ID.

'Who asked you to come?' He looked suspiciously at her bicycle, which had a wicker basket, not in keeping with his ideas about detectives and their transport.

'You're from Islandbridge, aren't you?' She made it sound accusatory. 'Fill me in while we walk.'

Trained to respond to briskness, the Guard answered, 'We got a call in from a phone box. Man said he'd been jogging in the park and saw a bleeding man. Gave us the whereabouts. We've found a young lad in the trees – in a bad way.'

They had reached the edge of the grouping of mature trees. Considine could make out a couple of Guards standing within, chatting. One raised a hand to his mouth and a puff of smoke rose through the dappled light.

'Detective coming through!' shouted the Guard beside her and they jumped apart guiltily. Islandbridge Garda station didn't have the best reputation, and here it was in action.

Considine stepped into the shade of the trees, and the noise of traffic and the city quietened. She walked slowly through long, sparse grass that thinned to nothing as she moved deeper into the trees, leaving just a dusty carpet of leaf litter. The two Guards they had interrupted stood and looked at her, their faces indistinct in the shade of the trees and the shadows cast by the brims of their hats. She felt a familiar unease – the unease of being in a remote place with men she did not know and the necessity of not showing what she felt.

'Where is he?'

'Behind that bush,' said the Guard.

The bush in question was a holly bush, solid and glossy. She walked carefully to the side of it and a space opened up in front of her, a dark clearing. A young man lay there, face down and one arm flung above his head as if he was swimming through solid ground. He wore jeans and a light-blue shirt. Another Guard squatted beside the man's head, one hand on his shoulder, perhaps in comfort.

'How's he doing?' asked Considine.

'Not good,' said the squatting Guard.

She turned to the first Guard who had brought her there. 'What's your name?' she said neutrally.

'Garda Mitchell.'

'Why haven't you called the ambulance men up?'

'They're on their way.'

'They're waiting for *you* to tell them to come up here. Don't you know the protocol?'

'Jesus, keep your hair on. Mikey! Stephen!'

The Guards who had been chatting obliged, running off at a fair pace towards the ambulance.

As Considine approached the young man on the ground, the Guard who had been with him drew back.

She checked the ground beneath her was clear – no footprints or unusual marks – then knelt and gazed at the side of the man's face, what she could see of it. It was covered in blood, dried and rusty blood, which had run down from a head wound on the front left of the skull, his dark hair matted there. Head wounds could look very bad and not actually be bad. She lowered her head to inspect the line of his skull. It did appear to be slightly indented, and that was not good. His skin was cold to the touch, but when she pressed her fingers to his neck, she found the soft beat of a pulse.

There was something small and bright on the ground, shining white under a coating of blood. She leaned towards it, then reeled back. It was a tooth, a broken incisor.

'Help is here,' she whispered, putting a hand softly between his shoulder blades. 'Just hang on.' She thought of Fintan and the danger he liked to flirt with. Men at the mercy of men.

Suddenly the ambulance men were around her, moving into their practised routine, talking to the man as they quickly felt his vital signs and checked for further injury.

'Has he been conscious at all?'

The Guards shook their heads.

Considine took the opportunity to look about. There were dark scuffs in the dust of the ground where the shoes of the police and ambulance men had turned up darker streaks in the dryness. This was not one of nature's unspoilt spots. She counted thirteen cigarette butts, some scraps of rubbish and what looked like a tissue. Near the injured man's foot there was something pale and long. It was an unrolled condom, flesh-like in the dusk of the trees, no debris or leaf scraps on it. She glanced among the roots of the holly bush and saw another condom, this one old and earth-spattered.

The ambulance men moved the victim onto his back, one

stabilising his head while the other carefully rolled the body. The side of his face that had been pressed to the ground was covered in leaf mould and earth, glued to his skin with blood. He must have been unconscious for some time. His shirt rode up his torso, and she noticed purple bruising on his side. The head wound was not the only injury.

'Garda Mitchell,' said Considine, 'did you call for forensic support?'

'Not yet,' he said tightly. 'That isn't usually my call. I need to talk to the station.'

'I've no intention of telling you how to do your job,' said Considine, which was always a good preamble to doing just that, 'but I'd get a photographer and a technician here right away. If this guy doesn't make it ...'

The ambulance men were lifting the stretcher. They had wrapped the young man in a blanket strapped down with black belts.

'He'll be fine with us!' one of the men said cheerily. She hoped they were right. She hoped someone would clean his face for him.

'I need to go and radio the station,' said Guard Mitchell, following after them, as if the idea was all his own.

Considine introduced herself to the remaining Guard, the compassionate one. He said his name was Hickey.

'Were you here when they found him?'

'Yes, I was first to stumble across him. Almost literally.'

'And did you talk to the jogger – the man who phoned it in?'

'He couldn't stick around apparently. We only had rough directions.'

Considine looked at where the young man had been lying. There was a darker stained patch where his head had been, a slight gleam on it.

'Did you notice that condom?'

Guard Hickey looked embarrassed. 'It was on the body.'

'What do you mean?'

'It looked like it had been thrown onto his back.'

'Does it look like a used one to you?' Considine asked awkwardly.

The Guard peered down at it.

'Well, we'll find out later. No one interfered with his trousers, did they?'

The Guard looked at her with a horrified expression. 'I'm not following you.'

'When the ambulance men moved him, his belt was buckled, his trousers closed. No one tidied him up – none of us, I mean.'

'No,' said Guard Hickey emphatically. He did not want to discuss trousers or condoms with her, that was plain.

Considine examined his face. He was not unintelligent-looking. 'What do you think happened here, so?'

'Eh, he could have been drunk, taking the air, met up with some bad boys. There was no money in his wallet, or in the jacket. So he was probably robbed.'

Guard Hickey appeared to search the ground around him, then walked heavily to the base of a tree and reappeared with a bundle of cloth. It was a light maroon jacket, beige on the inside, perhaps reversible. He offered it to her.

'Maybe we should have put this in the ambulance with him,' he said.

Considine carefully peered into each of the pockets; there were some coins, and in the breast pocket a fold of condoms in foil wrappers. Hickey took a wallet from the pocket of his own jacket and opened it for her to look at. There were no banknotes, but there were a few scraps of paper and card inside.

'Maybe I should run them both down to the hospital for him,' he said.

'I think it would be good if someone stayed here until the Technical Bureau arrive. They might want to look at those things too. Hang on to everything for now.'

Considine had another slow look over the scene in case there was anything she had missed, even though she had no real business being there. Not strictly speaking. She left Garda Hickey by the holly bush and made her way back out to the sunshine and her toppled bicycle.

A familiar dark-green car slowed on the road and pulled into the verge behind the patrol car. How did Swan find her? Garda Mitchell started to walk rapidly towards this new intruder, shouting at him to move away from the area. Considine smiled and let it happen.

Swan got out of his car and slammed the driver's door assertively. His light suit jacket flapped about in the breeze as he strode towards Mitchell, who had slowed at the sight of him. Considine watched the Guard touch his hat brim with respect. They knew each other, or else Swan carried his detectiveness more obviously than she did. Mitchell turned and fell into step beside her boss as they came towards her.

'Sergeant!'

Swan addressed her more formally than he usually would.

'Inspector!' she returned, and he smirked briefly.

'You've blood on your knee.'

She looked at her pale trousers – where she had knelt near the body there was a patch of red, already sunk into the material. She found a tissue and rubbed it over the fabric, but she would need a sink to be clean again. Guard Mitchell had wandered off into the trees.

'Who have you stumbled on, Gina?'

'Who told you I was here?'

'Barrett spotted you on the chase.'

'Some poor lad got the lights kicked out of him, looks like. I think it's a cruising spot. There were condoms among the cigarette butts. He was lying there for hours.'

Swan started to head towards the trees.

'Why would gay men use condoms? I thought that was the great advantage of same-sex attraction. No contraception.'

'Are you serious? Have you not heard of AIDS?'

'Oh, right,' he said, but she wasn't convinced Swan understood what she meant. 'Is it worth me having a look?'

'Not really. The victim's on his way to the Mater.'

'At least it was a warm night.'

Considine flashed on her memories of the previous evening, drinking in town with Fintan. It *had* been warm. When she left him at the Moonlit Gate she had walked home instead of taking the bus, listening to music pouring out of open windows en route.

'They've only just called the Tech Bureau.'

'Fancy, for a mugging.'

'I made them. He really did look in a bad way, Swan.'

Passing cars kept slowing for a look, the entertainment value of police work. Part of the sunny day. She squinted up into the uninterrupted blue and saw a small red balloon floating diagonally across the sky, having escaped from the zoo. A third police car pulled in from across the road, another squad car on the way to the depot. Guard Mitchell made his way over for a chat.

'Rubberneckers.'

'Not like us,' Swan said with a smile.

'I guess we should really get back to it.'

But they didn't move immediately, just stood taking in the scene. The sun baking their heads. Despite his joking, there was something tense about Swan, some odd mood.

'Are you all right?'

'Of course I am. Who called it in?'

'Someone from a phone booth, a jogger. But ... the place where he was lying was well hidden. You'd never notice him, in passing.'

'A jogger indeed,' said Swan. 'Probably someone after the same thing as he was. It's a murky world.'

Considine turned her face away. She didn't want to hear Swan's views on men soliciting men. She started to roll her bike towards the road.

Swan called, 'See you in the office?' and she nodded over her shoulder. He sounded puzzled. Never mind.

She liked Swan. She liked working with him. He wasn't a boor like some of them, but he wasn't as enlightened as he thought he was. With his settled life and his neat wife and his neat house, no doubt he'd have a low opinion of the deviants.

As she lifted her bicycle over the railing again, a Bureau van did a U-turn on the road. The advantage of proximity meant that the photographer and forensics had arrived in record time. She waved at them and made herself cycle away. Sadly, it wasn't her case.

5

'Why would I want that old thing?'

Swan stood on the doorstep of his old house, the empty wicker cat carrier held out in front of him. He knew that seeing Elizabeth again would feel like this – like a slap to the heart.

'I can't keep driving it around in my car. Besides, you might want to get another cat in time, a kitten maybe.'

'I knew you'd say that. It's not me who likes cats, remember? I only liked Benny.' She swallowed the end of his name, upset. Her eyes scanned the street for neighbours. 'You better come in for a minute, but leave that outside.'

She was already walking down to the kitchen, leaving the front door open. He put the carrier down on the porch. It was weird not to have Benny come running to inspect him, tail like a question mark. He hadn't been inside the house for two months now, and as he entered the kitchen he realised he was bracing himself against change, against finding things altered. He ran his eyes over the painted dresser, the kitchen counters, the oilcloth with its pattern of lemons; all was as it ever was, only the personnel had changed. There was no sign of the interloper he half expected, although Elizabeth kept denying there was anyone else.

She took down two mugs from their hooks.

'You've time for tea, though. Not rushing away?'

He pulled his attention from his surroundings to her face.

'No … okay.'

'You were too busy to talk to me after the vet's, is that it?'

'Sorry about that. I got pulled into something. Shall I tell you how it went?'

'I don't need any gory details.'

'Benny didn't suffer. I swear.'

She stared at him, and it seemed she was assessing his many faults and shortcomings. Something had hardened in her. Or was this what she was really like when the soft rub of daily intimacy was taken away?

'I wanted to know when he'd left the world, so I could think of him. Just a phone call. It wasn't a lot to ask, Vincent.'

He had gone to work and forgotten her. He was wont to forget her, that was one of their problems. She could do better than him, that was another, and she'd always made him feel it. But the lack of a bridge across their divides that children might have provided – that's what had proved the clincher.

In their five years together the only creature they had parented was an old tom cat. Elizabeth handed a mug to him, a corner of a teabag sticking up from the murky liquid. Swan wasn't sure if he should ask for a teaspoon to fish it out with or go and fetch one from the drawer. He didn't know the new rules.

He went to the sink with his mug. 'It was very peaceful,'

he said. 'They gave him a shot in his leg and he slipped away.' Swan plucked the teabag from the mug between thumb and finger, let it flop into the sink. 'I got to hold him while it happened. He was a good boy.' He thought about mentioning the purring but decided against it.

He heard a sniff at the table and turned to see her sitting with brimming eyes. He moved towards her.

'No!'

He chose a chair at the other end of the long table. 'There'll be other cats,' he said softly.

'You know your trouble, Vincent?' She was looking into her mug, not at him. 'You always think that you can fix everything. I've told you I don't want another cat – I want Benny back. But some things you want you can't have. And that's okay. That's life. We move on. If we're let.'

He wasn't sure they were talking about cats any more.

'Elizabeth—'

'I thought there was a chance the referendum would pass. You said it wouldn't, the polls said it wouldn't; but, you know, I couldn't help thinking that maybe this country would grow up for once.'

There had been a recent vote on whether Ireland would allow its citizens to divorce. The Church and its conservative followers had been out in force throughout the campaign, scaring the farmers that it would mean splitting the land, scaring women that their men would hare off at the first chance, leave them destitute with kids. Swan had voted for the amendment, of course he had, but in the booth his pencil had hovered over the ballot for a strange moment – it felt like he was voting for his own redundancy.

31

It was not easy, sitting in the kitchen that he had painted sunny yellow, across the table from Elizabeth's disappointment that she could not officially be rid of him.

'How's the music going?' he asked.

She looked at him briefly, scathingly, but went with the change in direction.

'I'm doing more with the chamber orchestra now, it's good.'

'Not so much teaching then?'

'How's your own work?'

'You don't want to know about that.'

'Maybe I do. Tell me something grisly. Something to make me count my blessings.'

She was in a funny mood: contrary, perhaps angry. It was hard to tell with Elizabeth; she thought anger was uncivilised, so she tended to twist it into strange silences or petulance whenever it arose. He had learned to tiptoe around her, only increasing her impatience with him. They had never managed a decent blowout. Perhaps it was time for some honesty.

'Well, there was a young lad this morning, found in the Phoenix Park. Not so far from our office. Someone attacked him – battered him in the head – and we think he lay there all night without help. He was barely alive when the ambulance came.'

'Merciful God!'

'You asked.'

Elizabeth stood up suddenly, thrusting the chair back. He rose in response. Something had happened between them, but he wasn't sure what it was.

'I better let you get back to it,' she said.

Swan found himself walking down the front path seconds later, cat carrier in hand, turfed out of the place. It was evening, but still light. He stood on the street, looked across the grass diamond at Kavanagh's pub. There was time for a drink before going back to his mother's house in Stoneybatter, where an evening straight out of his adolescence – tea on a tray and television – awaited.

6

As Considine put away the files on her desk, T. P. Murphy was trying to persuade Declan Barrett to come for a pint with him, on account of it being a lovely evening. She pulled her jacket off the back of her chair, knowing they wouldn't be asking her along. She didn't want to go for a drink with them; it was just that her head could never stop taking notice of the way that she was outside their circle.

All day her thoughts had kept looping back to the young man in the park. She wanted to know how he was doing, and she badly wanted to find whoever had left him there like that. Even the man who found him had not bothered to stay. And only one of the Guards had acted kindly towards him. Thinking about it made her feel that she had let him down too, in some obscure way. She had called the hospital at lunchtime – still unconscious, they said when she phoned, and no, they hadn't managed to identify him yet. She decided to make a detour to the hospital on her way home.

The Intensive Care Unit was on the top floor. Visitors entered through a wide wood-panelled corridor with soft chairs on either side and a low table with a box of tissues on it. The next room was a kind of antechamber to the ward proper, with a horizontal strip of window looking onto the beds beyond. A nurse at a long counter was staring at a computer monitor. Considine showed her badge and asked if she could see the young man found in the park.

'There's someone with him at the moment.'

'Someone who knows him?'

'No, she's one of yours.' The nurse pointed through the window at the row of beds divided by columns of limp curtains, each one surrounded by a huddle of trolleys and machinery, mostly obscuring the occupants. At the furthest bed sat a woman with curly hair tied back in a ponytail. She seemed to be peering very closely at the oxygen mask that covered the patient's face.

'Is that him? How is he doing?'

The nurse frowned. 'Stable.'

There would be no chat from her, that was plain.

'Could I pop in for a moment, though?'

The nurse cast her eyes around the empty room as if searching for a reason not to allow it. 'Don't talk to him, and wash your hands first.'

It was only when Considine walked up behind the woman at the victim's bedside that she saw she had a sketchpad balanced on her knee, over which her hand moved rapidly. She was rubbing out a section of her portrait's jawline, and flicking away the shreds of the rubber with a swishing sound, barely audible over the background machine bleeps and the hum of fans.

The woman had completed the outline of a face, with a competent rendering of hair, ears and eyebrows, but there was a blank where the main features should be.

'That doesn't look an easy task,' Considine said, to make the woman look round.

'Have you come to take the mask off?'

'No, I'm with the Guards. Like yourself, I believe?'

'Hardly. I don't usually do this kind of thing, I do court sketches, but they wanted something to show on *Garda Patrol* tonight.'

'That's great,' said Considine.

'Great if I can manage it. Half of his face is swollen, and I can't see his nose or his mouth properly. They said it would be okay to take the mask off for a minute.'

The artist handed Considine the sketchpad as a doctor appeared at the far end of the ward.

'I had to guess at the hair.'

Considine looked at the drawing, then at the patient. There was a large square of gauze strapped to one side of his head and the bandages obscured his hairline. The hair itself was brown, cut close to his head in a conservative style.

The doctor appeared on the opposite side of the bed, his short grey hair rumpled, his white coat looking in need of a good wash. 'Let's do this quickly,' he said.

He called over the nurse from the desk area to help monitor the machines. While they readied themselves, Considine stared at the sketchpad, thinking of how many people she knew who could fit that outline of a face, that brow – a bit like her cousin Conor, or several Guards she knew. She didn't hear the sketch artist ask for her pad back until the woman physically reached for it. The doctor was easing the strap of the mask from around the young man's bandaged head.

They had cleaned all the blood and debris from his face,

but the side that had lain against the ground for a long time was purple and distorted, not a match for the clearer left-hand side. She didn't envy the sketch artist her work.

The woman bent closer to the revealed victim, trying to angle herself and her pad to a workable place. Considine moved to the foot of the bed, still gazing at his face. There was a flash of something bright, and Considine saw that the woman was moving a rectangular mirror towards the centre of the man's face.

'A little trick I learned,' she was saying to the doctor. 'You know that faces are never completely symmetrical, but ...'

There was a moment, from where Considine stood, when the tilt of the mirror revealed a full and undistorted face. Unexpectedly familiar. She didn't trust herself to speak, but waited for the artist to tilt it that way one more time. When it happened again, it still looked like him.

'Did you see that?' asked the artist. Considine nodded, and swapped places with her so that the woman could sketch while Considine held the mirror at the right angle, her face unavoidably close to the young man lying below her.

She was almost sure of it. It was the Guard from outside the Moonlit Gate.

'Are we done here? Only he needs his oxygen.' The doctor was addressing Considine, and she nodded quickly.

'Wait,' said the sketch artist, 'I couldn't see one of his eyes, could I?'

With a slight sigh, the doctor placed his thumb lightly on one of the man's closed lids and rolled it back. His pupil was dark, the white deeply bloodshot. The artist took one last look, then sat down to work on her sketch as the nurse replaced the mask.

Considine replayed her memory of the night before. His face – this face – shadowed by street lights: 'Detective Sergeant …', the way he addressed her so formal, something he needed her help with. What had he been wearing? Some kind of dark casual jacket, jeans probably. The victim in the park wore jeans and a blue shirt, not a jacket. But a jacket was handed to her. It could have been a match.

The young woman was sketching fiercely now, her skill like a magic trick. The doctor stayed to watch, mesmerised.

Considine was no longer sure the face taking form on the page was the man she had met, but it could be. In the middle of darkening an eyebrow, the woman suddenly stood up and grabbed her bag.

'I've got to get to the *Garda Patrol* studio by six.' She rushed away, not even closing her sketchbook.

The doctor touched the back of his hand to his patient's brow, briefly, gently.

'How is he doing?' Considine asked.

'He's still with us,' the doctor replied, turning away, but his tone had been bleak.

'Okay?' asked the nurse, expecting her to leave too. Considine indicated that she would stay, and the nurse went to another bedside.

It could be him, she was almost certain. There was a strange feeling in her stomach, something like guilt. She should tell someone that she might have seen him in town at a certain place the previous night. But didn't that certain place incriminate her too? Superintendent Martin had warned her at their little chat: *You need to watch the company you keep, Sergeant.*

She practically slapped her forehead as she realised – panic was muddling her head: she didn't need to recognise him from last night, she could recognise him from their first meeting, that training course in Templemore. All that mattered was identifying him. He needed to have his family with him, whoever they were, and that was something she could help with.

The sun was low, shining in her eyes, as she cycled back to the office. People strolled slowly home, or stood outside the pubs to get the last of the warm air. Like a foreign place.

The lights were already lit in the almost-empty office. DI Ownie Hannigan was standing over by one of the windows, looking out at the yellowing sky, smoking. There was always someone on night duty, covering the phones, but the DIs usually managed to get out of that. Hannigan was sly, though. She always suspected he liked the time alone to check through everyone else's business.

'Lovely night,' she called out as she headed to her desk.

'If you like that kind of thing,' said Hannigan, turning with a sceptical look. 'What are you doing back here?'

'Something top secret, sir.'

She knew Hannigan was too crabby to play along with foolishness and, sure enough, he turned back to the window with a disgusted *pfff.*

It would be a mistake to go directly to the filing-cabinet drawer she needed, so she sat at her desk and flipped through a notebook in case he tried to engage her, but minutes passed and he was still window-gazing. Considine rolled her chair back and slid open the drawer she needed. At the back of various handbooks and procedural papers were the files where she kept her training coursework. Swan liked to tease her neatness, what he called her *convent-girl* tendencies, but he didn't realise that carelessness was a luxury afforded only to the favoured, and that the route of bar-room bonhomie was not open to her. Not that Swan was a great socialiser, but he didn't need to be. He'd floated up to the role of inspector by being smart and not fucking up, that was all.

She found the course folder she was looking for, and the list of twelve attendees paperclipped inside it. She ran her finger down the list, eliminating the names of people she already knew. That left her with three. One guy from the drug squad, one from Dublin district and one from Limerick. The man she remembered had worn a uniform, so probably wasn't drug squad. She couldn't recall his accent, but if that *was* him outside the Moonlit Gate, he was likely to be stationed in Dublin. That would make him 'Garda Kieran Lynch, Dublin District'.

'Would you mind the fort for a minute, Gina?'

Hannigan had crossed the office without her noticing. She kept her hands still on the pages. Any move to conceal what she was doing would draw his interest.

'Only a minute, mind.'

'Good girl.'

Hannigan had an unhealthy pall to him, worse than usual. He was a man much troubled by his digestion and liked to talk about his guts, if given the slightest excuse.

She reached for the phone and dialled Swan's home number. He might know of some way to narrow down where Kieran Lynch was based. If she could find his Garda station, she could establish whether he was on-duty or not – that would sort it out. The more she thought about it, the more uncertain she became about the resemblances between the Guard she remembered, the man in the bar and the young man lying in the hospital.

Swan's wife answered and told her he wasn't there. When she asked when he'd be home, Elizabeth offered her a different number, his mother's house in Stoneybatter, she said. Considine dialled quickly, her eye on the door. Swan answered his mother's phone himself.

'It's Considine. If I have a Guard's name, how do I find out where in Dublin he's stationed?'

'And good evening to you.'

There was something odd about his voice, sleepy or blurred.

'It's kind of a long story. There's no one in the personnel office at this hour, and I thought you might have a shortcut.'

'Have you tried Dublin headquarters?'

'Would you try them for me?'

There was a silence in which she thought she had lost him, then the noise of fumbling.

'Sorry, dropped the pen. If you give me the name, I'll see what I can do.'

He'd taken a few drinks, she realised, that was the difference. It gave her a disoriented feeling. Swan was not a drinker.

She was going to ask if everything was okay, but the sound of Hannigan's footsteps in the corridor meant that she only told him the name, promising to fill him in later.

'Where are you?'

'At the office, but I'm heading back to the Mater, so if you find out anything about him, could you call me at the ICU there?'

'Is this about the lad in the park?'

DI Hannigan entered the office, looking at her with interest.

'Bye now, thanks!' she said brightly.

Swan's protesting voice faded to an insect squeak as she took the receiver from her ear and placed it on the cradle.

7

Nobody likes hospitals, Swan reminded himself as he took the lift up to Intensive Care. He found Considine immediately, sitting with her elbows on her knees and her head in her hands in an empty waiting area. He thought she was weeping, but the face that she raised to him had no tears on it, only a weary strain.

'You didn't have to come,' she said. 'I said to phone me.'

'My curiosity got the better of me. How's the patient?'

'He hasn't woken up yet.'

Swan eased himself down on the seat beside her.

'Tell me what's going on. Who's Kieran Lynch?'

'I think *he*'s Kieran Lynch, with his head bashed in – he's a Guard. I didn't recognise him in the park, I couldn't see his face, it was all swollen. I wanted to be sure ...' Considine trailed off for a moment, then came back to herself. 'There was a woman here, making a sketch of him for *Garda Patrol*, and I recognised him when she did a thing with a mirror ... it's hard to explain. He was on a training course I did in Templemore: "Fostering Respect in the Community", or something.'

'It was only a drawing. You know what they're like – they leave a fair amount of room for doubt.'

'It wasn't just the drawing.'

'All I meant was: don't be hard on yourself.'

She shrugged off his attempt at sympathy. 'Did you manage to find out anything?'

'There's a Kieran Lynch at Pearse Street station. Does that help?'

She nodded.

'So I called Pearse Street and asked to speak to him.'

A flash of displeasure on Considine's face. He had gone beyond his brief.

'What did they say?'

'They said he was supposed to be on shift earlier today, but didn't turn up and didn't phone in to say why. I left it there.'

'I should call them. They would have his emergency contacts.'

'That might be an idea. Even if you're wrong, it does no harm. But it sounds like you're right.'

'If I'm wrong, I'll give them a heart attack.'

'Leave it to his colleagues – they'll handle it.'

She rubbed her eyes with her fists. It looked sore, and Swan put his hand on her wrist to stop her.

She slipped it out of his grasp and looked at him closely. 'Have you been drinking?'

'Have I been what? I'm not on-duty – you called me at home.'

'It's not like you.'

He didn't know whether she meant the drinking or the touching. Considine went to ask the nurse if she could use the phone by the desk.

Swan watched her, feeling vaguely aggrieved. Things

used to be much easier between them. Considine never used to treat him with suspicion. He suddenly realised that she hadn't phoned him at home, but at his mother's. That meant Elizabeth must have given her the number, because he hadn't updated his records at the office. There was a chance that Elizabeth had told her about their separation. The waiting room felt uncommonly hot. Maybe Considine was waiting for him to admit that his life had crashed into a ditch.

She was coming back down the corridor. He was not drunk. He'd only had two whiskeys, but nothing made you seem drunker than loudly insisting on your sobriety.

'I didn't get to use a phone,' she said. 'The nurse is busy in the ward.'

'Can we go take a look at him?' Swan made his voice steady and reasonable.

They wandered over to the broad window overlooking the line of beds, their green curtains casting an aquarium-like light. Considine showed him which bed the man from the park lay in. Two nurses attended him, their white dresses and caps luminous in the dim. They orbited their patient slowly, attentively. One moved aside a trolley, the other pressed some switches on a machine with tubes.

'They've taken off his mask,' Considine said, a hopeful note in her voice.

'I look forward to hearing what Garda Lynch was doing, wandering the park on his own.'

One nurse placed one of his arms under the cover, then moved round to the other side of the bed and pulled a cannula from the back of his hand and tucked that arm away too, then pulled the blankets smooth and wrinkle-free.

They both realised what was happening at the same time. Considine put a hand up to the window and made a small noise like a breath gone wrong.

The nurses were unhooking him from the air and the liquids and the monitors that had been supporting him. They were setting him free of all his tethers. Kieran Lynch no longer needed any of it, because Kieran Lynch was gone.

8

He has a lovely smile, says Jess, and I agree. I tell her it is beatific, because the boy is a saint. I hover my finger above the halo – the hoop that hovers over his head in the painting. It looks like it was drawn with a single hair dipped in molten gold.

Jess says she knows all about saints and martyrs. Says that, in the home, the nun used to read every night to them from a book called *Six O'Clock Saints*, then left them to nightmares of bodies lashed to wooden wheels, eyes plucked out, live immolation.

'He's smiling,' she says, 'because he knows he's invincible.'

The little painting shows some soldiers trying to burn the boy saint. We thought it was a girl at first, but his dress is too short, his chest too flat. I think it's a copy of something from the early Renaissance, on account of how they are dressed: pointy stockinged feet, strange hats and helmets, weird hills in the distance, everything flatly lit.

The boy is smiling because the flames refuse to touch him. They fan out towards the soldiers who started them, and the soldiers leap away, making strange shapes with their bodies, all astonishment.

We only took this one picture from the trunk. The

others were amazing things but unwieldy. Imagine putting drawing pins through an old canvas to keep it on the wall. This is only a loan to brighten up our attic room. Jess says no one will miss it. I tell her we need to put it back soon, because we don't want Kieran to get in trouble.

She rolls her eyes. Slowly. She managed to find some hash resin in one of the crates, big as a bar of soap. After some artful reduction with a penknife, she agreed to put it back. Jess thinks I'm a coward. I'm just not tired of living, I told her. She's not getting that key again.

Now she's moving her photo of Phil Lynott – torn from a paper on the day he died – and tacking it up further along the wall towards her guitar case. The little pink martyr gets pride of place instead, balanced on the upturned tea chest that serves as Jess's makeshift altar, a place for candle stubs, coins, pretty beads. I tell her to move the candle away from the painting. She tells me I am a nag. She flicks her hand at me to turn away and goes to the bucket in the corner to pee. I light my smoke and look up at the hole in the roof, trying not to listen to the trickling.

It is not a bad attic, and it was kind of Kieran to give us the key. He says he's a cop, but I wonder if that's a fantasy. Jess says it's true. A cop with keys to a warehouse full of stolen goods? In America maybe, but you don't imagine the Garda *Chickeeni* get up to much. Kieran did seem genuinely surprised when I showed him what was in the locked room. Couldn't get out fast enough. I only thought he should know, even if it means our eviction notice may be coming soon. I wanted to impress him, if I'm honest. He's very attractive, in a young Rock Hudson kind of way.

There's a fluttering noise and Jess shrieks from the corner, 'Look, Mottie, a dove!'

There's a pigeon strutting around on our floorboards, dirty thing, head doing the horizontal bob.

I wave a scarf at it. 'Shoo, shoo!'

It crouches, then jumps up with light flashing under its beating wings, disappears. I wish I could do that trick.

Jess asks when I'm going to fix the hole. We found the skylight shattered on the ground when we moved into this place, but we decided on this room anyway because it has a big bolt on the door. I tell her I'm never going to fix the hole; that she obviously has me mistaken for a handyman.

The sun falls in an interesting way through the skylight and onto the stippled accumulation of birdshit, bright as whitewash. I may be a little stoned. Jess throws herself down beside me on our shared mattress: a thick wedge of cardboard layers gleaned from the other floors of the building. It is a mattress of convenience. We're not intimate – in that way.

'Well, someone has to mend that hole before the autumn comes.'

'We need somewhere better than this,' I say. 'I have hopes that my gent in Henrietta Street will come through for us. He has so many antiques stuffed in that place, I'm persuading him he needs more onsite security.'

'For onsite favours?'

'He only likes boys.'

'Even better,' says Jess.

We dress for the day; we share the hand-mirror to do our faces and spend time on our hair. We never get out before lunchtime. We pack our little rucksack and take the guitar. The day is warm, but I pull on my jacket with the fur sleeves anyway. It gets chilly in the alleyways.

But when Jess finally unbolts the door and pulls it open, we hear a distant slam on the ground floor. I hope it's Kieran returned at last, but the footsteps are many and their voices are rough. They are coming up the stairs to the floor below. The floor with the goodies.

I stroke the crate that conceals our door, for good luck, and we push the bolt home once more. I tell Jess that we might need that hole in the roof one day as an exit, and we tiptoe back to the bed, poised and listening.

'I forgot to put the key back,' I say.

There comes a bashing and a crashing and a splintering of wood. The sound of a door hitting a wall with excess force.

'I guess they didn't need it,' says Jess.

We huddle and wait, for there is nothing else to do.

9

Considine was the only woman in the briefing room, as usual. Her close colleagues had stopped remarking on it years ago, which you could judge as something of a victory: this honorary status of sexlessness. But she never stopped noticing it herself. Some women in the force even claimed to envy her, imagining the heat of the attention paid.

'You wouldn't put on the kettle there, would you, Gina?'

Superintendent Martin was new to their unit, didn't understand that he was setting the clock back to Considine's first days, when she was expected to take care of all catering and clerical needs. Or maybe he understood very well. She walked to the corner where the sink was, passing a few smirks, counting heads along the way. From the Investigation Unit there was herself, Swan, DI Ownie Hannigan, DS Declan Barrett, DI Eric Joyce and the superintendent. Islandbridge station had sent two of their own detectives, and there was also an inspector from Pearse Street station, one of Garda Lynch's bosses. Nine mugs in all.

The discussion started without her as the second kettleful boiled. A plan was being drawn up, a standard dragnet of surveillance, forensics, a system to question regular park users. She listened and let the first round of teas strengthen in the cup, not bothering to take out the bags.

She short-changed everyone of hot water and presented the tray with a bag of sugar, one spoon and a bottle of milk. She might not be able to get out of making the tea just now, but Considine was damned if she would do it well.

'Help yourselves,' she said and took a seat at the edge of things.

Superintendent Martin pushed his glasses up his nose and sniffed at her. He looked more like a bank manager than a police officer, everybody said so: his little wire glasses, his thin lips. Their previous boss, Kavanagh, was a big blusterer, but in hindsight a popular fellow.

Declan Barrett, meanwhile, had been given blackboard duty, as the other lower-ranking officer. Martin was a stickler for hierarchies. Declan hung the sketch of Kieran Lynch on the board beside a map of the park. That was all they had for now. A forensics team had searched the grove of trees, a stone's throw from where they sat, but nothing definite had emerged from that yet – unsurprisingly, given the police and ambulance foot-traffic involved in taking him to the hospital. Also, Kieran Lynch had spent the day in hospital, where his person had been washed and tended to. 'So there may have been things lost there,' said Eric Joyce, who had been given the job of leading the investigation. 'In some ways, it would have been better if he'd been found dead.'

The inspector from Pearse Street winced visibly.

'From the forensics point of view is all I mean,' said Joyce, stubbing out the butt of his fag in the tin ashtray at the centre of the table, twisting it in a vaguely disgusted way. He was a lean, rabbity type of man, nearing retirement, who no longer bothered to disguise his crankiness.

Joyce went on to read out a list of injuries from the initial post-mortem report, cause of death being the subdural haematoma occurring after Lynch's skull was fractured. Hours of lying in the open while his brain died, in effect. There was damage to his jaw and extensive bruising to his ribs and torso, but that had not impacted upon his death.

'As you will all be aware,' said Superintendent Martin, 'that area of the park is used for some particularly unsavoury practices, and we do want to make sure that Garda Lynch's memory is not sullied by association.'

He lifted his eyes and watched a certain shifting embarrassment among his detectives. For a moment his gaze rested on Considine and she made herself not look away.

'Even if that is a relevant part of the investigation?' asked Swan.

'Don't mistake me. I am closing no doors at this stage. I am merely thinking of his family. His heartbroken mother. His comrades. We need to keep an eye on the press, particularly the lower class of rag.'

'We have to find what drew him to the area,' said Joyce. 'Maybe he was following some dodgy types, or was lured there. We need to interview the rent boys as well as the normal citizenry.'

'Like you'll get a straight answer from them,' said Declan Barrett.

'More like a bent one,' Ownie Hannigan said, smirking. Barrett hooted in appreciation.

The uniformed inspector from Pearse Street – Brogan, she thought his name was – stared at the two detectives. 'Kieran Lynch was one of the finest young men I have had the privilege to work with. He was honourable. He was intelligent. His preferences don't come into it.' A deliberate pause as he stared meaningfully at Hannigan and Barrett. 'Nothing must divert us from getting justice for him. Our own detectives have started to review every case he was involved with over the past months. There could be a grudge involved.'

'That's a laudable attitude,' said Superintendent Martin, 'but you need to coordinate your efforts with my team. These detectives present have precedence, now that it is a murder inquiry.'

Inspector Brogan looked down at the surface of the table in front of him, visibly upset. Swan was next to him, and Considine saw him lean towards him and mutter something. Brogan nodded, mouthed 'Thank you'.

The meeting puttered on with a certain lack of urgency, Considine thought, the superintendent laying out the groundwork while putting forward a variety of rough theories to see who would support them. Kieran Lynch was mugged, plain and simple; his empty wallet the key factor. A Guard would fight back, naturally. Or perhaps Kieran Lynch was doing some extracurricular law enforcement that had gone wrong. Or Kieran Lynch had been beaten up elsewhere and had been taken to that spot to frame him. Or Kieran Lynch had gone to the cover of trees to relieve himself and stumbled upon his killer.

'Or stumbled across two fellas in the act, who needed to keep him quiet,' said one of the Islandbridge detectives.

'We need to be wary of branding every gay as a potential murderer,' reasoned Swan.

'Homosexual, not homicidal, am I right?' said Hanni-gan, pleased with himself.

Considine was conscious that her silence might make her conspicuous, but looking around, she saw that no one except the superintendent was paying any attention to her. Her colleagues were gripped in an odd manner of conversing: the familiar assessment and planning of a case undercut with false jollity and strain. Usually the detec-tives vied to show how much they knew and understood the milieu under discussion, but now it seemed to her that they were trying to emphasise that they had no special interest in it, or else that there was nothing suspect in their knowledge of the twilight world of the homosexual.

Eric Joyce had begun to talk, in his pedantic way, about Dennis Nilsen, sentenced in England a few years back as a serial killer of young men. 'You think your average homo-sexual is all flouncy shirts and lisping voice, but there is real evidence that there are predatory, violent impulses among them.'

'He's the one who kept the bodies with him,' said one of the Islandbridge detectives excitedly. 'He used to put them in a chair to watch the television with him. Mad stuff.'

Considine stared at the man who'd spoken, his creak-ing leather jacket, his full moustache and bouffant hair. District detectives often went for a swaggery kind of dress. Too much American television, Swan always said.

'You don't even have to look abroad,' said Superinten-dent Martin. 'Wasn't the Grierson case one of the most savage killings we've ever seen?'

It was getting stiflingly close in the room, now that the

sun had moved round to fall through the windows. Considine got up and opened one of them, tilted the blinds, taking her time. She felt the need to take her face away from the discussion for a moment; her expression had gone rigid and unnatural.

The talk rolled on, Superintendent Martin trying to put a shape on the investigation, while Hannigan, Joyce and Swan threw in counter-suggestions – some helpful, others subtly undermining. Foreheads shone with perspiration.

Several times Martin stopped the discussion to emphasise that they could just be looking at a nasty accident. 'We need to ask the pathologist if his injury could be consistent with, say, stumbling into a tree.'

The short feature on *Garda Patrol* had brought in a lot of calls that would have to be followed up – Hannigan would sift through all of those. The Islandbridge detectives were to set up local interviews and checkpoints with park users, as well as running through the whereabouts of the usual gougers and likely lads. Detective Joyce would take charge of efforts to trace Lynch's movements on the night he was injured. Barrett volunteered to relocate and talk to the jogger who had discovered the injured Guard.

'Swan and Considine,' said the superintendent, 'I need you two to look at the *gay community*, as they call themselves. I'm not casting aspersions on Garda Lynch, but he could have got mixed up in something. We have to learn lessons from the Grierson murder, though. That's a shadow still hanging over the force; not just that you didn't find the perpetrator, but we alienated a lot of people who might have helped us.' The superintendent took a moment to look heavily around the table, radiating blame. 'This could be our chance to restore a bit of trust. That's why I thought it would be a good area for you, Considine – the softer touch.'

He smiled thinly and deliberately at her, and it felt as if someone had set her neck on fire. She scribbled tiny, illegible words quickly in her pad, so she wouldn't have to look at him, but then realised that Swan had a good view of the page. So she wrote down Sonny Grierson's name in large print, as if noting tasks to be done. As if his name was something new to her that she would need to remember.

'Thank you, gentlemen!' The superintendent stood up and whisked out of the room.

Swan tapped his finger on the name on Gina's pad. 'I know something about that. Catch you back at the office.' He pushed back his chair and left hurriedly.

Considine returned to the windows, closed the one she had opened, made a few trivial adjustments to the blinds. When the room was silent, when there was no further movement reflected in the glass, she turned back to the empty room.

Had there been a moment when she could have safely told someone she'd seen Kieran Lynch the night he was attacked? Perhaps she could have told Swan at the hospital. Or declared it in the meeting, despite the consequences. That gap of opportunity had now closed. Once you start hiding things, it makes you vulnerable. And culpable. And for what? Just so that no one would know she'd been standing outside a gay bar.

Kieran Lynch's face wouldn't leave her. His expression

that night was so keen and untroubled, as if he'd wanted her to come on an adventure with him. The way he had held his hand out and she had refused to touch it. If Superintendent Martin hadn't threatened her with exposure, she probably would have gone with him. Even if she'd kept talking to him for a few more minutes, it might have meant he wouldn't have been in that place at the wrong time.

The boy with the fancy jacket and the kohl around his eyes calling to him from the lane – he'd had a torch in his hand. What dark place had they been headed for? Was he Kieran's killer?

10

Swan was worried. No, worried was too strong a word. He was *concerned* about Considine. She said she didn't know the dead Guard well, but he saw how tough it was on her – what happened at the hospital. She hadn't said a word in the meeting yesterday. Not one. And she hadn't returned to the office afterwards, on the first day of a murder inquiry. Not that anyone else seemed to be champing at the bit to solve this one.

He came in on Friday morning to find her still missing, and finally had to resort to phoning Arlene on the switch-board to find out that Considine was in the file archive and had asked for calls to be rerouted to her there. Arlene was the depot's finest asset, if you could get her on your side. He knew immediately what Considine would be doing down there and wished he had been given the chance to stop her before she disappeared into the black hole of the Grierson files.

Sonny Grierson had been murdered in 1981, stabbed to death at his Dalkey apartment building. A taxi driver took him home from town that night with another man. He said they had been 'carrying on' in the back of the car. The Guards had searched for this mystery companion for a year and never found him. No one in the neighbouring flats had heard a peep, despite the body being discovered in the communal stairway. It appeared that Sonny Grierson had almost managed to escape from his attacker when he met his final end.

Grierson was well known in Dublin, an impresario. His speciality was staging musicals and TV extravaganzas starring popular entertainers. He had a wide circle of friends in Dublin and others in London and his home town of Edinburgh. Everyone who had ever known Sonny Grierson was interviewed over the course of that year, and many who didn't. The circle of interest kept widening until it wasn't within shouting distance of the original case. It took the commissioner to finally intervene and call a halt to it all.

Swan knew the files would be extensive, but he wasn't expecting that Considine would have to book a separate side room to accommodate the cardboard boxes of statements. At least ten were stacked on the big table that she sat at, elbow-deep in cardboard folders.

'Are you building a fort?' he called, and she gave him a distracted look. A squeaky trolley entered on his heels, carrying more boxes.

'This is nearly your lot,' said the records officer, a small man in a shirt and waistcoat with carefully combed hair. 'You better make good use of them, after me breaking me arse for you.'

Considine simply acted like she couldn't hear him, flipping over the pages of a stapled sheaf.

'She's not much fun, your girl,' the man said to Swan.

'Maybe your jokes need an overhaul.'

The archivist jutted his chin, but said no more, rolling his trolley away for the final load.

Swan tried to judge Considine's mood.

'What have you got there?'

'It's supposed to be an index of what's in the boxes. There must be a thousand names here. Did you get paid per interview back then or what?'

'It was an extremely brutal murder. We were under pressure.'

'You did some of these?'

'Only for the first two months. Looking for the blond man from the taxi. The driver changed his mind a few times about whether he was foreign or English or just very posh. It was my feeling that he left the country right away, but Hannigan and Murphy kept on it for a whole year or so, plugging away, contacting any gay man they could find in Dublin, it seemed like. There's more than you'd think, as it turns out. And quite a few who rejected the label, despite the circumstances in which they had been brought to our attention. Married men who happened to have sex with other men in public toilets. They made it sound accidental.'

She looked directly at him then, a look that was cool and subtly disappointed.

'Sometimes it doesn't work out,' he said. 'You know that.'

He went over to the line of boxes, opened one at random and pulled out a green file. Inside were sheets of typed-up statement with a photograph paperclipped to them. A handsome young man with moustache and curls looked morosely up from a mugshot, harshly lit with the subject close against a wall. The interview covered the young man's slight acquaintanceship with Sonny Grierson, then moved on to questions about his current job, his family circumstances and his first gay experiences.

Out of the corner of his eye he saw Considine draw another file from her stack, check the photo and flip quickly through the pages, as he had done, then reach for another.

'I remember this case,' she said. 'It was before I made it into detective training. I was down in Kilkenny, paying my dues, but I tried to follow the investigation.'

'I'm not convinced this is the best place for us to start, going through all of these. Five years is a long time. What are you hoping to find?'

'The superintendent was keen that we should *learn the lessons* from all this. I was wondering what those lessons might be.'

'Don't get distracted would be one.'

Considine granted him a brief smile. 'Do you knowingly know any gay people, Swan?'

'How do you mean?'

'Do you know any socially?'

'I don't know many people socially, to be fair. I know the odd fella to see. The obvious ones. But I've no dislike of them, if that's what you're getting at. I've always suspected my Uncle Tony was that way. My mother made out he was living in sin with his landlady across in London – that's why he didn't marry. He was an educated man, more to him than the rest of my family.'

'Where's Uncle Tony now?'

'He died relatively young, sadly. So I'll never know what his real story was.'

Considine had finished checking through the files in front of her. She returned them to their box, shoved it aside, then reached for another.

Swan pushed it towards her. 'What's your method here? Are we looking for previous Phoenix Park incidents or are you looking for someone in particular?'

'I'm just getting an overview.'

'I think we need to get out and talk to people. Like today.'

She didn't even look up.

'What's up with you, Gina?'

'It's depressing, that's all. Backward. Britain decriminalised homosexual acts years ago.'

'But we don't actually persecute anyone. We don't put plain-clothes officers up to entrap men. They used to do that in the Met all the time.'

'What do you call all this then?'

Swan pulled a chair out from the table and sat down. 'I don't want an argument. I don't even know what we're arguing about. But I do know we're not getting anywhere.'

He waited until she closed the file in front of her.

'What have we got?' he asked. 'A man beaten up in the park in an area used for sexual activity between men. Let's put aside the fact that he was a Guard, for now.'

'His wallet was there, but no money in it, so mugging could be a factor,' she said, crossing her arms and looking at him properly now.

'It was an unlikely place to be strolling innocently at night. Looking for sex is a possibility, though our colleagues don't seem keen to go down that road.'

'Did you notice Brogan, his boss, saying his preferences didn't matter?'

'So?'

'If he thought Kieran Lynch was rampantly heterosexual, he wouldn't be bothering to say that.'

That was a fair point. 'He lived in a flat on the quays,' Swan said, 'so not too far away. Lynch could have been walking, saw something suspicious or followed someone, not knowing what he was getting into. Or he could have been brought there. The road is so near those trees, you could bundle someone in a car and take them there as a convenient place to give them a private beating. It's a busy road, though, so it would be chancy.'

'And Kieran Lynch was a big guy. It's an excellent way to frame someone, though. Toss a condom down beside them and the sympathy vote really changes. No one's up in front of the cameras extolling Kieran's heroism.'

'What I can't decide is if they thought they'd killed him. Or if that was the intention.'

The trundle of the trolley in the corridor silenced them, and the records officer wheeled in more boxes. 'Here's your lot. Have fun.'

'Can we lock up this room when we go?' Swan asked. 'We're never going to get through all of these today.'

The officer went into boring detail about why this was difficult, but agreed that they could have a few days' run at it, as long as he kept hold of the key.

'Where are we going now?' asked Considine.

'We're going to go talk to the family. A pastoral visit combined with information-gathering. Apparently his mother was watching *Garda Patrol* and recognised her son from the sketch.'

'How awful. She rang the information line?'

'No, but she tried to contact him and couldn't, so … that's how they found out.'

Swan got to his feet.

'We can come back and look at these if we run out of options, but I'm thinking it might be more constructive to engage with the community as it is now, not what was written down five years ago.'

Considine put a file to one side, but stayed sitting.

'I'll get the parents' address and make sure no one else has been out to them today,' Swan said. He noticed her eyes slide back to the discarded file. 'So I'll see you upstairs in ten minutes?'

'I'll tidy up here a bit.'

Something was bothering her, but he couldn't fathom what.

11

She would have to be wary. Swan was not stupid, though he could act it when it suited his purposes. *Dim Dad* – that was her and Terry's nickname for him at home. Though that was partly a way to play down her fondness for Swan, so that Terry wouldn't be jealous of the long hours they spent together.

She waited until she was sure that Swan wouldn't suddenly return to the basement room before opening the file she had set aside. *Maurice Deegan.* She held it up to inspect his photo closely. She couldn't be a hundred per cent sure it was the person she'd seen with Kieran Lynch outside the Moonlit Gate. She was trying so hard to keep the memory crisp. His hair was very different in the photograph, short and dark, but that counted for nothing. The police interview had his age as eighteen, but he looked younger – a delicate and beautiful boy with small, sharp features and limpid eyes whose lashes were surely thickened by mascara. He looked like a Hollywood urchin. Pretty and defiant. He had the kind of face that certain rough men found difficult to bear, that would make their hands curl into fists.

The file recorded his height as five foot six; that fitted too. What were they doing measuring people, though?

What had any of this fishing expedition done to win justice for Sonny Grierson?

She remembered not just the case, but the ripples it caused among her friends. She had spotted an old flame of Fintan's in the first load of files. After he was interviewed, this man was worried the Guards would tell his family. He emigrated to New York a couple of months later. Many others emigrated too, and there were rumours of suicides.

It was enraging. But Swan had a point. Justice for Kieran Lynch was her job, not stoking the embers of the fate of Sonny Grierson. She needed to locate Maurice Deegan and talk to him before anyone else did. Find out where he was taking Kieran Lynch and what he showed him. She would work out how to protect herself along the way.

Considine slid the photograph from its paperclip, but left the clip in place, hoping that if anyone noticed, its loss might seem accidental. She slipped it inside a paperback in her bag. Fintan might recall Deegan better than she did, or know where to find him.

She put the files away as she had found them, switched off the room lights and stood for a minute in semi-darkness, just the light from the frosted glass of the door hitting her feet. She was no better than the rest of them now. The ones who bent the rules, the ones who told the lies. She held up her hand so that it was silhouetted against the light. Not a tremble.

12

'Joyce asked if we could show the family these.'

Considine started to lay out a line of small photographs on the dashboard of the car. They had been heading out when DI Joyce waylaid her, and Swan had waited, listening to the RTÉ news. There was no further mention of Kieran Lynch's death, or of the investigation, in the news bulletin he heard. Someone was doing an excellent job of keeping the story small.

The first photograph that Considine put down showed Lynch's wallet; the next was of the fold of three wrapped condoms. The last two photos showed a slip of paper printed with the words 'ONE DRINK' above a stamped outline of a swallow, and a small square photograph of a dark-haired man with sideburns, holding a baby in front of some jazzy wallpaper.

'They usually shove all the victim's belongings into one photo,' Swan said. 'This seems extravagant.'

'I think the Technical Bureau has a new camera.'

'It's nice to have the option of not showing his mother the condoms. It doesn't seem the best way to put her at ease.'

'Ease is overrated,' said Considine.

Swan smiled back. 'Isn't that one of mine?'

'We can certainly ask who this chap is.' She held up the photograph of the man and baby. His features were over-exposed, hard to distinguish. He wore a suit and a skinny little tie. The photograph appeared to be from the early sixties. Box-Brownie format.

'He looks like a Teddy boy. You too young to remember them?'

'There's quite a few old Teddy boys still knocking around my neighbourhood,' said Considine. 'Some men stay with their glory years through thick and thin.'

Swan laughed more than the joke merited, glad she was back to normal and slightly nervous that she was having a dig.

'Joyce also asked if we could get a photograph of the victim not wearing his Garda uniform.'

'Indeed,' said Swan. 'Something for the press?'

'He said it was to get a clearer view of his face, but I think you're right. They're trying to make a civilian out of him.'

They drove south, out past Donnybrook and the new dual carriageway past Booterstown until they reached the sharp turn that took them towards Blackrock and the coast.

'The house is called Valparaiso and it's on Frascati Terrace,' said Considine, reading from her notebook.

'As good as a foreign holiday, coming out here.'

'They must have named it after the poem,' she said.

'What poem?'

'It was in every school poetry book – *Tháinig long ó Valparaiso*, you know. It's a place in South America apparently, a beautiful port, but the poem's really about longing.'

'Isn't it always?'

They found Frascati Terrace eventually, in a knot of curving roads near the railway track. It was less fancy than its name – mostly garages and mews houses. At the very end of the road was a large wooden gate, solid and seven feet high. There was a little black box to one side of it that Swan recognised as an intercom.

He got out for a closer look, and indeed there was a small metal plaque with the exotic house name on it. He pressed the button on the intercom. After several tries there was a distorted crackle of a reply and the gate swung silently open. Behind the gate was a narrow stone bridge, just wide enough for a car, and beyond he could see a complex arrangement of tiled roof and what looked like a bell tower.

It was all unexpectedly grand. He got back into the car quickly, anxious that the gate would close against them in the same automatic way as it had opened.

'We're going across the railway line,' Considine said as he drove carefully over the bridge. The driveway plunged downhill in a curve around one side of the house, revealing bladder-tightening glimpses of rocks and white water, before levelling out onto a large gravel turning circle in front of an imposing open-arched porch.

They sat for a moment and stretched their necks to take in the gleaming house. It was painted primrose-yellow all over, and had many arches edged in white. It gleamed almost painfully in the full sea light. The windows had multiple panes, like Georgian ones, but the arches were pure Spanish villa. The tower that occupied one corner was shaped like a medieval round tower. There was also a double garage to one side, done up like a country cottage.

'It really is ... something. Hiberno-Hispanic-Hollywood,' said Swan.

'You're an awful snob,' said Considine and got out.

He had that sense – usually enjoyable – of having discovered a bit of Dublin that didn't feel like Dublin at all. The garden of the house was no more than scraps of green between giant boulders falling down towards the water. A very narrow path twisted down through them. It would be some place to see out a storm.

'Are you sure we got the right address?' Considine asked when he joined her, shading her eyes until they reached the dimness of the porch.

For want of a doorbell, Swan pulled a strange tasselled rope to the side of the gigantic carved door. Something akin to a church bell sounded in the house, and Considine chuckled.

'His parents might be the housekeepers,' said Swan.

The doorbell was answered by a meek-looking woman in a flowered housecoat.

'Mrs Lynch?'

'I'll tell her you're here. If you don't mind waiting in the kitchen.'

He exchanged a look with Considine.

They passed through an immensely high, circular hallway with an elaborate staircase and entered a kitchen, which took up half of the ground floor. White walls, white cupboards, a black-and-white chequerboard floor and a bright-red Aga. There were large windows, but here at the side of the house they mainly looked onto raw blasted rock and the edge of the gravel drive cutting across blue sky. They sat at one end of a massive farmhouse table and waited for Mrs Lynch to appear. Ten minutes went by and there was still no sign. The woman who had shown them in appeared at intervals, ignoring them as she put away something or other or wiped perfectly clean surfaces.

Swan asked eventually, 'Is Mrs Lynch on her way?'

The woman left the room without answering, but they soon heard voices somewhere above. A low arguing.

Eventually another woman appeared, her feet in marabou slippers, the rest of her in a pale-cream skirt and matching jacket, fastened with gold buttons. Her hair was also gold, a groomed mane of curls, and all her jewellery was oversized, as was the fashion. Her face was tanned, but set in lines of misery.

Swan and Considine stood and gave their condolences as she came towards the table. Her movements appeared elegant at first, but by the time she sat down, he realised they were unnaturally slowed.

The housekeeper placed a glass of water in front of her, shoved it an inch closer.

'Kitty, the guests,' said Mrs Lynch, lifting one hand in their vague direction, and the woman went to fill the kettle.

'Mrs Lynch, do you mind if we—' Considine began.

'Char-maine, please,' she corrected, drawing out both syllables. Swan wondered if she was on tranquillisers, likely prescribed in the wake of her son's death.

'Charmaine. We're doing everything we can to find out what happened to Kieran. I know it's the last thing you want, to be bothered by us at a time like this, but there are things you could tell us about Kieran that might help us piece together what happened. Is Mr Lynch home?'

'He's on his way!' said the housekeeper, Kitty, in a sharp voice.

'Are you Kieran's friends?' asked Charmaine Lynch.

'No, not … I mean we're … his colleagues,' Considine said. 'We care very much about what happened.'

Swan observed as Gina talked. It took him a while to realise that the woman was not actually looking at Considine, but at a spot beyond her, where the sun cast a reflection on the wall.

'Did Kieran have many friends?' Considine asked softly.

'Friends, yes, friends,' Mrs Lynch responded.

'Perhaps there's a name or two that you recall?'

'Have you asked the Guards – he was in the Guards.' And she shook her head sadly, as if such a thing was a mystery to her.

'No friends from school?'

The woman slowly tilted her head as if listening out for something. 'He didn't like school,' she said.

They heard an engine then, as she no doubt had before them, and glimpsed a car flash by the window and come to a quick stop, crunching the gravel. The bang of a door. Charmaine Lynch smiled briefly.

'Here he is now.'

The man who hurried in was white-haired, but youthful in his movements. A similar tan to his wife's. He was all brisk handshakes – *call me Robert* – and shouts for the housekeeper – *Mrs Duggan!* – to hurry up with the tea. His

76

three-piece suit was well cut. Of course it would be, Swan told himself. A place like this. He didn't sit with them but stood behind his wife, a hand gripped on the back of the chair as if bracing for more bad news.

'Our sincere condolences to you, Mr Lynch,' said Swan.

The man nodded briskly, his jaw clenched.

Mrs Duggan arrived with a tray of tea things and placed two striped mugs in front of Swan and Considine.

'I think you'd better leave us, Mrs Duggan,' said Robert Lynch.

'Thank you, Kitty,' added his wife in a singsong voice as the woman retreated to some other room.

'We wanted to tell you about all we're doing to catch the people who did this to Kieran,' said Considine.

'I thought maybe you were here to tell us you'd got them.'

Considine glanced at Swan and he took the cue.

'We have put all of our best resources on this case. We've detectives from Islandbridge and Pearse Street working on it, and the entire Investigation Unit. But we had very little to start with. No witnesses so far. We were hoping you could give us more of an understanding of Kieran's habits, as it were: who he hung around with, how he spent his weekends.'

Robert Lynch shook his head in exaggerated confusion, then took a chair at the table, every limb sagging. There was a kind of see-saw energy to him – prosperously buttoned up, but in turmoil. It was never easy, dealing with this raw stage of shock.

'My wife phoned me to get here quick. I thought you had some announcement.'

Mrs Lynch looked down at her immaculate lap and said in a very small voice, 'I'm sorry.'

'Let's start again,' said Considine. 'Tell us about Kieran.'

'Kieran was a grown man,' Robert Lynch began, addressing only Swan. 'He had his own interests, his own flat. He wasn't calling his mammy and daddy every half-hour. His friends in the Guards will know more than us.'

'Of course,' Swan replied. 'But you can tell us things his work wouldn't know. Like childhood friends – we were just asking, er, Charmaine about that.'

'You think he was killed by his childhood friends?' said Robert Lynch. A tiny flash of anger ran across his face, but he pulled back to politeness. Swan didn't hold it against the man; he'd be angry, in his place.

It was Considine's turn to smooth the waters. 'Before he joined the Gardaí, what were his main interests?'

'After school he spent some time in a seminary, but decided the Church wasn't for him. Then he joined the Guards. He's idealistic, you could say.'

Charmaine Lynch tipped forward in her chair. 'He was always a very good child, right from the get-go.'

'Well …' Robert demurred.

'No, but he was – he was very kind, for a boy, I mean. Very interested in helping others.' She beamed proudly, briefly, then remembered anew what had brought them all together.

'This is painful for us,' said Robert Lynch. 'Unless you have some pressing thing to ask us, wouldn't you be better off searching the city for the thugs who took our boy from us?'

'When were you last in touch with him?'

'He visited us on Charmaine's birthday, a fortnight ago.'

'And phone calls,' said Mrs Lynch.

'How was he when you last spoke?'

She was trying to remember, her eyes unfocused. 'When was it—'

'He was fine,' said the father, exasperated.

'Did he have a girlfriend?' Swan asked quickly.

'I … I'm sure he had … it wasn't our business.'

'Girls loved him,' said Charmaine Lynch, looking directly at Considine. 'Simply loved him. Kieran has great charm.' She put her fingers to her throat, ran them along the links of her necklace. 'Great charm.' She began to cry, very softly.

Considine took the evidence photographs out of her bag and slid one across the table. They were rushing through things now, feeling the time was running out.

'He had this in his wallet. Is this you with Kieran?'

Their heads bowed towards it. Robert Lynch's came up quickly. 'No, that's his godfather. It's an old photograph.'

Charmaine Lynch was still looking at the photo closely, Swan noticed.

'Where did you get this?' she asked.

'Kieran had it in his wallet.'

'He had this in his wallet?' said Charmaine Lynch, her fingers still twisting at the necklace.

'Kieran was fond of him,' Robert Lynch said to his wife, then straightened and regarded them with a hard look. 'Is there anything else?'

'I was hoping you might be able to help us access

Kieran's flat. Or provide the name of the landlord. Twenty-six Essex Quay, I understand. We didn't find any keys with him.'

Nobody spoke.

'We can gain access by forcing the door, but we like to avoid it.'

'I am the landlord, in that I own the building. I can give you the relevant key on the way out,' Robert Lynch said, standing up.

'Oh, and do you have a recent photograph of Kieran?' Considine asked. 'The official one we have doesn't show his face that well.'

Mrs Lynch made a sound between a hiccup and a sob.

'It would really help.'

'I keep one in my bureau,' she answered, glancing at her husband, but he paid her no attention. Considine stood by her as she rose slowly and led the way to another part of the house. Swan heard their footsteps echo on the curving stair.

Robert Lynch appeared to be listening also. When they could no longer hear the women, he took a step towards Swan.

'I don't trust any of you dozy fucks to get this right, so don't think I won't be taking actions of my own. By God I will.' He pointed a finger close to Swan's face. His voice had lost all its worldly smoothness to become pure Dublin staccato. It would be a mistake to act the bantam back at him, so Swan opted for a priestly mode.

'Mr Lynch, I realise you're grieving, and grief makes us wild when it doesn't flatten us. Please leave it with us. That's what Kieran would have wanted.'

He placed a hand on Robert Lynch's expensive sleeve and pushed his pointing arm down. The fact that Lynch let him do this was reassuring, though Swan could feel that the man was shaking.

'If you could look for those keys I'd be very grateful.'

Lynch led the way into a room off the kitchen. There was a very large boiler in it and various cabinets. He unlocked a shallow metal cupboard and Swan got a glimpse of lines of keys on hooks with matching plastic tags on them, all very orderly. Lynch quickly snatched a set of three keys from among them and handed it to Swan.

'Entrance door, Chubb and Yale for the flat.'

'You have a lot of properties?'

Lynch shrugged. 'It's my profession.'

Considine was waiting for them in the kitchen.

'I don't know what's in his flat, what stuff he keeps there,' Robert Lynch said.

They made polite goodbyes and assured him that the family would be informed right away if anything of substance came to light.

Swan noticed Considine holding tight to the door handle as they drove up the driveway and over the narrow bridge, first gear all the way. The gate opened for them automatically. They must control it from the house somehow. He drove along to the sea front at Blackrock and parked behind an ice-cream van.

'Debrief and a ninety-nine?' he offered.

They queued together for their cones and went to sit on the sea wall.

'I wanted to see how much of the vulgar villa you could

see from down here,' Swan said, but the view was mainly of the abandoned pools and diving platforms of the old swimming baths, streaked with rust and grime. The only visible part of Valparaiso was the roof of its tower peeping over a scrubby headland.

'I've never met a Guard whose parents were that rich,' he said.

'If I was rich, I wouldn't spend my money on that house. It feels wrong to be hanging off the edge of the land like that. When I went upstairs with the mother, the place was weirdly empty, like they were rattling about in it. There was a sofa in a room that I passed all wrapped around with cardboard, like it had just arrived. I can't make out if they're moving in or moving out.'

'There are all kinds of ways to make money, and I'm pretty sure Robert Lynch didn't inherit it. He got a bit aggressive with me – veiled threats about how if we didn't sort it, he would. Bit of a gangster touch for the mourning father of a policeman. He had the keys to dozens of other properties.'

'Some subtle enquiries wouldn't go amiss.'

'Indeed.' A trickle of ice cream hit Swan's skin and he fumbled for his handkerchief.

'I thought it was interesting that Kieran moved from the Church to the police.'

'Fond of an institution, or doing it to piss off his parents,' said Swan. 'How long had Kieran Lynch been in the Guards for?'

'Just a year and a half.'

'Do you think he was gay?'

'I think it's likely.' She tossed the end of her cone in a nearby bin, so he followed her example.

'There was no definite answer on the girlfriend front, and his mother seemed to think him a dote.'

'I noticed. But I was more struck by the father saying he didn't know what Kieran kept in the flat. Like he was expecting us to find something that might compromise him in some way.'

'We can only hope. What kind of photo did the mother give you?'

Considine wiped her hands with a tissue before she took it from its envelope. You wouldn't know it was the same boy as the clean-cut recruit in his smart uniform. Kieran Lynch was smiling in the sun, a whitewashed wall, a distant harbour. It looked like Greece, but the misted pint glass he was holding bore a Harp logo. Some Irish seaside town on a blessed day like this one. He was looking straight down the lens, eyes squinting with pleasure. He wore a blue T-shirt and his hair was longer, wavy, haloed by sun. There was something like love in his smile.

13

'Vaguely.'

'C'mon, Fintan. You were mooning over him outside the Moonlit Gate. It was only a few nights ago.'

'And this is the dead Guard?'

'Keep your voice down!'

Fintan had agreed to leave his work early to meet Considine in the Bailey, near his office. She hoped the pub would be quieter, but Friday afternoon was part of the weekend these days. And his memory was proving less accurate than she had hoped.

'I thought a fine legal brain like yours was specially honed. Photographic, even.'

'Ha bloody ha.' Fintan tilted the photograph in its see-through envelope. 'He's familiar, that's all I can say. Handsome, in a rather obvious way.'

'He came out of the pub when we were arguing and you went all swoony. His hair was shorter than the photo and he's thinner. *Was* thinner. There was a short guy with him, a little glamour-puss. Make-up and all.' Gina took out the police ID photograph of Maurice Deegan. 'I think this is him, but a few years ago.'

Fintan reached for it, but she pulled it back. She didn't

want him seeing the official stamp on the back. She held it up in front of his face.

'Oh yeah, I know *him*. Everyone knows him. He hangs around with a girl, mixed-race, cloud of hair. They busk badly together. Sometimes he does mime in the clubs. Tragic. You'll have seen them on Grafton Street or the bridges.'

Considine couldn't recall any pair like that. But not much of her work took her to Grafton Street.

'He calls himself something stupid ... Tattie – no, Mottie. He was away from Dublin for years; claims he did mime in Paris and one of those punk circuses in LA.' Fintan chuckled. 'Camp as Christmas, balls of steel. Can you imagine the grief he must get, looking like that?'

'You don't know where he lives at all?' Considine asked.

'No idea.'

They suspended their conversation as two men came by to consider the empty table beside them, then moved off towards one nearer an open window. The street outside was a cacophony of voices. She felt far too hot in her work suit, but the blouse underneath was not one she wanted to reveal after a day's perspiration.

'You're not going to want me to testify to any of this stuff?' Fintan asked.

'Hopefully you won't have to.'

'Seriously, Gina.'

'This is just you and me. I need to talk to this guy, that's all.'

'I suppose you saw the papers? "Pervert Park" in the *Independent*, with an actual map of where people go to.

And the Guards seem to be doing a pretty good job of disowning their boy – I've never read the phrase "off-duty" so many times. Do you think you could catch one bastard for us, Gina?'

'That is the idea.'

'I guess Kieran Lynch won't be receiving the Scott Medal for bravery.' It was a standard honour for Guards killed in the line of duty.

'We don't know why he was there. We don't even know he was gay.'

'Yeah, right. Want a real drink?'

'I need a clear head. Just get me another Coke.'

Fintan went up to the bar, and Considine looked through her bag until she found the photograph of the drink token discovered in Kieran's wallet. When Fintan came back, she showed it to him.

'Does this look familiar?'

'Oh yeah,' he smiled. 'I'm better with drinks tokens than faces. That's the same as the ones they give you at Tabú at the gay centre. It's not a bad night there. The music is very good.'

'I know. We've been there *together*, ya dose.' She took a big swig of the Coke. The sharp burn of alcohol bloomed in her throat. She banged the glass down and shoved it away.

'Fintan, you fucker.'

'I didn't want to drink alone.'

'I'm going back to work!'

'Ah, it'll do no harm.'

It hit her plain in the face that Fintan had a problem. He

wasn't only an enthusiastic drinker, but a desperate one. Everyone had to join in. It was a betrayal if you didn't. There was no point in addressing it now; it would do no good. And she needed him, she thought queasily, because Kieran Lynch's association with Mottie Deegan could be reported to Swan as coming from Fintan rather than herself.

'Ah – here she is!' Fintan jumped to his feet and held his out his arms towards the doorway. Terry was standing there, a slightly confused look on her face.

'Why aren't you at work?' she asked when she got to the table.

'Sit down, sit down,' said Fintan.

'I am,' said Considine. 'Seeing Fintan is the work.' She put away the photograph lying on the table as Terry sat down beside her and stroked her thigh briefly with her palm.

'No kisses?' said Fintan.

'Voyeur,' said Terry. 'He rang me at home, said I had to come in for a drink, that there was someone I just had to meet.'

'But it's only me.'

Terry performed her *Stop it* sigh. 'Why the cloak-and-dagger, McNulty?'

'Been so long since I've seen you two together, I wanted to be reminded of all I'm missing, being only a poor bachelor.'

Fintan gave them an acid smile and went up to get a drink for Terry and another refill for himself.

'Have you noticed how much he drinks these days?'

'No,' said Terry.

'I don't know why he did this. I'm sorry. I have to get back to the depot. I don't know when I'll be home even.'

'It's fine. I was coming into town anyway. Some of the girls at work, they wanted to see the karaoke at the Harp.'

'Right.'

'They say it's a laugh. You're welcome to join us. Most of them know who you are to me. They're fine with it.'

It was good that Terry's fellow teachers were mainly tolerant, but on the occasions she had met them, Considine had found she had nothing in common with them. In fact they made her nervous; they were mostly married, glamorous and raucous. They hit a good time like a skidding lorry and inevitably flirted with Terry when drunk enough. *I've always wondered what it would be like …*

'As I said, I'm on this new case. Sorry.'

Terry made the shape with her lips that she always did, part pout, part holding back some words that were trying to escape. God damn Fintan and his interfering.

Considine looked over towards the bar, where Fintan was now talking to a lithe, short-haired girl and a man she recognised. The girl looked like a dyke, but not one Gina had seen before. They all started to walk over to the table.

'This is Miriam,' Fintan announced grandly and proudly.

Considine smiled and held out a hand. 'Nice to met you.'

Terry limited herself to a gruff 'hi'.

'And you know Denis.'

Considine vaguely remembered a night out somewhere; she remembered that he was nice. 'Sure. How'ya, Denis.'

'Gina is Terry's girlfriend,' Fintan said in a bright voice.

As Miriam pulled over a stool to join the table, Considine snuck a look at Terry, who was peering at the far side of the room. Fintan had a smug-looking smile on. Whatever this scenario was, she didn't want to spend another moment in it.

She checked her watch. 'Oh. Sorry, I have to leave you.' She gathered her bag under her arm, stood up, pushed roughly past Terry's knees and headed straight out the door.

The fact that Fintan had named her as Terry's girlfriend meant that Terry already knew this woman. Yet she couldn't remember the name 'Miriam' ever being mentioned. There was no good dwelling on it. Considine pulled down a mental roller shutter between herself and whatever was going on in the pub. It was what she always did when she needed to focus. She was good at focusing.

Mottie Deegan. Surely a boy as flamboyant as Mottie would be out on the town on a Friday night?

Considine walked up towards Stephen's Green, looking for buskers, but then detoured by the newsagent's on the corner to buy a packet of Silk Cut and a box of matches. Lapsed again. She had arranged to meet Swan at the office at six, after he had looked through Kieran Lynch's flat. She had lied about being in a hurry, to get away. Away from her girlfriend. *Pull down the shutter, Gina.*

She smoked as she walked down Grafton Street, paying attention to every face that passed. She needed to find this Mottie before anyone else did.

14

Swan parked outside a new restaurant on Fleet Street selling 'Traditional Irish Fare' – *lamb stew*, *boxty* and *coddle* spelled out in Celtic lettering with extra dots and flourishes. He didn't think he'd ever eaten coddle in his puff. Stew with pale sausages and rashers in it. Must be for the tourists who knew no better. Temple Bar was sprouting definite signs of enterprise – he passed a gallery and a record shop on his way to the quays. Rents were cheap here, but short-term because the whole area was going to be redeveloped into what CIE was calling a 'transport hub'. A gigantic bus station, in other words. Swan was fond of these narrow cobbled streets and tall sooty warehouses, just as they were. He tried to make his brain swerve the adjective *Dickensian*, but the cliché was apt.

He wasn't against modern architecture in general, but he was against how it was practised in Dublin. The high-rise bunkers of the Central Bank and the offices they built over the Viking remains at Wood Quay were great galumphing travesties of everything he loved about the city – its breadth, its warm brick, its liveable scale. The silver lining of the current economic slump was that no one had the finances to move forward with their gleaming visions. Meanwhile the free-market bohemians were colonising the place.

He turned towards the river, heading through Merchants' Arch. A girl with a big guitar was regaling the empty passageway with a sad song. It took him a moment to recognise it as a Thin Lizzy anthem turned into a ballad. In her version, the boys being back in town was a cause of trepidation rather than glory. She was very good, but the smell of piss and pigeons after the heat of the day wouldn't tempt you to stop there and listen. He flipped a ten-pence piece onto her guitar cover, noticing another figure sitting in the shadows, head on knees, long blond hair – asleep or intoxicated. He hoped it was just the drink. It felt like the city was starting to get too familiar with heroin.

Swan emerged onto the quays and the Friday-evening traffic roaring along; the pavement was rammed with bus queues, everyone eager to get home for the weekend. Swan expected to be working through the weekend, which was better than clearing his mother's garden or hoovering her loft, or whatever strenuous job she could think up for him. He soon found the door he was looking for, sandwiched between a travel agent's and a cobbler's shop, and took out the keys that Robert Lynch had given him. The stairway beyond was dark, with old but clean lino worn through in patches on the stair treads. He climbed three floors where the doors were padlocked and thick with dust, before reaching a final door on the top floor with gleaming paint and a bristle mat to wipe your shoes on. There was a whiff of bleach in the air.

Kieran Lynch's flat was exceptionally homely and neat. There was a bedroom to the rear and a living room with kitchenette to the front. Between the two rooms was a small, spartan shower room. The brown carpet tiles throughout were spotless, the table wiped clean, with a small stack of heatproof mats placed in the centre. Very domesticated.

Swan found a Garda uniform hanging in the wardrobe, brushed and buttoned. In the top pocket of the jacket was the dead man's Garda ID. He took his time looking through the rest of Lynch's clothes, drawers of neatly balled socks and conservative clothing. No fishnet tights or boas to be seen. Not that he was making assumptions, he just hadn't expected such dullness. It would almost make you suspect that someone had been doing a clean-up job.

The shelves in the front room had a few books on sport, two editions of *The Guinness Book of Records* and a thick book of film reviews – *Halliwell's Film Guide*. No fiction. The small fridge contained only a block of Cheddar, a pint of milk, some spreadable margarine and a packet of rashers.

Swan went to the window and looked down at the mucky Liffey surging quietly between its stone walls. The houses opposite on the north quays did their best to glow in the day's last light, but many were missing panes or whole windows. There was a new gap site where something had collapsed, and big buttresses of wood propped up its former neighbours. His grandfather had had an auction room on Arran Quay, before they moved the whole shebang to Phibsborough. It was a shame, the state of the inner city, but developers never wanted to restore what was there, they only wanted bigger.

He turned to look at the room again. Why did the neatness of the place seem so melancholy? It reminded him of an institution rather than a home. It was a room like the kind of blank expression some people give you, to hide what they're really thinking.

He went back into the bedroom and started to search around the bed. It was a double bed, which at least was less depressing than a single. The young man in the photograph the mother gave them looked happy, sociable with his pint, but this looked like the flat of a recluse. Swan looked under the bed, pressed around the edges of the mattress. He located a suspicious lump on the far side of the mattress, near the pillow, and lay across the bed in an ungainly way to push his hand down the crack and seize hold of what felt like a thick book. He was hoping for a diary, but when he finally wrestled it out to the light – knuckles scraped on the wall – it was only a Bible. A New Testament, to be exact, with an abstract dove in orange and yellow on the cover.

He wondered why a Bible would be hidden as though it was porn. It could be as embarrassing, he supposed, if your love life was more liberal than your creed.

The Bible was well used, broken-backed, with pencil underlinings throughout. Swan flipped through some of it to try and see if there was a particular pattern, but there were too many marks. He left it by the bed and went back to the front room.

Kieran Lynch was a puzzle. A kind boy, a charmer, according to his mother. A disciplined man, according to his flat. An honourable, intelligent young man, in the words of his boss. A little too good to be true or someone to whom goodness mattered? Did anyone join the police in order to be good? Not in Swan's experience. He found himself back at the window, watching the mesmerising drag of the river and the endless flow of cars, bicycles, pedestrians. Maybe that was why the flat was so bland; you would spend all your time here, watching everything roll by.

He went back to look at the shelves again and took down one of the sports books, one documenting the Moscow Olympics of 1980. He held it so that the pages would fall open where they might. They opened on a double-page spread of photographs of male gymnasts. One hanging from rings like a crucifixion, his muscled torso caressed by light. Swan tried again and the book fell open at a colour photograph of a glistening runner breaking the tape, genitals creating a prominent outline in his spandex shorts.

Or was that what Swan was making himself see? He put the book back quickly. Once you tilted your mind that way, the most masculine things looked homoerotic.

It was the kind of thing he would be interested in talking to Considine about, if it wasn't so embarrassing. Being younger, she had a better understanding of these things. She had fresh ideas, she'd been to college and she had gay friends, by the sound of it. Maybe she was back at the office already. Swan looked around and found the phone on one of the front-room shelves.

Never pass up the chance of a phone call when you're out and about, that was a cardinal rule.

But it was Declan Barrett who answered. Considine hadn't been around.

'I don't know what she's up to.' Barrett never passed up the chance to infer that Considine was some kind of loose wheel.

'What are *you* up to?' Swan responded.

'I'm off to the park with Hannigan to talk to the smack-heads and perverts.'

'That's a bit dark, even for you. Any progress?'

Barrett didn't reply.

'Any sign of the jogger?'

'Not yet. No.'

'I'm at Kieran Lynch's flat. He was very neat, signs of piety. No obviously gay materials. I mean porn or that kind of thing.'

'Why are you telling me this?'

'Because it's useful information for someone investigating his murder, Barrett.'

Answer came there none. Just the sound of Barrett's adenoidal breathing.

'Well, it's great to catch up,' said Swan.

'Sorry,' said Barrett, 'it's a long night ahead.'

It would be a long night for Swan too, but he heroically refrained from pointing that out. Putting down the receiver, he noticed the phone had a little pull-out drawer underneath, and inside it a slim book for phone numbers. He gave it a cursory flick: *Brian B*, *Roger McK*, *Gerry (Drimnagh)*. Almost exclusively male names, few of them in full. Interesting. Swan slid it into his inside jacket pocket.

He decided he had time to drop by his mother's. It would be good to walk for a stretch and think; he could pick up his car later on or not at all. He crossed the river to the Four Courts and picked a wandering route through Smithfield.

Lynch's death might just have been bad luck: running

into some nasty thugs on a dark night in the wrong place. Either because he was gay or because they had assumed he was. It had happened before and would again. Boys proving themselves to each other by attacking the thing that terrified them all – softness. At least that kind of thing seldom stayed secret, because boasting was an important part of it. Unless there was only one assailant: someone strong, because Kieran Lynch was tall and fit.

Swan found himself examining the faces of all the young men he passed on the streets, as if they could hold a clue to who Kieran Lynch was, because he could make no sense of him at all.

He reached Stoneybatter and walked up towards Manor Street. Larry Mulligan's pub had its doors propped open, and Swan passed through a miasma of heat and smoke that issued from its dark interior.

The sound of a woman laughing followed him as he passed on, feeling virtuous. He seldom went into pubs when he was married – mostly to prove he wasn't like his father – but now that he was on his own, well, it was more of a temptation. He picked up the pace to shake off the shadow of his unbeloved father. Sometimes he'd catch himself unawares in the mirror and find the old goat there – something in the set of his jaw or some new furrow. The ancestors are within us, eager to emerge again through a wild-growing eyebrow or new ailment. He turned the corner of Kirwan Street and unlocked the door of the modest terraced house – 'artisan cottage' in the estate agent's parlance – that his mother had bought after his father died. She had been quick to shake off the old family home and seemed happier in a solo life.

It was a shabby little neighbourhood in many ways, but his mother liked the people and the life of the street.

'Hello!' he called towards the kitchen.

'Hello, yourself,' said his mother from the sitting room. She was seated by the unlit gas fire, her glasses on her head and draped in the blanket she was knitting – had been knitting – since he moved in with her.

'That's coming on great guns,' said Swan.

'I didn't make you anything to eat,' she said, flicking her head neatly so that her glasses fell from the top of her head down onto the bridge of her nose.

'I'll fetch something myself, don't worry.' He had spent his first weeks here persuading her not to cater for him, to break with the past; he was not a schoolboy. They had wrangled and struggled and worn each other away with false politeness. Now he had won and there was no dinner.

He went and kissed the top of her head.

'Fetch me the remote, Son, I'm too cosy to get up.'

'I'm surprised you're not melted.'

He looked into the crowded fridge for a while, thinking of the contents of Kieran Lynch's fridge, the strange neatness of his flat, then pulled himself together and made a ham-and-tomato sandwich with mustard and a pot of tea.

He re-joined his mother with his food and a cup for her. She was flipping through the *RTÉ Guide* to see what she had circled for evening viewing.

'Are you not staying in?' she asked, casting an eye over his suit jacket. She had knitted him a cardigan for his birthday, a strange thing with a belt, and longed to see him in it. This had become their new micro-war.

'I'm going back to the office. There's a case on.'

'Of course there is, sorry.'

She kept frowning at him.

'Will that sandwich be enough for you?'

'Mam – was Uncle Tony gay?'

She looked quickly at her needles, as if there was a problem with the stitches. 'Where does this come from?'

Swan took a slow sup of his tea, extra-casual. 'He just popped into my mind, today. I didn't know him so well, and you used to make jokes about him and his landlady, but, you know, there was something very ... sensitive about Tony.'

'He almost got married, you know. He was engaged.'

'What happened?'

'Don't leave your crusts, Vincent – honestly, you're a grown man.'

Swan put aside the plate. 'What happened?'

'Well, actually, I warned her off.' She threw the blanket to one side, her face flushed with warmth now. 'You're right, of course, he was homosexual. I mean he was my only brother, and of course I knew he was different from other boys. My mother thought that getting married would cure him, not that anyone said that straight up – it was the fifties after all, we didn't even have words for things. Tony was very much under her thumb and so he started doing a line with a nice, shy girl, but I thought it was heading for disaster. It wasn't like they could get a divorce or anything when it didn't work out. Neither of them would be happy, and I thought it would be an awful waste. So I told her. Marie Cronin. Still a friend, as it happens.'

His mother stopped short and gave Swan an odd look.

'Are you sure there's no particular reason you're asking me about Tony?'

He didn't like that look. He had been subject to it constantly as a boy, when it usually preceded a dreaded 'talk'.

'No reason at all. He just came into my mind. Anyway, I better get to the office.'

'Take your plate!' she shouted, and he had to double back from the hall for it.

15

Swan would be here soon. Considine put the file photograph of Mottie Deegan into her drawer, then opened the case notes and other photographs on her desk, so that she would appear occupied. What she was really thinking about was whether to recruit Swan into her quest.

He arrived at a quarter past six, later than they'd arranged. His suit jacket was wrinkled, his hair disarrayed around the temples. He was often late these days.

'Is it windy out there?' she asked.

Swan turned to the large window to check.

'Doesn't look it,' he said, as if he had no recall of the world he had just passed through. She estimated he was in his mid-forties now – not old at all, though she sometimes treated him as such, their bit of fun. But he was increasingly distracted of late. That still made him more acute than most of the others in the unit, but she didn't like considering that he might have burned out or short-circuited or something. The officers of the murder squad enjoyed a kind of survivor mythology – the idea that the weaker colleagues constantly fell by the wayside because of the toughness of the work. In reality, Considine was still surrounded by the same faces who had greeted her with disbelief when she was hired four years before.

The girl was what they called her then. How ironic would it be if *the girl* was the first to be forced out of the unit? She wished Superintendent Martin would be more exercised by incompetence than lurid rumours.

Swan rolled his chair over to the end of her desk, took out a floppy handkerchief and mopped his brow.

'Strange aul' weather,' he said. 'The heat is still coming off the stones.'

'We're not good with the heat, are we?'

'We're not built for it.'

They smiled at each other in the silence of the office.

'Do you have that photograph of Kieran Lynch the mother gave you?'

Considine extracted it neatly from the papers in front of her.

'Where would you say it was taken?' asked Swan.

'Ireland, like you said. Some coastal town in the west?'

'There's so many boats—yachts, I mean. I think it's Kinsale.'

'I've never been there. I've heard it's nice.'

'See that little peninsula with all the coloured houses. I'm sure it's there. How have you never been to Kinsale?'

Considine shrugged. There were a lot of places she'd never been. They tended to spend their holidays in Donegal, where Terry's aunt had a house in Portnoo.

She took the photograph from Swan's hand and looked at the landscape one more time, even though she knew there was nothing new to be discovered in it.

'It's his face, though,' said Swan. 'I mean, he's so damn happy. He's like a different person from the photo on his Garda ID.'

'It's like his smile's not for the camera but for the person behind it.'

'It might be good to know whether it was a female person or a male person he was looking at in that way.'

'Just because Kieran Lynch might have been cruising doesn't make it any less of a murder.'

'You know that wasn't what I was meaning. It's about his reasons for being in the park at all. And this boy in the picture doesn't look like the type who would live in the flat I saw. It was so sparse. There were no personal touches, no photographs that I could find. And he had a Bible tucked under his mattress like a dirty secret. It was as clean as a monk's cell. And the building itself was odd. Some kind of office building, with no other flats in it.'

'No one to notice comings and goings.'

'There's that. There's also this.' He took a slim notebook from his pocket. Fake black-leather cover. Considine took it and looked inside.

'Fuck, is this his?'

'Found it under his phone in a little drawer.'

She put it down quickly. 'Brilliant. But what about forensics?'

'We can't wait for days. We've nothing. There'll be prints all over his flat if there were prints on that.'

That was true. She took up the address book again and looked quickly under D and M – no Deegan, no Mottie, no Maurice Deegan. This book wasn't going to help her track him down.

'What are you looking for?' Swan asked.

It was time to tell him a version of the truth. Two sets of

eyes were better than one, after all. She had to rely on the assumption that Mottie would not remember her. And if he did, well she'd deal with that when it came.

'I talked to someone in the gay community,' she said. 'Someone who knows that scene. He says he thought he saw Kieran Lynch the night he died, in the Moonlit Gate pub, which is very popular with gay men. I believe.'

Considine took the photograph of Maurice Deegan out of her drawer and passed it to Swan.

'He was with this man, I was told.'

'He's just a boy.'

'That was taken five years ago. The name I got was Maurice Deegan, known as Mottie.'

She noticed Swan stroke his finger over the indentation that the paperclip had left. His eyes flicked to hers.

'Okay, I took it from the Grierson files.'

'Do you have the file itself?' He was looking at her with a kind of intensity that she didn't like.

She shrugged lightly. 'I didn't want to annoy the dungeon-master. But I know what it said.'

'This is reckless behaviour, all the same.' He smiled.

'Let me sum it up for you. Deegan was living in a hostel over by Busáras then, so it's unlikely he's still there. I rang them anyway; they don't know of him. He had received a warning for soliciting in the previous year, but denied taking money for sex when interviewed. I couldn't find anything more up to date on him.'

'That doesn't mean he's given up soliciting, though,' Swan said.

'There's been nothing in five years.'

'We mostly turn a blind eye, you know that.'

Considine stopped herself from saying something sarcastic.

Swan picked up the colour photograph of Kieran Lynch on holiday and placed it beside the stark black-and-white photograph of Mottie Deegan, taken in police custody.

'What do you think, Gina? Would these two have gone off together to the park, for a little knee-trembler in the woods? Unless he's put on a lot of muscle, this little feller doesn't seem capable of beating anyone – let alone a tall Garda – to death.'

'Kieran Lynch's flat is directly en route between the Moonlit Gate and the park. If they were sexually involved, they could just have gone to his flat – no need to go to the park.'

But even as she said this, she was thinking of Fintan and his love of dark and dangerous places. Maybe Kieran Lynch had a similar penchant. Neat home, responsible job, messy sex life. It wasn't a thought that she was tempted to share.

'I don't see them as a couple, but they were definitely going somewhere together.'

Swan gave her an odd glance.

'That's what I was told.'

'This person who saw them together, is he or she willing to talk to us more formally?'

'I doubt it. There wasn't any more to it than that. He saw them together, he saw them leave the bar together.'

'So we need to talk to this guy.' Swan tapped the photo of Mottie Deegan.

'Yes, we do,' said Considine, back on more certain ground. 'Oh, and he told me something else.'

'Your informant.'

'Well, it's pretty common knowledge. That drinks token in Lynch's pocket – it's from Tabú disco, a dance night at the gay community centre. It happens every Friday, they tell me, so it wasn't something relevant to the night he was attacked, just something he had left over in his pocket.'

'It's Friday night tonight,' Swan pointed out.

Considine was aware of her armpits prickling with sweat. It was a strangely muggy night. She pushed her chair away from the desk and made a show of flapping the hem of her shirt about.

'Have they kept the heat on, do you think? It's so close in here!'

She went over to one of the windows and pulled it up, but the night air was hardly cooler than inside. On the other side of the depot yard the trees of the park stood still, not a leaf moving in the humid dark.

'We can do this, Gina – it's not going to be like the Grierson case!'

She turned back to look at Swan. He'd taken off his jacket and was on his feet, pacing. As he moved, she noticed suddenly that his shirt was baggier on him than usual. His eyes burned with intensity and she found herself wondering if he was sick, if that was why he'd been a little odd lately.

'Listen to me!'

She sat down, trapping one hand with the other in her lap, resolving to be cool, to hear him out.

'We should go out to that pub, not as police, but as punters. Chat casually, no big pressure. There's a lot we can find out just by being among the gay people, I'm thinking. There'll be talk about the case, if we're lucky. We don't call anyone into the station, we keep it all low-key. We redeem ourselves with anyone who thinks we're the enemy. We could even change our clothes and go to that disco. What are you smiling at, Gina?'

'It's quite an image.'

'We serve everyone or we serve no one. It was you who said that to me once. There's nothing to be nervous about.'

'Are you thinking I'm prejudiced? Me?'

But Swan was putting his jacket on, full of enthusiasm. If they went to the Moonlit Gate there might be people who knew her in her other life. Perhaps Terry and Fintan would decide to do a pub crawl. She'd have to take him to The Earl. She didn't often go there, so it would be safer.

'Can we take your car? I've left mine in town.' He was already heading for the door.

They were supposed to be driving straight into town, but Considine felt in no rush to get there. As they passed the main entrance to the Phoenix Park, she pulled a sudden right turn and drove in, heading for the grove of trees where Kieran Lynch had been found. Beyond rose the Wellington Monument, its stone needle relentlessly black against the grainy twilight sky.

Swan looked at her in surprise.

'I just want to take a look at the place again,' she

explained. 'I've never been in the park at night. It was probably darker than this when he was attacked.'

There was one car parked on the side of the road, exactly where the ambulance had been on the morning they found Lynch. Right where she wanted to park. She drifted the car slowly past, and they could see that there was one person sitting in it. He turned his head as they drew level. It was Declan Barrett. Considine braked to a stop, and Swan rolled down the window on his side to talk.

'All right, Barrett?'

'Fine, boss.'

'Are you all on your own, so?'

'I amn't. Eric Joyce is away in the trees somewhere. Call of nature. Or so he says.' Barrett had to laugh at his own quip, since no one else did.

'Has it been quiet?' asked Swan.

'There doesn't seem to be anyone looking for trade, not selling it anyway – I think word must be out among the rent boys. There's a fair few slow cars doing the rounds, though. Mercedes and all sorts. Old fellas mostly. It would make you sick, so it would.'

Gina revved the accelerator in annoyance.

'Shall we take a stroll around?' Swan asked her.

It seemed to her that there was no point, if they were going to be watched by Barrett and Joyce. She realised she had wanted to be alone in there, among the trees; she wanted to think about Kieran there, but it wasn't the kind of urge she could easily explain.

'I think it's better if we get on,' she said to Swan, as if it was he who had insisted on the detour.

'Bossy little thing, isn't she?' Barrett said.

Considine leaned towards the passenger window, brushing Swan back with her shoulder. 'Fuck your nonsense, Declan,' she said, then roared away, the night air streaming into the car.

'You're in a strange mood,' said Swan after a minute.

She forced a laugh, but didn't dare look at him.

16

I drop Jess off at her evening gig at the Cabin – she doesn't like to walk alone with her guitar in case some bastard nicks it from her, and then what would we do for cash? Also she's been understandably wobbly since we found out that Kieran was killed. Looking after her makes me feel uncomfortably masculine.

The sweet guy in the restaurant kitchen makes me a sandwich in a little bag, and because I'm starved, I eat it in the street on the way back – though my mother would die to see it. I'm chewing on the last crust by the time I get to the warehouse. When I go to unlock the outer door I discover it is slightly open. We didn't leave it that way. I toss the crust for the birds and slip inside. There's a smell in the stairway: a cheap cologne that reminds me of the worst days at school: Brut. I'm curious more than scared.

The warehouse staircase is made of such solid wood that you can climb without making a noise. I trained in silence, and it has proved useful in all parts of my life. Like a kid off the Bisto box, I sniff my way up to the first floor, where the room that was once a treasure trove is lying open. There's only a dim spill of light from the street, but I don't see anyone inside, so I take a little look. A couple of empty cardboard boxes, an old suitcase. The trunk of paintings and all the dodgy stuff seems to be gone. They've been coming and going for days, but I'm still surprised. I hope they haven't emptied our attic too. I turn to go and a man is standing in the doorway. Someone else has the gift of silence too. It takes me a moment to recognise Mr Brylcreem, the watcher in the street.

He starts breathing heavily. 'I don't suppose *you* know who took the stuff?' It's more a statement than a question.

'Is this the gay centre?' I make my voice fey, gossamer.

'Don't give me that. I seen you here before.'

He takes a step towards me, big shoes crunching on the plaster flakes and broken glass. I don't know whether he wants to have me or hurt me. I'm judging the angles of possible escape when I catch a sniff of something sharper than cologne. I smell paraffin. I know it so well from my fire-eating circus days.

'I can see you're a serious man,' I say, 'but the thing is, I'm not. Look at me. I didn't take your things. I don't even know about any things.'

'But I saw you, you little fuck, with that copper. You've no idea what you started.'

His eyes are shifting to and fro, like someone reading a page. I think he's considering what he's going to do to me. I'm ready for his lunge, I can dodge a lunge. And I've noted the position of several glass shards on the floor, in case it comes to that.

There's a bark from the stairway: 'Badger!'

The man's eyes go wide. 'On my way!' he shouts, turning, raising a hand as if to tell me to wait right here for my beating while he attends to his summoner. He clatters down the stairs. The scary man is scared of someone else. I wonder if *Badger* is some kind of code.

I should run, but this is such a heady scenario, how can I help but sneak a look out of the window. Yes, they're on the pavement together, Mr Brylcreem talking to another man under the street light. This man has a slight comb-over and is wearing a Crombie coat with a velvet collar. Very fancy, if a bit tight on him. He has backed Mr B up against the post of the street light and seems most displeased. The man in the Crombie suddenly punches Mr Brylcreem in the side of the head, fast and vicious, so that his skull bounces off the metal post. I mean, *yikes* – the sound of it.

Mr Brylcreem holds his head and starts to stutter apologies. 'Sorry, Mr Barry,' I think he says. Everyone seems very angry that the treasure is gone.

I pass three cans of paraffin on the stair landing as I run to the attic. I shove back the crate that still hides the door – *phew* – and stand there under the dim light of the roof hole, thinking what to pack. It would be a bore to lose all our stuff again. The old painting is still propped on the tea chest, which is a relief, but also a problem.

There isn't much time left, if any. I don't have the flame resistance of our little martyr.

17

Swan had thought that a gay bar would be gayer, exotic and lively. But the pub that Gina brought him to looked like any other one at first. The music was offensively loud, but that was often the way on a Friday night. There were far fewer women than normal, and more solo drinkers, it seemed. The glances that came Swan's way were veiled and bored-looking. He and Considine had been identified as alien the minute they walked through the door. Perhaps they had been taken for a married couple who had lost their way, but more likely, he realised, they were spotted as police.

He leaned in towards Considine's ear. 'Do you think all these people are gay?'

'*I* don't know.'

She was in some kind of strange mood.

'Why don't I get us a drink? I just go up and order as normal, right?'

Considine rolled her eyes elaborately.

By the time Swan returned from the bar, a lager in either hand, she had disappeared. He experienced a small flash of panic and worried that he was not as urbane as he fancied himself to be. He wasn't prejudiced, not all, he was merely uncomfortable. A squeal of laughter rang through the bar as a group of four young men fell about laughing, but not at him, thank God – at their own joke. The most lissom one was gesturing wildly, his hands a performance. *Stop staring*, Swan told himself. At least there were a few other men of his age and older. The nearest was dressed in a soft suede jacket, with a large scarf swathing his neck, a bit theatrical. Perhaps Swan should have changed into something more casual for this, other than his work suit. Not that he had anything outré in his wardrobe. Elizabeth had quite conservative taste.

He'd be doing all his own clothes shopping from here on, he reminded himself.

He found a place to settle, two stools at the end of the long bar, with a good view of the room. He would have preferred a corner, but all the tables were taken. He spotted Considine at last, talking with a group at one of the tables at the back. He saw her flash the photograph of Mottie Deegan briefly. One of the group, a skinny chap with a generous moustache, started to nod emphatically. At the table next door to Gina were five women, mainly short-haired and sombre-looking, as if they weren't enjoying themselves at all. One of them spoke while the rest listened – except for one, a girl with a puff of curls above her closely barbered nape. She was staring hard at Considine, but Considine didn't appear to notice.

Swan watched her move away from the men and look around to locate him. He waved from his end of the bar and she re-joined him, taking a swig of the beer before she spoke.

'They all know Mottie – to see, at least. But no one's seen him recently.'

'Did you ask them about Kieran Lynch?'

'Do you want to go over yourself for the full interrogation? Be my guest. Only I thought we were befriending the community, not grilling them.'

'You were the one running about with the photograph. Speaking of befriending, one of those girls was giving you the eye.'

Considine wouldn't look over to where he was indicating 'Really?' she said tightly, staring into her glass.

'Ah, Gina, don't be annoyed. I'm not disrespecting these people, you know that – I'm as liberal as they come. It was a joke.'

Swan saw her eyes slide quickly to the table of women, then flick back to him. Maybe she was nervous, he thought. Maybe she wasn't as confident in these surroundings as he assumed.

'Do you want *me* to go and talk to the women?'

'No!'

And off she went again. He couldn't get anything right. He ordered another beer; Considine still had plenty in her glass. Then he got the barman to cash a cheque for him, as the night would be long and possibly expensive. The floor of the pub was filling up now, and he couldn't clearly see how Considine's conversation with the lesbians was going. She had her back to him. The women still looked unfriendly, but one, with spiky black hair, was speaking and gesturing.

As he was trying to keep track of what was happening, a heavyset man in a denim shirt and chinos walked into view and caught Swan's eye. Swan didn't recognise him, but the man continued to stare. Was it a threat or a come-on? He turned his attention to his drink. That disco music popping little electronic beeps into his ears seemed to be getting more insistent.

Considine arrived back and squeezed up onto the stool he'd saved for her. 'Okay, that wasn't a complete loss. Those women know Mottie, and say he busks regularly on O'Connell Bridge and at the bottom of Grafton Street these days – he does mime and some circus stuff, and he works with a black girl who plays the guitar. She's known as Jess or Jessie. Not so hard to find the pair of them, you'd think.'

Swan remembered the singer he'd seen at Merchants' Arch, near Kieran's flat. She had had someone with her – he had thought it was another girl, but it could have been the two of them.

Considine was ordering more drinks. Swan thought of refusing, but it had been such a long day, and this was such an odd place. A place that looked completely normal in so many ways. After she paid, Considine twisted in towards him and rested her forehead on her propped-up hand.

'Is everything okay with you, Gina?' He knew no good would come from asking, but he'd felt out of step with her all evening, so it had to be addressed.

'I was just about to ask you the same.' She gave him a wan smile and took a swallow of her beer.

'Actually my cat died this week,' he said.

'Are you serious?'

Swan shrugged. 'He was a good age. What can you say?'

'To Benny,' said Considine, and they clinked glasses. He was touched that she remembered his name.

They sat and drank and tried not to look like they were scanning the clientele. As the drink took effect, Swan found that he could tolerate the music. It took the pressure off chatting. He marvelled at his own levels of relaxation in what had started out as an alien place.

'You know what I love?' He leaned into Considine's ear. She shook her head minutely. 'I like being surprised. There's the Dublin we see every day – the gangsters, the sad homes, the fanatics, the bedsit suicides. You start to think that's the city, that your version of things is the whole. I like to be proved wrong.

'One Sunday morning I had to go to the Stella cinema to talk to the manager about a series of raids on their box office. This was a few years back. There was a film on, and I stuck my head in at the back, thinking it would be some kids' thing. But the place was full of Indians, I mean every seat in the house: ladies in saris and kids running up and down the aisles, men in jackets and shirts. All of them chatting away over the film, which was some kind of Indian musical.'

He jiggled his hands beside his ears to make her laugh, but she didn't.

'I was the only white person there. It was great.'

'Why was it great?'

'Because I never knew there were enough Indian people in Dublin to fill a cinema. It threw me back on myself. And it was … joyful. Sometimes, in this job, all you see is the bad side of the city.'

'There's an original thought.'

'All I meant was, this is nice. Here. This is unfamiliar

and it's nice.' He held his arms out to indicate his appreciation. 'Seriously, what's up with you?'

'Nothing. You don't have to talk so loud. I'm sure everyone's very appreciative of your tolerant attitude.'

The group of women were leaving the bar, passing close to where they sat. 'Good to see you working hard!' one of them called to Considine, and the others smirked.

Swan turned to bid them a good night and thank them for their help, but Considine stopped him. 'Don't say anything.'

'Do you think we should move on somewhere else?'

'The minute we leave, Mottie's bound to turn up.'

Their glasses were empty again, but it was only ten o'clock and the nightclub at the gay centre wouldn't start up until later.

'Orange juice?' asked Swan.

'I think we should split up. We look more like Guards as a pair. You go on to the disco and I'll look at some other places, maybe check out the late buskers when the pubs close.'

'We could do both.'

'We'll cover more ground separately.'

'I don't feel good leaving you on your own.'

She gave him a sceptical look.

'Okay, I haven't been to a disco since before they were called discos, let alone a gay one. I'm not exactly dressed for it.'

Considine smiled at last. 'I'll tell you what to do.'

The barman came up then and removed their glasses and wiped the bar in front of them. He didn't look at them or ask if they wanted another. Their welcome was running out.

'Not all gay men are like Dick Emery,' she said. 'Plenty look just like you, Vincent. They live outward lives of normality, married with kids, but there's part of their life that no one knows about. Sometimes this life never manifests outside their head, but plenty of them crack. Drink lowers their inhibitions and they do risky things – make a clumsy pass at some boy or turn up at a gay disco half-cut, still wearing their office clothes,' she gestured at Swan's suit, 'their ties in their pockets,' she dipped into his jacket pocket and pulled out a loop of the tie he had discarded, 'and with their wedding rings removed.' She lifted his left hand. 'Oh.'

She drew his hand closer to inspect the groove where his wedding ring usually sat. He could feel her breath on his fingers. A feeling of shame crept through him.

'I see you've done that bit already.'

'Let's just go get another drink somewhere,' he said. 'Somewhere normal.'

She dropped his hand like a stone. 'What is going on with you? Why are you always at your mother's house when I try and reach you?' Her hand shot up to cover her mouth. 'You've split up with Elizabeth, haven't you?'

Swan looked away, trying to catch the eye of the bar staff, a finger poking the air. The barman saw him wave but pretended he didn't, walking away to the far end in search of other custom. Swan noticed that the further end of the room was really packed now, but there was plenty of space around himself and Considine.

'Why didn't you tell me, Vincent?'

'It's not your problem.'

'No, but it explains a lot.'

'I've been perfectly normal; if anything, it's you who's been acting strange.'

'Oh, let nobody cast doubt on your utter normality. If you don't want to go to the gay club, that's fine. Maybe you'd be better off at home with your mother!'

'See? That's exactly what I mean. You're not yourself – you're ... angry. Why don't *you* go home and I'll find this Mottie character.'

They were both off their stools by now, almost squaring up to each other. Swan couldn't understand how things had got so heated between them. Some completely sober part of his brain was on the sidelines, marvelling, amused even. The barman appeared beside them.

'I think we're done here, folks,' he said in a polite voice.

They found themselves out on the pavement, staring off in opposite directions and breathing the nice cool air.

Considine lit a cigarette and they started to walk slowly down towards Dame Street, a careful gap between them.

'Let's just stop here on the corner,' Swan said after a while. 'We've as much chance of seeing him on the street as in a pub – probably more.'

There were plenty of people out and about, high heels clicking on the pavement, the occasional shout and laughter in the distance. Buses swept past like lit galleons, ferrying tipsy passengers home to the suburbs. Down in Temple Lane someone was putting things in a van, and a stuck car was beeping behind it.

'We'll stick to the plan: I'll go to the gay centre disco on my own, like a sad case – a role I seem qualified for – and you check out any other likely bars or clubs. If you find yourself still out in the early hours, I'll head for the Graceland Café between one and two. Fair enough?'

Gina nodded, dropped her cigarette butt and stomped it out with a swivel of her shoe.

'I should have dressed up,' she said.

'You don't have some sparkly earrings in your pocket, do you?'

'You know I don't.'

'Borrow my tie. You could fashion it into a hairband or something.'

'I'm sorry about you and Elizabeth. That can't be easy.'

Four students came along the pavement, arms linked. They were trying to do the Monkees' walk, stepping their feet out one way, then the other, laughing and tripping each other up. They banged into Swan as they passed, but he let it go.

'It was a long time coming. Sometimes the anticipation is worse than the calamity.'

'Your mother is probably glad to have you there.'

'Don't know about glad. She has her own life now, and it's a small house.'

'Do you think you'll get back together?'

'No. I used to. We'd still have the same problems. Just because you've invested years in a relationship doesn't mean it's a good idea to keep going. Elizabeth said we could both be happier.'

'And are you?'

'Not yet, but I have my modest hopes.'

'I want you to be happy.'

Out of the corner of his eye, the flashing neon of the *Why go Bald* sign switched a man's head between white scalp and orange tresses in a never-ending sequence. Swan noticed how it cast its warm, then cold glow onto the side of Considine's face. She reached out a hand and he took it in his, not daring to look at her face now, but keeping his eyes on their joined hands under the lamplight, wondering at the warm knot that their fingers made and what it might mean.

18

Gina shook Swan's hand loose from hers eventually, when she realised he might never let it go. The poor man was in more of a state than he knew, but his neediness made her nervous. What if he did something awful at the disco? At least she wouldn't be there to see it.

After a quick goodbye, she headed up South Great George's Street, edgy with discomfort. Of course she was sorry for him, but she was also sorry she'd asked about Elizabeth. They were good together in a work situation, but that was the limit of it. He so obviously needed a friend to talk to, but it couldn't be her.

She zigzagged through the narrow streets around the Powerscourt Centre, stopping at every corner to check the alternative vistas, expecting the elfin figure of Mottie Deegan to catch her eye at any minute – his blond-tipped hair gleaming under the lights. But the streets were almost deserted. She stopped across the road from the Moonlit Gate, lit another cigarette and reimagined her way once again through Tuesday night's encounter with Kieran Lynch. Was there something she had missed? Mottie and Kieran had headed north towards the river, perhaps to another bar, or to Kieran's flat. The gay centre was that way too. She should check if there had been any event there on Tuesday.

She looked down towards the alleyway where Mottie had waited, squinting with the effort of recalling him exactly: how he danced with impatience, the lit torch in his hand. Were they going to a break-in? Or somewhere without electricity?

A young man in glasses, conservative-looking in a neat beige jacket, was making his way along the opposite pavement. As he neared the pub door, he checked all around him and saw her standing and looking. Considine could have sworn he was about to enter the pub, but he walked on with hurried steps, frightened off by her presence. It made her think of the first time she had gone to the women's night here, a Tuesday gathering in the upstairs lounge. Women's events were always held midweek, the weekends too precious to be expended on those unprofitable lesbians.

Nothing in her police work had been as frightening as stepping across that threshold. She'd hoped the women might be friendly to her, but they weren't. Silence had dropped like a scene in a western saloon. She stood alone at the bar and drank her pint while feeling the eyes bore into her. Then an older butch dyke came over. *Don't look so terrified, there's a first time for all of us*, she said. Considine had been so grateful for her company, even though it came with heckling from the woman's friends, making out that she'd take advantage of her. Then another table started slagging the first table off for 'objectifying' Considine, and all she wanted to do was disappear. There was nothing sexy about the situation. And that was the whole point of being there.

Her saviour was starting to monologue about her

troubled love life, and her own coming out. The space between them was growing smaller with every sway. Considine was ostentatiously looking at her watch, inventing an exit, when Terry walked in, and all she could do was gawp.

Terry had spotted her immediately and, after a moment's hesitation, smiled and walked straight over.

'Hello, Gina.'

'Miss Murray!' Considine couldn't help saying, though it had been years since Terry had been her teacher.

And that was that. It felt like a revelation and a homecoming. Who could ask for anything more?

Considine stubbed out her cigarette in the gutter, walked across the road and straight into the pub. There was a certain rustling among the clientele as she made her way to the bar. She blamed her beloved Michael Mortell trench coat, with its belt and little leather trims, for marking her out. It helped project authority on the day-job, but was less suitable for mingling with the evening crowd. She recognised a couple of faces, male friends of Fintan. Well-to-do, the gleam of good watches and belts against the neatly laundered denim.

She leaned on the edge of the bar and waited for the manager to spot her. She fished his name out of her memory – Matt – an old-school Dubliner, not gay himself, but wise to a profitable clientele with an aversion to fist fights, if not drama.

He gave her a glance, then finished up his conversation at the other end of the bar with a man wearing a fedora and came to serve her.

'Just yourself?'

Considine ordered a gin, even though she hadn't quite intended to. He put the glass in front of her and the opened tonic beside it and waited, because he knew there'd be something else. She slipped him the photograph of Mottie Deegan and asked when he had last seen him.

'He's not old enough to be drinking.'

'The photo is a few years old. He was here the other night – Tuesday: furry jacket and longer blond hair. Make-up.'

'Is this an official investigation? My customers aren't much given to being questioned, if that's what you're intending.'

He looked pointedly at the gin he had served her.

'Who said anything about questioning, Matt? Aren't we just having a chat?'

He flinched when she said his name and looked at her more closely. Considine could see he was trying to place her, to weigh her importance. He was probably raking his mind for past run-ins with the Guards, rather than his occasional visits to the upstairs lounge on a women's Tuesday.

'I can't help you.' He moved off to take someone else's order.

Mottie Deegan wasn't here. The rope across the stairs indicated the upstairs lounge was closed. There was no point trying to talk casually to the clientele with the landlord's eagle eye on her, and an incriminating amount of drink inside her. She scanned the drinkers again and realised she'd been half hoping to run into Fintan and Terry, if they were still out. She drank her gin quickly and left.

Now that Grafton Street was pedestrianised there were

sometimes buskers performing at night, leaning against the roller-shuttered shops or starkly lit in the entrance bays of the larger shops. Considine had plenty of time to kill before she was due to meet up with Swan.

She walked around to Chatham Street, passing Neary's pub. Laughter leaked from behind the etched glass of the windows. The bars would be emptying soon, but for now Grafton Street was relatively quiet. A few couples and knots of young people passed, some girls bare-armed in the mildness of the night. As she got towards the bottom of the street she heard a soulful, but not exactly tuneful, voice:

Love is teasing, love is pleasing
Love is a pleasure when first it's new
As it grows older, love grows colder
And fades away like the morning dew …

It was a song she had known all her life, but echoing off the night buildings in a man's strangely accented voice, its sorrow outweighed its sweetness. The singer was sitting on a cardboard box outside a shoe shop, wrapped in a scarf and an army greatcoat. He had a pointed black beard and long tendrils of hair escaped from his small knitted hat.

He finished his song and held a hand out towards her, trying to make the gesture feeble. Considine took a coin from her pocket and dropped it into the McDonald's cup in front of him.

'Thank you, lady.'

'Where are you from?'

'Chile. You know Chile?'

'I could point to it on a map.'

'That is something. Can I sing you another song?'

'No, but you can answer a question.'

She showed him the photograph of Mottie and he hesitated over it, sneaking an assessing look at her. He finally admitted to having seen him about.

'Do you know where he would be tonight?'

'I hope he is inside in the warm with a full belly.'

'But it is warm. This is summer.'

'This is no summer.'

A laughing group passed them, boys in shirtsleeves this time. Considine gestured to them as evidence of her point.

The singer shook his head. 'Irish are crazy.'

'I thought South Americans were crazy too.'

'We are crazy in the same way. You are all crazy in different ways.'

He said his name was Rafael, and insisted that he sing her another song. It was in Spanish, a heartfelt lament that he seemed to give more care to than the Irish ballad that went before. A half-dozen passers-by stopped to listen, but as the song rose to its crescendo it stopped in the middle of a phrase and Rafael was gone. Only the cardboard box and the rolling paper cup remained. Two Gardaí were walking down the street, taking their time. Although they were obliged to 'move on' the buskers, it was less work if the buskers moved on of their own accord.

The little audience dispersed, but Considine waited for the Guards to reach her and flashed her ID.

'Evening, lads. Quiet night?'

They agreed it had been, but looked wary. They towered

over her, one young and outrageously freckled, the other with mean-looking eyes and a puffed-out chest. She might as well just plunge in.

'You're from Pearse Street, yeah?'

Freckle-face looked at the other, who confirmed it with a nod.

'Did you know Kieran Lynch?'

They exchanged a glance, but answer came there none.

'I'm actually working the case,' she said.

'On yer own?' said the tougher-looking one. She wondered if they could tell she'd been drinking. It had been a long time since she had checked her appearance in a mirror. Her hand automatically went up to smooth her hair and she jerked it back down, making an odd little wave, which drew their eyes.

'No, of course not on my own. The whole squad is on this, night and day. I'm trying to find a witness right now. But it's good to run into you. I was hoping you could give me a better idea of what Kieran was like, what he did when he wasn't on-duty. Anything that helps us catch a Garda killer, right?'

'He wasn't killed for being a Garda, though, was he?' This from the freckled one.

'How's that?'

'He was off-duty, and in a place he shouldn't have been.'

'There's any number of reasons why he might have been found there,' said Considine.

The bigger Guard's lip curled minutely and the other tried and failed to suppress a small snort of disgust.

'Sorry, I didn't get your name.'

'Philbin,' said the senior Guard.

'And?' She turned to the freckled one while retrieving her pen and – thank God it was there – her notebook from her shoulder bag.

'Byrne.'

They watched her write their names in her book.

'Look, Miss ... Detective ...' Garda Philbin leaned closer, his voice low. 'Don't get us wrong. What happened to Kieran shouldn't happen to anyone, but he was very – what's the word? – zealous. I always tell the young lads: *Look and learn and shut the gob.* Don't I?'

He turned to his colleague, who recited obediently: 'Look and learn and shut the gob. Yep.'

'But young Lynch always knew better. He was all set to save the whole bloody world. He was so keen, he'd almost annoy you. He was the type to walk up to the point of a knife and offer the sign of peace.'

'You think he got himself into trouble?'

'I didn't say that.'

'We better get on,' said his younger partner.

Considine pulled out the slightly creased photograph of Mottie Deegan and asked them if they had seen him lately.

Garda Philbin took it and made a play of tilting it under the light of the street lamp to see it properly.

'I know him to see, or should I say *her* – it's all a bit unisex hairdresser with that one.'

'Have you. Seen him. Lately?' She made her voice slow and deliberate, someone patiently talking to the thick.

'He performs with a girl called Jess. Sometimes here, often down at Merchants' Arch.'

The other policeman suddenly swirled his hands around his head, like he was swatting mosquitoes in slow motion. He held his mouth in a wide grin.

'That's all he does. Hand-dancing. And people still give them money.'

'I'd give him money to stop. She has a lovely voice, though,' said Philbin.

'Do they ever busk at night?'

'I haven't seen them do that, and we're by here most nights.'

Considine thanked them and bid them goodnight. She might have got more from them with a bit of charm, but she was thrown by their lack of solidarity for a colleague they worked beside day in, day out. As if Kieran had gone looking for his own death. Or as if the circumstances were so tainted that he was no longer a Guard to them.

She stood for a while outside the bright windows of McDonald's as the street livened with people kicked out of pubs, wandering home or loitering for a feed. A queue formed in front of her, a screen of tipsy people. Over the slurred chatter she heard a sudden laugh, high-pitched and raucous. So familiar it was as though someone had twitched a thread to her heart.

She glimpsed Terry and that girl Miriam passing in front of her, on the other side of the queue, caught up in some joke, shoulders bumping together. Considine turned away quickly, but she could still hear the laughter.

There were people just on the other side of the glass window, sitting brightly lit on white plastic seats, shovelling floppy chips into their mouths. They looked up at her in alarm, but did not stop eating.

She hadn't heard Terry laugh like that in a really long time.

Her ears rang with it. She waited a minute there, then slipped away from McDonald's and headed to the dark streets behind Switzer's, making sure that Terry was not in sight. She looked very deliberately at the steps her feet were taking. There was more than an hour to kill before the rendezvous with Swan, and she could really do with another drink.

19

Swan reached for another leaflet from the rack in the corridor of the gay community centre. The room with the disco didn't open until half eleven, so he waited, reading about craft fairs and theatre shows and alternative hairdressers and the like. He felt like he had swallowed a copy of *In Dublin*.

A man with very short hair, wearing braces and a grandfather shirt, kept passing by with crates of wine and beer. He had already refused Swan's offers of help. A smell of cooked meat came out of the doors every time he passed through, which was strange. Swan would have happily gone home to his bed, except that he had to prove to Considine that he was a man free of every prejudice. He reached for another leaflet – black, pink and white, *Gay Health Action* emblazoned on it and, in smaller letters, *Your guide to safer sex*. He fumbled it back into the wire rack.

The doors to the club burst open from the inside, and the legs of a table preceded the man with the braces. He set it down, then arranged some tickets and cards on the table, a petty-cash box and a stamp and inkpad. He waved Swan forward.

'No discounts for the early birds, I'm afraid.'

'How much is it?'

'Three pounds entry, dinner is extra.'

'Dinner?'

'With simple dinner, you get two tokens for beer. With deluxe dinner, you get a token for a bottle of wine. Three pounds or nine pounds.'

'Simple dinner. What's the dinner?'

'Nobody cares.'

Swan wasn't convinced this was strictly in keeping with the licensing laws. It was hard for any club to get an alcohol licence, so imaginative workarounds were common. The man handed him two little slips of paper stamped with swallows. The very same as Kieran Lynch had had in his wallet. Swan thought about asking this pleasant man if he knew Kieran, but there was the chance he wouldn't be let inside if he did.

The big room he entered was stark in its ugliness – just an old factory floor with some plywood nailed over the boards and the brick walls painted black. But someone turned off the fluorescent tubes as he reached the bar counter, and the place transformed – soft-coloured lights fell on battered tables and glitterball dots reeled on the now-indistinct walls, making it acceptably mysterious, if not glamorous.

Swan set himself up on a stool in a prime corner between the bar counter and a wall, jokes about watching your back flicking unhelpfully into his head. The man with the braces and clippered hair appeared behind the bar.

'You get about,' Swan said.

'I do indeed. What can I get you?' The man winked at him.

Taken aback, Swan pushed one of his vouchers across the counter.

A bottle of German lager was put in front of him, then the man disappeared through a door and came back with a plastic basket containing a burger and chips in a nest of napkins. So that was the smell. Swan was immediately ravenous and ate the whole thing, while the door to the club let in a slow but steady stream of people, men mostly, in casual but well-considered clothes. He felt terribly self-conscious and his beer was already empty.

The barman appeared again.

'Are you doing all right, my friend?'

'Thank you. Another beer would be good. It's been an awful week.' Swan surrendered his second token and leaned towards the young man. 'A son of a friend was killed in the park, did you hear?'

'You're a friend of Kieran Lynch's dad?'

'Eh, more of a friend of his mother.'

The barman went to get the second beer. Other customers were pressed against the counter, tokens in their fingers, trying to get his attention, but he ignored them. He placed the bottle in front of Swan but didn't let it go.

'Kieran was the best of us – one in a million. He helped so many people.'

'What did he help them with?'

'He manned the switchboard, he was a health advocate. He never stopped.'

Swan had learned enough from the downstairs notice-board and leaflets to get the gist of this. Kieran Lynch had found time for community work. More saintliness.

'So he was gay?'

The barman looked at him carefully, frowned. 'Who did you say you were now?'

'Michael,' said Swan, 'just call me Michael. I'm on my own.' His voice sounded pitiable in his ears.

'You're not a journalist?'

'Absolutely not.'

The bartender decided to accept him as a sad sack. 'You sit there, Michael. I can tell you're new to this. I'm Bert. We don't bite. Unless that's your thing.' He grinned.

'Can I just ask you, Bert ...' The barman was turning away to serve people next to Swan, so he put his hand on Bert's sleeve to stall him. The barman looked at it significantly and Swan snatched it back.

'Did you know that Kieran was in the Guards?'

'Oh yeah, we all knew that. But I believe he was closeted at work.'

'He was what?'

But the barman's attention was on others now. A teenage girl in a big apron appeared out of the kitchen with a tray of food baskets. She put a bowl on either end of the bar, one at Swan's elbow. He thought they were some kind of condiment in silver sachets, but a second look and he realised they were condoms. He picked up one labelled *extra strong*, like the ones in Kieran Lynch's pockets.

He put it back immediately. He couldn't get over the oddness of seeing contraceptives openly displayed. Even if they weren't contraceptives in this context. When Swan was young, *frenchies* could only be got hold of when someone brought some in from Britain or Northern Ireland. Boys would carry them around in their pockets, flashing them to each other to demonstrate their worldliness. And although they were legal now, you had to get them through a doctor, not just pick them up like this.

An alarming noise ripped through the air, resolving into hundreds of violins swirling over a bassy beat. A DJ stood behind a couple of record decks, fat earphones clamping down his permed curls. The volume was incredible to Swan, he could feel it vibrating his eyeballs, his intestines, his groin. He watched Bert the barman leaning over the counter, talking to two lads. His mouth moved, but the music obliterated everything. In the semi-dark, more bodies entered the room, some solo, some in groups. They strolled, they leaned against walls, they narrowed their eyes at him if he stared too much.

Swan lifted his bottle, sipped it to make this one last. He'd expected the club to be something out of the ordinary, but already couldn't remember the anticipated version clearly. He had expected flouncing and great dancing, he realised, but there was a feral intensity that was new to him.

A very good-looking man in a tight sleeveless T-shirt leaned against a wall on his own. His jacket was tied loosely around his hips in an insolent way, one foot was held flat against the wall and his expression was one of infinite boredom, though his eyes scanned the room sharply enough. Swan watched as a series of men paused near him or went up and asked for a light.

Swan wondered whether he was selling drugs, but could see nothing being exchanged. He could only conclude that he was watching the belle of the ball, the most desired man in the club. Then all at once the dance floor filled with bodies and he lost sight of that particular drama.

He smiled to himself as he remembered that another of his assumptions was that he himself might be the target for attention – his irresistible heterosexuality. There were a few other gents of his own age, as in the pub. A couple of louche fellows in waistcoats and one with a fancy paisley-print shirt had commandeered a long padded bench. They looked relaxed, convivial, cupping their ears to catch some chat or nodding their old heads to this awful, engulfing beat.

All Swan knew of disco music was what he heard snippets of, before turning over the radio station in the unit cars. Elizabeth was a real musician, a classical one. He'd known nothing much of music before they married, and was proud of all he'd absorbed from her. But she used to say that dance music was 'bestial' because it catered to the lowest of instincts, embodied in the beat. God help us. He should have seen the writing on the wall long ago. A wife who thought sex was the lowest instinct, and himself with too little experience, or confidence, to persuade her otherwise.

Two young men were kissing on a bench under a boarded-up window, arms wrapped tight around each other, legs entwined in a way that made it hard to tell whose were whose.

A hard tap on his shoulder made him jump, but when he looked round it was only Bert offering him another beer. He might have seen Swan watching the young boys.

Probably had him down as a paedophile now. Swan refused the beer because he really had no intention of navigating the toilets – that would be a novelty too far.

The girl with the apron was selling vouchers at one end of the bar, then people would walk five paces along and give the vouchers to Bert. It didn't seem like the kind of scam that would bear any scrutiny, so the licensing board probably left the gay centre alone. The odd basket of food still emerged from the back kitchen, and chips were strewn on the floor under the bar stools.

He'd give it another ten minutes in case Mottie Deegan turned up, although the place was so crowded now that the boy could be here and Swan wouldn't know it. He scanned the faces of the dancers and tried to imagine Kieran Lynch among them, with his regulation haircut. A sudden flash of whiteness and commotion drew his eye to a woman in the middle of a circle of dancers, who had taken her top off and was now dancing in a glossy black bra, an ecstatic look on her face. He wondered if she was a lesbian, but she kept approaching different men and shaking her creamy breasts under their noses, taunting them to appreciate her.

Bert slipped out of his enclosure and went to capture the woman, picking her blouse off the floor and draping it in front of her breasts. He steered her to the edge of the dance floor, where a tall boy in a satin shirt came to claim her, shaking his head and wagging his finger, but the woman was tossing her head and laughing, still eager to be undressed.

Bert arrived back at his post behind the bar, leaned over to yell in Swan's ear. 'Happens all the time in here. Girls realise no one is going to hassle them and they go wild. Start to become the hasslers.'

Swan nodded. He leaned towards the barman's ear. 'Fascinating!'

'Wha?'

'I said it's interesting – to watch.'

The bartender laughed as if Swan had said something risqué and put a small glass down in front of him, ignoring the press of people trying to order. He took a bottle from under the bar and poured a shot for Swan, nodded encouragement. It was very decent of him to be so welcoming, thought Swan, he could hardly refuse.

Not being able to hear made exchanges very basic. He took the shot glass and held it up, smiling a nod while he tried to get a whiff of its contents. Something fruity, not unpleasant. He tipped it down his throat and the bartender grinned back at him, said something that sounded like encouragement.

It lit a heat in Swan's gullet to match the heat of the room. He wanted to take off his jacket, but couldn't see anywhere to put it. The black walls were starting to shimmer with condensation. At one of the low tables he noticed a group of three men who were watching the dancing. The one in the middle was thin and pale, his cheekbones like blades. His two companions each stretched an arm behind him on the bench and seemed to enclose his frailty as they talked over him.

The thin man looked out at the dancers with a desperate expression. Swan experienced a pang of uneasiness, realising this man could well have the illness that threatened this community. He didn't feel in direct danger, it was just that he had never come across anyone affected before. He was touched at the way this man's friends protected him.

Bert the barman was dancing behind the bar as he worked, clinking bottles, pouring measures. Then a new song came on, greeted with a cheer, and the place went a little wilder, people stretching their arms out to point and sweep around whenever the singers sang 'Go West'. The cooler customers against the far wall ignored the raucous dancing, caught up with their serious flirting.

Swan found himself smiling at the antics, nodding his head. There was something infectious about people having fun. He hadn't realised there would be so much fun.

Bert was deep in conversation with someone down the other end of the bar. Swan leaned forward and looked along a line of customers to where the barman was talking. He caught a glimpse of blond hair and the impression of delicate youth, before a person leaned in to obscure him. Bert stepped backwards, looking worried, and disappeared through a door behind the bar, to the outrage of all those waiting to be served.

Swan saw the blond boy turn away from the bar, a swirl of dark material. He definitely had the look of Mottie Deegan about him. Swan abandoned his precious place at the bar and went in pursuit, squeezing through the press of thirsty bodies.

20

Meanwhile, on Wicklow Street, Considine stepped out in front of a bicycle, causing it to weave wildly, though both the cyclist and the friend perched on his back carrier managed to stay on.

'Lights!' shouted Considine after them, noticing they had none, although the fault had been entirely hers.

Knots of friends, ousted from the closing pubs, stood on the pavement, deciding what would come next. Some carried clinking bags to bring home for sessions, others assembled at bus stops. Town was emptying. Only those flush with money to spare could afford to go on to the nightclubs and restaurants where you could drink at inflated prices. All she wanted was one more drink. How could she go home to Terry – or, worse, to no Terry – just yet?

Then she remembered the Cabin, a late-night restaurant on the edge of Temple Bar. It was kitted out more like someone's front room than a proper restaurant, with a fireplace and an Irish dresser. The proprietor was notoriously cranky and you got whatever was on the menu for the evening, no concessions. Both things seemed only to increase its popularity among a certain crowd.

She walked down the dark canyon of Temple Lane,

glancing up at the gay centre's boarded windows as she passed, hearing the dull thud of the music and wondering how Swan might be getting on. She'd love to take a peek at him, probably glowering in a corner, but she couldn't risk her private and professional lives overlapping any more than they already had. The thought occurred to her that Terry and her new friend might also be there. Her stomach hurt.

The restaurant looked closed as she approached, but there were telltale lines of brightness where the curtains didn't quite meet. She opened the door to a clamour of music and stamping, but saw nothing until she wrestled aside the heavy curtain that formed a small curved space between the restaurant and the door. Heat and smoke and rich cooking smells enveloped her. The tables had been pulled together to make one big table, and no one noticed her come in since they were all watching a girl standing on a box in the corner, playing a guitar and singing some rousing song. The remains of a large cake lay devastated in a litter of white icing and yellow crumbs.

Seamus, the owner, appeared magically at her side, greying curls circling his head under a grimy chef's toque.

'No problems, I hope.'

He never forgot a face – one of the elements that made this eccentric place successful. She had been there twice, once as a customer and again in the course of an investigation, but here he was, greeting her like a slightly unwelcome family member.

'More of a social visit, Seamus.'

'It's a private party tonight. But just you wait there.'

He slipped into the kitchen. Considine leaned against a wall, the door curtain draping against her side like a light, comforting embrace. Nobody from the raucous party paid her a blind bit of notice. Seamus reappeared with a large glass of red wine and put it in her hand.

'Would you like a slice of cake? I have some put by.'

'You're very kind. But no.'

'Well, give us a nod before you go.'

She smiled. It was a polite way of saying she wouldn't be getting another drink out of him. *My road to corruption is going at a rapid pace*, she thought. *First the omissions, now the backhanders.* She took a gulp of wine, rough-edged but perfect.

The singer finished her song and most of the room clapped loudly, though some were so deep in their shouted conversations they didn't even notice. The girl had on a bright dress, made of some vintage fabric printed with loud fruit and flowers, and she also had some silk flowers tucked into the scarf that wrapped her head and gathered her curls like a bouquet. She was a delight to look at.

She started to sing something slow, and Considine felt it soak her. The girl's voice was beautiful, low and clear. It was a familiar melody, but she couldn't name it. Her throat felt thick all of a sudden. She should put the wine down. She lifted it to her lips instead. The chatter at the big table carried on, polluting the poignant song.

Considine watched the girl's face. Although her voice was full of heartbreak, her eyes scanned the people in front of her, appraising. Suddenly she spotted Considine in her corner and decided to focus her gaze there. *Oh, great.* Now the love song was being sung straight to her, the sad weirdo at the back.

The curtain beside her billowed as someone entered, a puff of night air. The singer's gaze shifted away to the newcomer, and her eyes slanted with pleasure. *Well, that romance didn't last long.* Considine looked around at her usurper.

It was him. Mottie Deegan, the boy she had worn her shoes out looking for all night. Stand still and they will come to you.

He was wearing a loose black outfit and was carrying several bags. His long hair was tucked up under a tweed cap, but there was no mistaking him. A face both innocent and wily, his poise consciously elegant. He held an arm out towards the singer, tapped its wrist with a finger. *Hurry up.*

The girl was still singing about her yearning heart, but nodded mid-note to say she had got the message. She had to be Jess, Considine realised, the girl he busked with.

Considine pretended to study the traditional dresser that stood beside her. She couldn't question him here, shouldn't even acknowledge him when she was half pissed, but she couldn't just let him get away.

Up on the tiny stage, Jess strummed a loud flourish to indicate that her song and her set had finished. Everyone looked around then and applauded or banged their hands directly on the tables, setting cutlery dancing and wine shivering in the glasses.

Mottie kept fidgeting and looking at his watch. He was only a foot away from Considine now. He had a green bag over one shoulder; she recognised it as an old Aer Lingus flight bag. The strangest things became fashionable. On the other side of the restaurant, Jess was zipping her guitar into a soft case, and Seamus had come up to talk to her.

'Come on!' Mottie shouted above the diners. Jess half turned and made a quick gesture for 'money'. Rubbing her thumb quickly against her fingertips.

'She's a wonderful performer,' Considine found herself saying.

Mottie turned and looked at her, dipping his chin and raising his eyebrows.

'Have you got another gig to go to?' she persisted.

He looked at her glass of wine, then at her face again, and something changed in his eyes. She felt him recognise her.

'Oh, *now* you're curious?' he said.

'I was hoping we could talk about that.'

'I need to go.'

Jess appeared beside him.

'Please—' said Considine, but her reaching hand touched only air. With a quick swirl of curtain, they were gone.

She took a last gulp of wine, abandoned her glass to the dresser and set off after them. They were already haring along Fleet Street, guitar and bags swaying and bumping against their sides. They were shouting at each other, arguing as they ran. Considine couldn't tell if they were running away from her or towards something else, but after a few minutes of hugging the walls and dodging pre-emptively into doorways, she was convinced they were not aware of her at all. They headed for Westmoreland Street, occasionally walking to catch their breath, then trotting once more.

Four lit-up buses were waiting on the curve of College Street, and Mottie and Jess dodged through the sparse traffic towards them. They clambered onto a number seven and disappeared up the stairs while Considine was stuck on a traffic island. *I see you*, she muttered. She made it to the bus just as the driver closed the doors. She knocked sharply and managed to find and press her Garda ID up against the window glass. He grumpily pressed the lever and the doors opened with a mechanical sigh.

'Thank you.'

He didn't answer. The bus was fairly full of people, mostly young and merry. At that hour, it was probably the last bus. She decided to stay downstairs, hoping they didn't spot her getting on. She felt a bit dizzy from the chase, and hung on to the bars as she made her way down the bus to the last free seat, her palms clammy on the metal. It was a huge relief to sit down, but she looked up to see Mottie Deegan stepping off the bus, alone. The doors rattled shut and the bus started to move off before she could react. She half rose, not wanting to get into some argument with the driver in front of this crowd. The drink hadn't made her stupid, but it did make her vulnerable. Mottie was standing on the pavement, waving up at the top deck and giving a good-luck thumbs up. He didn't seem aware that Considine was there at all.

The bus gained speed as it rounded Trinity College, its engine roaring. Jess must still be upstairs. She could either get out at the next stop and go back to try and find Mottie or wait until the girl got out and follow her, perhaps learn where she lived or talk to her; that could also lead to

Mottie. Considine had more than an hour to spare before she was due to meet Swan. It seemed better to have a bird in the hand than nothing at all.

21

Swan was dancing. Not that others would recognise it as such. He moved from one foot to the other and worked his arms like a runner getting nowhere. The music was loud enough to take you over. He stopped being mortified once he realised that no one gave a damn. The truth of alcohol was upon him. Two lads twirled by, imitated his effortful moves for a moment, then smiled and twirled on.

After looking for Mottie Deegan in the crowd, he had lost his prime position at the bar counter. Maybe it hadn't been the boy at all. He stood near the dance floor, gathering himself to leave, but got caught up watching the gyrations of the youth. It had all been ballroom in his day, the misery of a bad foxtrot, so he couldn't help feeling a kind of admiration for the fact that everyone here was doing their own thing. There was a small posse of punks near him, holding their cans of Carlsberg and affecting to look down their noses at the line of people doing the hustle in front of them. Swan knew it was the hustle, because the song they were dancing to kept exhorting everyone to 'Do the Hustle'. He felt very with it, for once.

He may have been smiling. In any case, something caused the extravagantly drunk girl with the penchant for striptease to appear in front of him with a pouting look.

'C'mon, dance!' she shouted and pulled him out onto the floor. He looked around for someone to pass her on to. She shimmied in front of him with an impressive flexibility and rubbed her hands through her masses of hair, lifting it in a sensual way. She arched forward and her breasts brushed against his shirt front, making him take a sudden step back into the sharp elbows of a particularly committed dancer.

The drunk woman's friend appeared behind her, took a look at Swan's expression, mouthed 'Sorry' and steered her away. Some young men smiled at him in a charitable way. The music really was rather good. It had a lot of 'go' to it. Blasts of brass and that addictive beat. So Swan kept dancing to a song about young hearts running free. His heart was not so young any more, but it certainly was free.

He swayed and stepped, and he tried not to think about how ridiculous he must look. His mind wandered to Considine, to that moment when they were holding hands on the corner of Dame Street. Considine ... what if the world still held some surprises for him? She was too young for him, he knew that, but when their hands locked, it seemed as if some strong emotion was moving between them. It would be easy to love her, as easy as opening a door. She didn't like to talk about boyfriends, but she was an extremely good-looking girl, she must have had relationships.

The track ended, and silence followed. Puffs of dry ice slid from under the DJ's rostrum and the crowd that had been dancing moved into a semicircle. A fanfare blasted out of the speakers and a woman stepped into a sharp-edged spotlight.

She was tall, with a candyfloss cloud of blonde hair, and she wore a full-length black sequined dress and a white fur stole. A blast of old-style jazz and the woman started to lip-synch along with Marilyn Monroe, singing 'My Heart Belongs to Daddy'. While she pretended to sing, she wiggled and pouted, she blew kisses and sensually peeled off one evening glove. It was only gradually that Swan realised the performer was not a woman. And even when he was sure, he couldn't quite put his finger on why. Her height, a certain breadth to her shoulders. Maybe it was just the air of a shared joke that prevailed between artist and audience.

The song ended as the second glove was pitched into the audience, and the club descended into blackness and cheering. The dry ice was catching at his throat now, and the place was already pretty full of cigarette smoke. When the disco lights came back on, they created cones of coloured mist.

A light flickered above him, and when he looked up he noticed smoke pouring down from some ceiling vents. Not dry ice, but thick black stuff.

Swan made a dive for the DJ's desk. 'Stop the music!'

The DJ squinted at him, not hearing. Swan made a frantic throat-cutting motion and the man pressed a button to stop the backing tape. Broken shouts filled the space that the music vacated. Everyone was scanning in different directions, aware something was wrong. Swan looked up again and saw a line of orange near the back wall, sparks falling from a ceiling vent.

The smoke was thick, ugly, tasting of burnt plastic. Bright

lights rattled on, illuminating the smoke haze and the press of bodies around the door. Swan looked for another exit, remembering the door behind the bar. Bert the barman was somewhere in the crowd – Swan could make out his voice, calling for calm. A few people sat on the banquettes in a daze and Swan went up to each of them, pulling them up and urging them towards the exit.

There must be another way out. He dashed behind the bar and opened the door he had seen Bert go through earlier, but it led upstairs, not down.

Just then the fluorescent tubes went out with a sizzle, leaving the club in darkness. There were a couple of emergency lights, but you could barely make out the glow of them, so thick was the smoke now. He could still hear the voices of people trying to get out of the club. *Stop pushing!* they cried at each other.

Swan was torn. Go over and try to calm the crowd – a shouter among shouters – or check that upstairs was empty. Perhaps the air would be better upstairs. He stepped onto the staircase and closed the door behind him.

The lights were still working on the floor above, a rough warren of storerooms. One room had a couple of mattresses on the floor, blankets bundled on them. Swan quickly kicked the bundles to make sure no one was under them. Smoke seeped through the gaps in the floorboards.

There was a sink in one corner of that room and, over-taken by the instructions of some half-remembered safety film, he quickly went and wet his handkerchief and tied it cowboy-style around his face. The last room was an empty dressing room, with a gap-toothed line of light bulbs around a vast mirror and someone's make-up scattered on the counter. A cigarette was propped in an ashtray, but it was impossible to tell if it was still burning, since the room brimmed with smoke from below. There was a head sitting on the counter, but when Swan squinted his stinging eyes, he saw it was a blonde wig on a block. Ah, Marilyn. Where had she got to?

The stairway that led to the roof was a mere wooden ladder, but Swan climbed it anyway. He could see the night sky through the open hatch at the top, and his lungs were longing for relief. He tumbled out onto patchy asphalt, sucking in great gulps of fresh night air, then coughing it out in spasms. The city rang with the whoops of sirens approaching. But smoke was billowing from the hatch he had just left. He kicked it shut and got to his feet.

He found himself standing in a roof valley between two shallow slopes of slates. On top of one of those slopes, a strange figure was silhouetted against the smoky glow. This person was tall and wearing nothing but a pair of fishnet stockings and a strange nylon cap. But it was the face that terrified Swan: huge, dark eyes like a demon, a mouth that looked bloody.

'I'm no good with heights,' said the ghoul, metamorphosing into a man in make-up. Marilyn.

'Did you look for a way down?'

'I think you just came up it.'

'I mean another way.'

'Won't they come with ladders?' the man shouted over the noise of the sirens.

Swan didn't want to voice his doubts over whether you

could get a fire engine down the narrow canyon of Temple Lane. Smoke gushed from the end of the roof that was nearest the river. Swan ran in the opposite direction to the low wall that separated the gay centre from its neighbour. There was a nauseating gap where a narrow alley ran between them at ground level. Something a film hero might leap across, or hang by his fingertips from, but not Swan, though the female impersonator might be more agile in his tights.

He made his way up to the ridge where Marilyn was. The roof ran straight off the front of the building, with no retaining wall to stop them from falling. He could see the reflections of blue-and-red siren lights playing on the brickwork of the building opposite, but they couldn't see all the way down to what was happening in the lane.

'Where are the ladders?' asked Marilyn.

'Where indeed?' Swan said. He set off to look at the back of the building. Smoke had started to flow from under the slates in places. When he looked over the top of the second ridge, he felt a wild blast of relief. There was not only a low wall that they could hold on to, but he could see two dark metal hoops of an access ladder straddling that wall. He slid down to look closer. Thank God, there was an intact ladder there, leading into a dark void that was probably a light-well for the back of the building. There was no smoke rising from the void. Yet.

'Hey, Marilyn!'

The man in the make-up appeared above him, balancing gracefully on the slates. 'It's Paddy, actually.'

'Do you know what's down the back here?'

Paddy looked around to get his bearings. 'I've been out in a yard back there for a smoke. I think it does lead to an alleyway, but don't sue me.'

There was a sound like a gust of wind, and water started to fall on them, a waving swathe of water coming from fire-hoses at the front.

'Come down from there!' Swan shouted, and Paddy duly slid on his arse down to the narrow cleft between the slates and the perimeter wall. Swan caught Paddy's arm as his legs crumpled against the stone blocks.

'You okay?'

Paddy nodded, but his eyes looked terrified.

Swan grabbed hold of the ladder hoops and shook vigorously. They stayed put. The fire-hose stream had moved off to concentrate on where the smoke was thickest, but it could be back to wash them off the roof at any moment.

'There aren't great choices here, Paddy. We can hang about and hope they put the fire out before the roof collapses, or climb down into the dark.'

'I'm not great with heights,' Paddy said and began to scramble towards the ridge. He jerked his hands back. 'These slates are hot!'

'We've got to go down,' said Swan, 'or try to.'

'They won't see us back there.'

'They won't see us if we fall through it, either.'

Far beneath them came muffled collapsing sounds, bricks tumbling onto softness. Paddy made the sign of the cross.

'I'll go first,' said Swan. 'Then you can fall on me.'

It was supposed to be a joke, but Paddy's face was set

in grim determination. Swan swung one leg over onto the first steel rung.

He didn't think about the distance to the ground or the hungry, yawning space. He thought about the bar he held fast to, the stones of the wall he straddled, the first rung, then the next. He ignored the wind at his back. When only his head remained above the parapet, he made Paddy follow, talking him through the motions of getting onto the ladder, loosening a hand to help place his stockinged feet onto the first rung, then the next. It was good to have someone to help, it kept his mind away from panic.

In terms of the rickety ladder, it might have been better for them to go one at a time. But he couldn't have sent Paddy into the unknown or, worse, left him on the perilous roof. Swan could barely see the dirty brick passing in front of his face. He wished he had counted the rungs from the beginning.

These were the thoughts he was thinking when his foot hit air.

A curse escaped him, followed by a kick in the head from Paddy, who was on top of him in an instant.

'Back up a bit. There's no more ladder!' said Swan.

'Can't see a fucking thing,' said Paddy. 'Do you have anything in your pocket?'

Swan was tentatively moving his foot about on the bricks, hoping for a touch of metal. 'What do you mean?'

'To drop.'

'Ah.'

Swan dug into his trouser pocket and came up with a few coins. He dropped one – they heard nothing. Nothing at all. Panic took a cold clutch on his heart. He felt they were suspended over a bottomless hole, some place of illogic.

'It probably fell on something soft,' said Paddy calmly.

Swan dropped the second and third coins together, casting them outwards. After a moment there came two distinct small sounds, splashes.

'How far down would you say that was?' said Swan, trying to sound normal. He really didn't want to climb back up to a burning roof.

'Too fucking far,' said Paddy.

22

Considine was regretting her choice. The bus had passed Ballsbridge and she was now headed deep into south Dublin along Merrion Road. She should have got off the bus just after Mottie Deegan did. Was the girl still upstairs even? Tiredness was making her doubt the most basic things. Soon after they passed St Vincent's Hospital a bunch of young women got on, and Considine followed them closely up the stairs.

Jess was still there, in one of the front seats, her guitar like a thin-necked companion beside her. Considine took a seat behind the girls she'd followed, then went back downstairs with them three stops later and retrieved her original seat.

The bus had passed Blackrock when Jess finally came bundling down the stairs, laden with her bags and guitar. She rang the bell and waited an inch from Considine for the middle doors to open. Once she was gone, Considine went to nip out after her, but the doors slammed shut in her face and the bus started off.

'Hey!' Considine pulled her way to the front of the bus and demanded that the driver stop immediately. He took his time, signalling elaborately and slowing. She couldn't afford to lose time. Jess had headed in the opposite direction and might be gone.

She pulled the emergency door lever and jumped out. The street was empty, all the shops and pubs closed, but as she jogged back to the bus stop, rounding the curve of the street, a telephone box appeared, and illuminated beside it was Jess, recognisable at any distance with her bright orange headscarf. She was piling her guitar and bags up outside the phone box, and Considine noticed the light falling on a small green bag, the one Mottie had had over his shoulder.

Why did she have so much stuff with her?

Considine waited in a doorway while Jess made a call involving excited gestures with her free hand. There were still a few people out and about, dog walkers mainly. They greeted each other with nods and quick words. A civilised neighbourhood. Jess suddenly left the booth, looking cross, and started to gather up her stuff again. She would be easy to follow, weighed down with all that, so Considine let her get a bit of distance before she set off in pursuit. It was odd to find herself back in Blackrock again. Was it yesterday they had talked to the Lynchs? No, she realised it had been only that morning. Surely this was longest day that ever was. She looked at her watch – half-past midnight. Technically yesterday then.

She walked after the girl, keeping to the shadows, eyes on the pavement in case Jess happened to look round. When the girl turned down the road towards the Lynchs' house – the very same road Considine had driven with Swan that morning – Considine felt briefly triumphant. This had been worth doing.

But the street was quiet and mostly walled, with no

parked cars or trees to conceal her. She had no choice but to hover behind the concrete trunk of a street light and watch Jess make her way towards the Lynchs' wooden gate, half visible at the end of the street.

There were still a few lit windows in the upper storeys of the mews houses along one side of the road, old coach houses of the fine red-bricks that lined a parallel avenue. After Jess got some distance from her, Considine paced slowly down the road to where an untrimmed hedge ballooning over the pavement offered some deep shadow. One hand undid the buckle of her leather bag, the one that Swan was constantly bemused by, as he never found the need for more than pockets. *Were you a girl scout, Gina, is that it?* She found her bicycle lamp and gripped it.

She could not think of Swan without guilt. Not guilt that she had left him sitting waiting in a café, for that couldn't be helped. No, it was guilt that she had stopped being honest with him. About herself; about meeting Kieran Lynch the night he died. The thought of Swan's too-warm fingers clutching hers on the street corner earlier was disturbing. He had never been a needy man before, nor had he ever talked about his marriage. All the others did. Making their wives into the butt of their comedy routines.

Jess seemed to be waiting at the Lynchs' gate now, her bags at her feet. Considine stared at the gate, waiting for the moment it opened, wondering how close she could get once that happened, if she could slip in after Jess. She rubbed her eyes to refresh them and Jess was gone. But the gate hadn't opened.

Considine sprinted to the end of the road and discovered

a laneway on the right, running alongside the railway track and bound by high walls on both sides. The lane appeared to be empty. But there were various doors – the back doors of gardens and garages – in the right-hand wall, and she could just make out a huddled shape, like someone crouching, in one doorway. Considine switched on her bicycle torch and made her way slowly forward.

It was only Jess's guitar, a carrier bag and a strappy rucksack. She toed the luggage, nudging it apart. The green bag was missing, as was Jess, but the door that she had left them at was firmly locked. *Where is she?* Considine suddenly noticed an archway on the other side of the road. A concrete bollard guarded its entrance from cars, and the ground ran down steeply inside. It was a passage under the railway, leading to the sea, probably. There was an old sign for a swimming place on the wall.

The little tunnel was unlit, but short; she could see dim light from the shore on the other side. Her torch would make her too visible, so she turned it off. Considine listened hard – only the sound of waves – then walked into the tunnel. It was not as simple as it first looked. There was a branch off to the right, and also a strange light-well with a portcullis on top. She stopped to listen again and heard steps approaching on the damp cobbles, but it was hard to tell from which direction. She threw herself into the passage that branched off the main tunnel just as Jess passed.

Jess didn't notice Considine. She was agitated, talking to herself. Considine waited until the girl got far enough away to trail again, but as Jess stepped out into the lane,

Considine noticed that she didn't have the green bag. She was picking up the other pieces of luggage now. The bag definitely wasn't there.

Had she met someone on the shore? Considine decided to take a look.

The tunnel ran out onto a concrete sea wall and a rocky shore beyond it. She could make out a line of white foam where the tame waves lapped the rocks. Out on the bay were the red lights of ships and the dark bulk of Howth. The DART trains had stopped for the night, all was quiet. There was no one on the shore that she could see, but up on the sea wall the rudimentary shelters meant for changing bathers could conceal someone.

Considine walked out on the rocks as far as the water, so that she could turn back and get a better look at the shore. She lit her torch again and let it play weakly over the shelters, back at the tunnel entrance, along the wall and the narrow shore of stones. To her right, rolls of barbed wire and an ugly metal fence discouraged intruders from the gardens of a private house.

She suddenly realised that she was looking at the Lynchs' house, its bulk pale in the warm night and an upper bay window blazing with light like a warning to ships at sea. And yet she couldn't see any way in – no gate, no break in the fence. Jess had not been down here long enough for any elaborate manoeuvres.

It was only by patiently scanning the whole area with her torch that Considine found the bag, a patch of green tucked between two boulders below the sea wall, the waves practically spitting on it as they rolled nearer.

She picked her way across the stones and pulled it gently up by its strap – it was lighter than she expected. Which was good. No firearms or explosives, no small bodies. It crinkled lightly when pressed. She cradled it under her arm and retreated to a bench in one of the swimming shelters. She put her light on the bench and carefully unzipped the bag. Inside were crumpled newspapers massed around something flat and solid, also wrapped in newspaper. It was the size of a large bread board. She slid it out and rested it on her knee. She should wait, bring it back to the depot, but she badly wanted to know whether it was worth the trouble, and the wind was already unwrapping it for her, fluttering the loose sheets apart.

It was a panel of wood. Dark wood with strange brass nail heads dotting it and an old, torn label. She eased the board out of the paper. The ink on the label was too worn to read in the dimming light of her bicycle torch. Its glow was yellowing by the minute.

She flipped the board to look at the other side and was dazzled as the colours hit her eye. It was a painting. Almost cartoonish. A sweet-faced figure in the middle of a circular bonfire. Soldiers outside that circle reeling away from him, from his beauty, it seemed. He had a gold halo – real gold leaf pressed on top of the paint, it looked like. She shouldn't have touched this thing with her bare hands; it was obviously very old, probably valuable. She peered at the little face under a layer of clear varnish at the centre of it. Held in time. But she knew so little, it could be a fake.

The wind whipped up then – plucking one of the pages away and up in the dark air. She heard stones clinking together and cowered into the corner of the shelter. But it wasn't a person, just the rising tide, rolling rock over rock. She quickly wrapped the remaining page around the painting and nestled it back among the newspaper clusters.

She checked her watch and made her way back along the sea wall. A last glance back before the tunnel. One in the morning, and the lights in the Lynch house were blazing still.

23

Swan stood among the evacuated clubbers and watched the fire progress. They had been pushed back to halfway down the lane, behind a makeshift barrier, but the firemen made no effort to disperse them, being fully occupied. Paddy, the female impersonator, was at his side, with Swan's jacket over his shoulders for the slight chill in the air. He stood in his ripped tights on a square of cardboard that someone had fetched for him, but refused further offers of clothing from the small crowd, who all appeared to revere him.

Swan now revered him too.

Stuck up on that ladder, with only air below them, Paddy had filled his lungs and bellowed, loud as a car horn. Swan had joined in, for there were no cunning tricks left, no intelligent strategies, just animal howling. And they came – pale beams whisking through the yard below them, an endless clattering of ladders, then rescue in the form of pale-helmeted men approaching from the gloom, guiding them to the ground rung by rung. The moment Swan's soles struck the solidity of concrete, his knees had started to shake uncontrollably.

But now he had a hold of himself. Shocked sober and more wide-awake than he had been in months.

It was hard to leave the spectacle of the fire. The warehouse adjacent to the gay centre was also alight, and sparks fountained from the roofs and windows in a hypnotic way. A cumulus column of black smoke slanted into the night sky, south towards the Castle. Even though he stood at a distance, fragments of burnt paper and smuts floated down on his hair and shoulders like dark snow.

Around him, people were either weeping —*We could have been killed* — or outraged — *The bastards can't even let us have one fucking building. One dangerous kip.*

The ground beneath their feet rumbled as another wall inside one of the buildings collapsed.

As far as Swan knew, there were no flats in this street, it was all commercial property or abandoned, but a pair of firemen were knocking on doors and shining their torches over grimy windows. One panned his beam over the row of watchers, stopping at Swan.

'Didn't we fish you off that ladder? G'wan home, man.'

Swan reached for his inside pocket to show his badge, but he wasn't wearing his jacket. Of course he wasn't. He turned to Paddy, who had clasped his hands under his chin, like someone praying. The light of the flames was reflected in his doleful eyes, and the dried mascara-tears on his cheeks made him look like some strange icon.

'I need my jacket back.'

'And you can take your girlfriend with you,' the fireman muttered as he walked away, low enough for only Swan to hear.

He wanted to grab the man, wipe the smirk off his face, but Paddy was handing the jacket back with a wry smile, and it suddenly seemed crass to be taking on a fight that wasn't truly his. Or was it?

There was another roar of falling masonry from the burning buildings. A fire engine that was jammed into the top of the lane was contracting its extended ladder, preparing to get further away. It might be all they could do now to contain the fire from spreading more widely.

It was after one – Considine could be waiting in the café on the quays. She would know about the fire by now, perhaps be worried about him. There were still about a dozen clubbers standing around, many of them soot-streaked or wet from the hoses. One had a sprained ankle held delicately lifted as he leaned on his companion's shoulder. In a doorway a man was watching on his own, smoking a cigarette. His oiled hair and baggy jacket looked odd amongst this crowd. As he noticed Swan noticing him, he threw his fag down and moved further away, just as a hatchback car came reversing fast up the lane towards them.

Badger Stacy, thought Swan, *what the hell is he doing here?* The proximity of Badger and fire did not seem like a coincidence.

Bert the bartender got out of the hatchback and opened the boot.

'Everybody – help me lift this stuff!'

Swan watched while Bert mobilised the remaining clubbers to move a pile of boxes and files that had at some stage been brought out of the gay centre and left on the pavement.

'What's happening?' Swan asked.

'I couldn't let the office stuff burn. The switchboard

173

files, the photographs, the newsletters. That's our history, that is.'

'I'm amazed they let you in to get it.'

'I didn't ask for permission,' said Bert, watching the removal of what was left of the gay centre's records, along with a fax machine and a tea urn. 'We'll take them down to the Project!' he shouted. 'Some decent bloke has the key and says they'll store everything for us.'

Swan remembered something he'd seen earlier, before the smoke even started. 'Before you go, Bert, there was a young guy – longish blond hair – talking to you at the bar. And you went upstairs straight afterwards. What was that about?'

'I'm not sure I remember.' Bert looked up and away, as if thinking deeply.

'His name might be Mottie Deegan?'

Bert looked back at Swan, moved closer. 'You didn't hear this from me, right? He told me to check my fire exits – I thought he was warning me of a break-in. Thank God I did.'

'That's interesting.'

'You're not going to go question him?'

Swan felt mildly annoyed that Bert had spotted him for what he was. 'I will, if I have to.'

'Come back and see us sometime,' Bert said, 'though where we'll be, I don't know.'

Swan started towards the quays. He was hoping to catch up with Badger Stacy. Badger was a foot soldier in the criminal ranks, mainly associated with Dan Barry's lot. Something of a pyromaniac in his teens, he'd been fairly low-profile in recent years. It could be because Barry had taught him how to keep a low profile. Barry was Dublin's premier crime boss, though Swan didn't like to give him the credit of a title. He thought himself a kingpin, but Barry was just a common psychopath who'd learned the trick of getting other people to do his dirty work, including intimidating any witnesses who might point the finger. Robberies and drugs were his main business lines, with arson and death as occasional diversions.

Swan saw a figure disappear round the corner of East Essex Street and broke into a run. He didn't make it very far before his lungs failed to meet the demand of his legs and he had to stop to cough and spit. He'd inhaled more of the dirty smoke than he had realised.

He located a crumpled handkerchief in his jacket and wiped it across his mouth. Badger Stacy had vanished. No matter. He could be located again. Swan leaned for a minute against the wall of the Granary pub. There were filthy streaks of rust and soot on his trousers and jacket, and he smelt like a kipper burned in its paper wrapping. He would see if Considine was at the café, then go back to his mother's house and change.

The Graceland Café was a Dublin institution. Its plate-glass windows were fogged with condensation despite the warm night, blurring the handwritten menu and signs for ice cream and *Italian Coffee*. The smell of fried food cast its lure into the street.

All the tables and booths were occupied, some to over-flowing by friends crowded in together, others by just one nighthawk. The Graceland was where the society of the sleepless gathered; not only a police haunt, it attracted taxi drivers, musicians and all sorts of merrymakers who wouldn't go to bed. Despite the poster of Elvis in his jumpsuit pomp, the café was named for its owner and presiding spirit, Grace Mangan, a lady of substantial but indeterminate age.

Swan entered, stepping over a fiddle case that had slid into the central aisle, and spotted Declan Barrett and Ownie Hannigan at a back table. Considine wasn't with them.

Grace herself – enormous, raven-haired – bore down on him with four groaning plates of food: fried-bread triangles, black pudding and rashers layered over the skirts of fried eggs. She brushed against him as she passed, paused to look down at his dishevelled clothes and frowned.

'What's happened to you?'

'Sorry. Occupational hazards and all.'

With a backwards tilt of her head, she indicated that he should go and sit with his colleagues.

Barrett had stopped eating, cutlery frozen, to watch Swan approach. Hannigan twisted round and reeled back in mock horror. Swan slid in beside Barrett, so that he could keep a watch on the door.

'You smell like an ashtray,' said Hannigan. 'Were you at this fire? Don't tell me you were in the gay place. Does your wife know?'

'I was passing by. Shouldn't you two be up at the park?'

'We've been there all evening. Nothing doing. The rent boys are wise to the fact we'd be there.'

'Maybe they were out dancing with Swan.' Barrett grinned, spearing the last piece of a sausage on his plate.

'I thought you were on a health kick, Barrett – all that cross-country harriers stuff you do.'

'That's why I can eat like this,' he said equably.

Grace appeared, taking her notepad out of her pocket and licking the end of her pencil stub. Her husband, Larry, shouted something about orders from the kitchen hatch in the back.

Although Swan had eaten the hamburger 'dinner' at the disco, he found himself hungry again. Something to do with cheating death. 'I'll have the mixed grill,' he said. 'And a mug of tea.'

'You can wash your hands in the lavatory. I don't mind you using it.'

He looked down. His hands were absolutely filthy, black soot under his nails.

As he got up to obey, Hannigan said, 'Can't wait to hear this story. Two more coffees please, my darlin'.'

Their plates were empty, dulled by smears of cooling fat and streaks of yolk. The tin ashtray was half full of butts. They must have been here for some time. Swan headed for the small jacks beside the kitchen with the *Staff only* sign on the door.

He cleaned himself up as best he could with soap and bits of wadded toilet roll, then re-joined the table to find a mug of dark tea already delivered. Hannigan and Barrett were silent, grinning in anticipation.

Swan had no inclination to entertain them. Stalling, he added an unaccustomed spoon of sugar to his tea.

The booth across from them was occupied by men that Swan recognised as having been at the club. One of them was talking intently, stabbing the table with his finger for emphasis while the others listened, leaning in.

Hannigan followed his gaze. 'Someone's not happy about something.'

'They were evacuated from the fire.'

'Should be glad they got out,' said Barrett.

'Really, Declan? Glad?'

'Could have been worse is all I meant. Buildings round there are death-traps.'

'The fire engines did seem to be struggling to get close enough.'

Hannigan asked, 'I suppose it's too early to know if it was arson or accidental?'

'It is,' said Swan. He wasn't going to say anything about seeing Badger Stacy in these surroundings, and Hannigan himself was never the most discreet.

'You're a real raconteur, do you know that?'

Barrett laughed. 'Where's herself?'

'I thought she might be here,' said Swan.

'Ach, you didn't leave her in the fire, did you?'

Swan's ears were ringing – either from the music he had danced to or the commotion afterwards. Hannigan, thwarted from the banter he was seeking, started pontificating to Barrett about 'that lot' – very obviously indicating the group of gay men still engaged in furious discussion.

'I'm not a prejudiced man, not at all, but it's a health issue these days.' Hannigan seemed to Swan to be deliberately loud, but no one was paying him any heed. Declan

Barrett looked embarrassed. He was a lot younger and was likely to have more progressive ideas than Hannigan, though he hid them well.

Someone at a table of folky types, also waiting for food, flung his head back and warbled out the first line of 'The Aul' Triangle'. he was immediately hushed by his table-mates. Grace did not allow singing in her establishment and disobedience would only delay their food further.

A plate was lowered past Swan's eyes onto the table, a bounty of rashers, a glistening chop, mushrooms and tomatoes. He shook the paper napkin off his knife and fork, said inner words of thanks.

'I mean Plato himself would be embarrassed by the things I saw in those trees,' Hannigan continued.

'Plato, is it?' commented Barrett.

'I thought you said it was quiet up in the park,' said Swan.

'Everyone knows what goes on up there. It's no wonder they get ill from it.'

'Detective Swan! Phone!' Larry the cook was shouting through the hatch, a sweating gargoyle. All heads in the café swivelled to the detectives' table. Swan put his cutlery down and made his way back to the kitchen door, where the restaurant phone hung.

'I'm sorry, Grace,' he shouted, to where she was taking plates out of the dishwasher, and lifted the dangling receiver.

'Hello?'

'It's me. I'm kind of stuck.'

He'd known it would be Considine.

179

She gave directions to a phone booth in Blackrock, and Swan promised to get there as soon as he could get hold of a car.

'A taxi might be quicker,' he suggested, thinking mournfully of his food.

'There's no taxis out here. I'm quite near the Lynchs' house.'

'Is that where you were?'

'Come get me and I'll tell you.'

His heart-rate quickened – not for the Lynchs, but for what he felt was something intimate in her choice of words. He remembered how he had felt about her when he had been dancing. Something momentous might be happening between them, or nothing at all.

Hannigan said he could borrow their radio car as long as he hurried back with it. Swan put money on the table, took a fresh napkin and wrapped it around the bone end of the lamb chop so that he could take it with him. 'Help yourselves to the rest.'

There were only a few cars parked outside and he spotted the unmarked Ford Granada immediately. He stood to take some quick bites of the lamb. Wouldn't do to get the steering wheel greased up. What had taken Considine out to the south side anyway?

A small blond figure, carrying bags and wearing a cape, emerged from Merchants' Arch and hurried over the Ha'penny Bridge. The smell of the fire still hung in the air. The city was full of oddities this summer night.

Swan dropped the chop regretfully in a drain and unlocked the car.

24

That woman who helps Desmond run his house answers the door. What's her name? Majella. Like 'margarine' and 'jelly' mashed together.

'Look at you,' she says, plucking at my cape. 'Are you doing *The Phantom of the Opera* tonight?'

She takes one of my carrier bags as if it is precious and we go along to the big cloakroom. The hall is lit by candle-light: red walls, gold frames, floorboards shiny as treacle. Mr de Courcy loves his creaky glamour.

'Have you brought your real costume now, he was very particular about the gold shorts.'

'I'll bet he was.'

'Cheeky boy!' She mimes a face-slap and hurries off to her canapés. She is a bit like one of my holy aunts, and completely unshockable at the same time. What can she make of Desmond's soirées?

I get ready in the little cloakroom off the big cloakroom. I wash, then rub oil on my pale skin and wish I had invested in a bit of fake tan. I'm thinking about Jess as well. I hate it when we disagree.

I thought we should just dump the painting, let someone find it on a doorstep, like an infant. It's worth a lot, that's my guess. It's worth enough to hurt people for. To burn down

181

buildings for. *He saw me, Jess.* But she thinks it should be with the other paintings, and she says she knows who has them. When the men were moving things out during the week she took a peek from the roof. I don't know whether to believe her, frankly; she's as bad as me with the stories.

'Maurice, my boy!'

Here's Desmond. He's growing his hair out and has it parted in the middle. Oscar Wilde has a lot to answer for.

'You don't mind serving a few drinks, do you?'

'Just to start with?' We've been through this hundreds of times.

'You look *edible*, darling.'

He hires me as a dancer – he pays Equity rates – but I end up circulating with a tray while his guests make propositions that range from gentle to obscene. We somehow never get to the dancing bit. I think Desmond is too short-sighted to realise I'm too old to be a twink.

I like it here. His living room is stunning – two Venetian chandeliers, flaking walls, cascading linen curtains on floor-to-ceiling windows, statuary everywhere, beautiful threadbare rugs. Outside, the rest of Henrietta Street is dark and abandoned. There would have been a hundred people living in a house like this at the turn of the century, two families to a room. Now there is only Desmond, and Majella in her basement flat. Jess and I would be doing him a favour by moving in.

I move through the crowd, kiss cheeks, have my bottom patted. Get called *darling, girleen, Mottie love*. There's only a couple of younger boyfriends, one sulky, the other condescending.

I gave Jess some money for a taxi to get back, but where is she going to sleep tonight? Our home has burned down – I saw it go.

My tray is filling up with empty glasses. I don't mind giving out the drinks, but I hate being a depository. There are a few new faces, people from out of town, antiques dealers and louche businessmen. Desmond thinks that he runs sex parties, but it's just a lot of double-entendres and groping. I could tell them about things I saw in San Francisco that would make them choke on their cravats. Silly old queens.

At least they don't stay up late. Drink up, everyone.

Then I'll take my money and my tip, and peck Desmond's very soft cheek and pretend to leave. This big house will have room for me somewhere.

25

Considine waited on a low stone wall, the Aer Lingus bag on her knee, her satchel at her feet. From there she could see the entrance to the road that led to the Lynchs' house. She kept her eyes on it in case Jess turned up again. As she'd passed their gate on her way back up from the shore, she was sure she had heard the slam of a large metal door, like a van door. What could be happening there at this hour?

It couldn't be coincidence that Jess had left the painting so close to their house. Mottie knew Kieran, so Jess probably did too. And she couldn't have got a bus back into town, so she could still be around here somewhere. But why did she dump the bag where the waves could get it? Once Swan arrived, Considine would persuade him to go and look at the tunnel and the shore with her.

At last a dark car pulled in at the phone booth. The passenger door opened and Swan leaned over from the wheel to call to her.

'We've got to get this back right away.'

'Wait till I talk to you.' She went round to the back of the car, opened the boot and put in the two bags.

She swung herself into the passenger seat, but left the door open so that Swan wouldn't drive off. 'Something's going on at the Lynchs'. It's getting on for two in the morning, but their lights are on ... What in hell is that smell coming off you?'

'There was a fire.'

'What?'

'I'm fine. But the gay centre is pretty much destroyed. What are you doing out here without a paddle?'

'I found Mottie Deegan – briefly – and ended up following his friend Jess out here. Which must mean something, I just don't know what.'

'That's odd, all right.'

'I wanted to take a closer look at the house with you.'

'I need to get the car back. I borrowed it from Hannigan.'

'Are you not over the limit?'

'I wouldn't be driving, if it wasn't for you.'

That was fair. Considine considered getting out and continuing to keep a watch on the Lynchs' on her own, but then she'd still be far from home with no car. 'Okay, let's go.'

His arm reached across her, hand grasping for the door. She moved her feet into the car and shut the door herself. When she turned back, Swan was still close, still leaning.

'What?' she asked, but he didn't answer. After a strange, drawn-out moment of eye contact, he sat up behind the wheel and started the car. As he pulled out on the empty main road, she took a sideways look at him. He looked wrecked.

'How close were you to this fire?'

And so he told her about what happened in the club: that he'd talked to someone useful who knew Kieran; that smoke had filled the space and no alarms had sounded;

that no one seemed to be hurt in the end; and about the surprising appearance of Badger Stacy. Swan's voice was tense and tired.

They sped towards the city on empty roads, sitting impatiently at the few red lights. Her attention was half on what Swan was saying, and half on the bag in the boot.

'... when we got out of the place,' Swan said, 'I realised that the warehouse next door was on fire as well, so it wasn't necessarily aimed at the gay centre.'

'It's always been a target for hate, though,' she said. 'They've had a lot of vandalism in the past.'

'I bow to your greater knowledge.'

She squinted at the street lamps scrolling by. What did he really mean by *greater knowledge*? Was Swan hinting that he knew? She should just tell him and get it over with. Maybe he wouldn't even be surprised; they'd been working together for years.

They drew up at some lights at Ballsbridge and she could feel him taking quick glances at her. She grasped for the right words, but he spoke first.

'We've always kept private things separate ... but tonight, telling you about Elizabeth, I was really glad I did it. I think the world of you, Gina. The job wouldn't even be bearable without you—'

'You're right, we should be honest with each other. Hey, light's turned green.'

Swan did a kind of double-take and shoved the car into gear. 'I think that you and I—'

'There are reasons I don't tell you about what's going on with me.' She made herself smile. Her hands were shaking.

She was really going to say it. But he started to talk across her.

'Maybe it's a bad idea. You're a lot younger than me, for one thing, and if it didn't work between us, that's our jobs and our lives gone to shit.'

She stared blankly at the windscreen. This couldn't be happening – not Swan. Yet the sentiment in his eyes when they were in the bar and she was holding his hand, that strange departure on the street corner. Dear God, no. Not Swan. Swan, who she actually liked and needed.

They crossed the canal, speeding up as they neared town.

'Nothing's going to happen between us,' she blurted out loudly. 'I just don't feel that way.'

The thrum of the engine, the lights flicking past. Her stomach cold.

He nodded excessively. 'Of course, of course.'

A squawk of radio noise filled the car: '… mobile units in the Phoenix Park vicinity. All mobile units – report of injured person, unresponsive. Wellington Monument …'

They looked at each other as the new horror overtook the one they had created. Swan switched the siren on.

'We'll have to pick up Hannigan and Barrett,' he said. 'They're supposed to be in this car, and in the park. There must have been other patrols there.'

'What a fucking mess,' said Considine.

26

The advantage of being crazed with tiredness, Swan thought, was that it took all his resources to concentrate on what was going on around him; there was no energy left to rake over the embarrassment of whatever had happened between himself and Considine. There'd be plenty of time to examine his recklessness and humiliation once this night was over. It already felt like it had lasted a week.

He looked over his shoulder as they hurried across the grass. The eastern sky over the city was brightening, but ahead of them it was still night.

They had collected Hannigan and Barrett from where they were wearing hollows in the seats of the Graceland Café. Considine had gone in to get them while Swan kept the engine running. She was back out in a second.

'They were eating ice cream in little dishes. You should have seen their faces.'

The car radio was alive with comings and goings. Some Islandbridge police had arrived at the scene, an ambulance was on its way, and Considine had confirmed their imminent attendance from the squad.

Hannigan and Barrett rushed out and got into the back seat, effing and blinding and claiming that it was only Swan that had prevented them from being on hand. It was during

Hannigan's tirade on this subject that they learned from the radio that the injured person in the park did not need an ambulance. The injured person in the park was dead.

Swan couldn't find the gap in the railings that would bring them close to the monument, so he parked on the edge of the road and they pelted off on foot across the expanse of grass. The soaring needle of the obelisk ahead of them reflected some of the dawn light. In front of it was a grassy bank that led up to the monument's flat lawn. A Garda car was parked up there with its lights shining yellow across the grass. The Islandbridge Guards knew all the best routes.

Declan Barrett was furthest ahead, shadowy; Considine followed him at a trot, her coat flapping pale in the gloom; Hannigan trundled a few feet ahead of Swan, breathing heavily. On a normal night, Swan could have passed him easily, but his legs felt extraordinarily heavy and his lungs were still not right.

Hannigan stopped for a minute to lean his hands on his knees. Swan paused beside him. 'Never a good idea to go running on Grace Mangan's cooking, what?'

Hannigan drew himself up and there was a ferocity in his eyes. 'If this blows up, if the young fella and myself get the blame for not being here, I'm telling them you took the car.'

'Aren't you a prince? Always thinking of the real victim.'

Ahead, a Guard beside the police car started to shout at them to move away – to come round from the side, he seemed to indicate. Barrett and Considine went out wide towards the road, and Swan sighed and followed. He was feeling a bit short of compassion himself. A sleep and a shower would help his professionalism enormously.

As he got near the grass bank, the sight of what they were approaching banished all rumination. There was a small flight of stone steps set into the bank, and on those steps was the body of a man who looked like he had collapsed in the act of crawling up them. Considine and Barrett were near him now, and the Guard was flashing his torch beam about, lighting up the grass leading to the steps, then flicking it back to the poor unfortunate who lay there.

The man wore a dark suit, and the knuckles of his hands were skinned and bloodied. The steps around him were smeared with crimson.

'There's tracks all the way from over there,' the Guard was saying as he swung his torch beam over the grass. The morning dew had cast a silver coating over the meadow and you could clearly see a dark trail running through it, where multiple feet had obliterated the fine drops. It was a trail that would disappear once the sun came up.

'Did your colleague follow it?' Swan asked.

'He did.' They could just make out a small light moving in a line of trees, far away. The trees led directly to the thick copse where Kieran Lynch had been found.

Wailing sirens filled the air as two patrol cars turned in through the park gate.

'Hannigan,' Swan said, 'would you get two of those lads to join yer man in the trees. The others can come over here and help guard the scene.'

Hannigan stood for a moment, probably debating with

himself whether to allow Swan to call the shots. But they were all tired, so he went quietly for once, towards the cars that were pulling onto the verge.

'Can we borrow your torch?' Considine asked the Guard.

'All of you are detectives?'

'We're travelling in a pack tonight,' said Swan. 'Don't worry. We won't mess up your scene.'

With Barrett and Considine beside him, he moved slowly towards the steps, scanning the ground as they walked. When they were close enough, he tilted the light onto the body.

The man's dark hair was longer than the fashion, curling over the white shirt collar that peeked from his jacket. He was formally dressed in a suit that looked black, and wore polished dark shoes with smooth soles scarcely marked by use. Apart from all the blood, he was very neat, for a dead man.

'Did you turn him over?' Swan called to the Guard.

'We did, but we rolled him back when we were sure he was dead. He looks like he has knife wounds in his front.'

Swan ran the torch beam slowly over each step. There were plenty of footprints stamped in blood over the stone, a veritable dance pattern. Different pairs of shoes, it looked like – trainers and perhaps a boot or heavy-treaded shoe.

'Are any of these yours?'

'We had to go to him.' There was a wobble in the Guard's voice.

'Of course you did,' Swan conceded.

'I'll go call the Technical Bureau,' Considine offered. 'There might even be someone in the depot ready to go.'

Swan peered at his watch. It was five in the morning. Chances of anyone being in the labs were slim.

'Can I have the keys of the car?' she asked.

'That's our car,' said Barrett.

'I won't *lose* it.'

Swan threw the keys a short distance to Considine and she caught them with a clap of her hands. He watched her run back across the grass, then took a moment to mourn the stranger, and to mourn other losses of his night.

Declan Barrett was staring mutely at the far copse of trees. The sky had grown too light to make out any movement with torches.

'You all right there?' Swan asked, his weariness making him feel suddenly paternal.

Barrett didn't appear to hear him, and Swan was about to repeat himself when a scream ripped through the park. A scream that sounded first like someone in deadly fear, but resolved itself into a kind of crazed wolf howl. A chorus of distant whoops joined and answered, a pack of youths wanting to be heard. The cries came from the opposite direction to where the Guards were searching, over towards the vast spaces of the sports fields.

Considine had already driven off. He had no transport. Swan shouted to the newly arrived Guards – *Go! Go!* – waving his arms, urging them back to their patrol cars and into the chase.

27

Considine unlocked her front door and tiptoed to the living room, holding the Aer Lingus bag protectively under one arm. Terry should still be asleep, but sometimes took the notion for an early jog along the Dodder before work. Then Gina remembered that Terry had spent the previous evening drinking with Fintan and that girl, so she was unlikely to make an early start. The memory of Terry's laugh echoing around Grafton Street seemed paranoid fantasy now, another delusion of a very strange night.

She craved some caffeine, even a cup of tea, but the kettle would make too much noise. In the half-dark room she placed the bag on her coffee table. She was dazed from lack of sleep, but she needed to look at the picture properly before she went to bed, to work out what it was, and what the hell she thought she was doing, bringing it home with her. She had intended to tell Swan about it, but that was before his odd declaration and before the second killing in the park.

There wasn't yet enough light coming in the balcony window, so she turned on the reading light by the sofa, re-angled it and unzipped the grubby bag. One by one, she took out the crumpled pages of newspaper that cushioned the picture. They were all from an *Evening Herald* dated a week ago, so it hadn't spent very long in this packing. She lifted the panel carefully onto her lap and examined the back of it. The labels were still fairly legible. One was written in sepia ink in a hand so refined she couldn't decipher it. The other was half ripped off, with only 'School of …' inscribed by a very old typewriter.

She flipped the wooden panel over delicately and tilted it towards the light. The glaze on it threw back a honeyed reflection until she got the angle just right. The little face was even more striking than at first sight.

All the other elements of the picture submitted to the force of that face. The flames, which were like waving red grass, bent away from the figure and scattered the attending soldiers, the ones at the front crawling, the ones behind leaping. This boy saint was like a mighty wind. He wasn't looking at the devastation around him, he was looking straight out of the picture, eye-to-eye with the viewer, it felt like, full of bright certainty.

The robe that he wore was the exact pale pink of a party dress Gina was made to wear as a child. It was either a very old painting or a very good fake, yet the colours were uncommonly vivid, and the boy's face glowed with inner light, staring at her in the way a film star would stare into a camera, full of his own charisma. Her fingertip hovered over his perfect cheek.

She thought of Kieran, how he looked the night of his death – something of the same bright eagerness. It had been annoying to her, that over-confidence. He was a Guard, and it seemed he was a gay Guard. He had no right to be naïve or think the world would bend to him.

She resisted the urge to touch the surface of the picture and laid it carefully on the table, studying it, wishing she knew more about art. After a minute the flames started to twist and flare. The boy smiled more broadly. Considine realised that her eyes were shut and what she saw was only her imagination. She hauled herself awake. A quarter to seven, by her watch.

Two hours' sleep would have to do. She could slip into the warm sheets as Terry vacated them. She ought to be up for her work by now. No. Considine remembered it was Saturday.

Quickly and quietly she took a couple of pillowcases from the cupboard in the hall and put the painting inside one, folded it gently, then put that inside the next one and folded it in turn. It seemed like a more gentle wrapping than crumpled newspaper. There was a pile of folded blankets on the top shelf of the cupboard that wouldn't be used until winter. She slipped the painting into the middle of this stack and hid the bag and papers behind the ironing board, telling herself that she would take it into the depot exactly as she found it. Just not yet.

She stripped down to her pants in the bathroom and pulled on an old T-shirt that hung on the towel rail. When she pushed open the bedroom door she was surprised to be hit by sunshine blazing through the window. The curtains were open and the bed was empty. Made and empty.

It was suddenly difficult to draw breath, so she went and sat on the bed. Tried to think. Had Terry told her she'd be up early? Was there some ordinary explanation she had forgotten?

The skin of her thighs and arms prickled with goose-bumps, although the room was warm. That girl Miriam and Terry walking down Grafton Street together. Terry wouldn't do that to her. She had very strong feelings about infidelity. In their early days together, Terry had talked a lot – far too much – about what her previous partner did to her, and how Gina had to swear (there were many passionate swears in those weeks) that they would never be dishonest with one another.

Considine never found it difficult to be faithful to Terry; she was just grateful to be living a life that no one had told her was possible.

She started to phone around all the hospitals as if it was a work task, though her voice shook the first time she had to say Terry's name. Terry wasn't in a hospital. Using her contacts, Considine established she wasn't at a morgue, either. Aside from the man they found last night, there had been no fatalities in Dublin since she last saw Terry.

Or none that they knew of. She was being ridiculous. There would be a simple explanation.

Considine dressed again and started to make coffee. She was tempted to call Swan; he would know what to do next. Except that she hadn't told him about Terry, although she had meant to.

Swan. Aside from Terry, he'd been the steadiest person in her life. Together they had seen the worst things a person could see – all manner of harm, bodies broken and starved. Up until yesterday she would have said she knew him very well. How dare he hold her hand like that. How dare he feel things she didn't want him to feel.

She poured the coffee black and burned the roof of her mouth trying to drink it right away. No one was acting the way they should act.

The rasp of a key in the door made her freeze. She didn't turn round until Terry said her name. The way she said *Gina* was all Considine needed to know, slow and sorrowful, heavy as a stone. She turned and disaster was confirmed by the expression on her girlfriend's face. Solemn, determined.

'I never wanted to hurt you,' said Terry, doing just that.

Considine thought about throwing the coffee, thought about screaming or shouting, but she couldn't move.

'Gina ...'

Was Terry going to say that it hadn't mattered, that she had been drunk? What would she say to try and make it not so terrible?

'... we've had a good run of it.'

Oh.

'Aren't you going to say anything?'

Considine poured the coffee down the sink. What was there to say? She felt so exhausted. Exhausted and very stupid. Her eyes had started to fill, and she needed to be anywhere else.

The phone began to ring and she went towards it eagerly, hoping it was Swan, hoping he would take her away from this moment.

28

Swan edged past the fire engine that was still jammed in the neck of Temple Lane. A few weary firemen in blackened rubber coats watched the smoke and steam rising off piles of burnt rubble inside the ruins of the gay centre. The façade was still intact up to the second floor, but the top storey had gone – those rooms where he had run about looking for people just hours ago – not to mention the roof he had left from. You could look through the square gaps of the windows and only see the insistent blue of the morning sky.

After their adventure in the park, and the capture of three teenagers by some nimble Islandbridge Guards, he had returned to the depot and had a quick wash in the Gents and felt, if not restored, at least improved. He couldn't find Considine anywhere; she had given the impression that she'd be back, but her car was gone from the yard. Maybe she'd been sensible and gone for a bit of kip. He should do the same. And change his clothes. God knew if the dry cleaner's could ever resuscitate the suit he was wearing.

He got a lift into town to collect his car from Temple Bar, but couldn't resist this little detour to see whether the fire was out and what damage it had done.

When he asked one of the firemen if there was anyone

from the Gardaí about, the man pointed at the next-door warehouse. It was more intact than the gay centre; half of the roof still hung on precariously on the side furthest away from the blaze. The glass and frames had burned out of all the windows, but the bars on the ground-floor ones were still intact. A tall, familiar figure was walking softly amongst the ash in a white overall and hard hat, talking into a miniature Dictaphone.

Swan stepped into the empty doorway of the building, a reassuringly solid structure of stone blocks and lintel.

'John,' he called. 'John Moran!'

The man turned in his direction, pushed his wire glasses up his nose and shook his head, still talking into the machine. John was very fastidious, like most in the Technical Bureau. He wouldn't want to chat in the middle of his inspection.

'Just a moment of your time.' Swan raised a foot and leaned forward, as if he intended to stride among the remains.

'Don't!' Moran shouted. He pressed a button to stop his recording.

Swan called out his apologies, and Moran made his way over. Swan explained that he was investigating a case that had led him to be on the spot when the fire had broken out. Moran – a thin man with a pious look to him – seemed to be paying more attention to the state of Swan's clothes and person.

'… I'd be interested in any initial impressions,' Swan finished.

Moran looked at his watch. 'You know that isn't how it

works. But by the cut of you, I'll accept that you may be in the middle of some sort of crisis.'

'This is me cleaned up.'

'God help Mrs Swan.'

'C'mon, I won't hold you to anything, John.'

'Okay. I'm in the way of thinking – at the moment, it could change – that it started on the first floor of this building and moved to the one where the people were.'

He indicated an area of the wall above them, where the bricks were not black but pale grey, where the fire had burned fiercely.

'There are some indications of accelerant use there. Also there were big wooden props between this building and the next across the gap – supposedly for stability, but I think they provided a perfect bridge across for the flames. The wind was blowing from the north last night.'

'I don't remember there being a strong wind.'

'I didn't say strong. There's always a breeze,' said Moran, 'always a direction.' He moved his hand delicately through the air to demonstrate. 'Also the discotheque had fans to help with air circulation on this side. Fans to draw fresh air in, which might have drawn the flames in too.'

'That's pretty shocking. Can I perhaps help you in return? Among the crowd that were here last night I happened to see our friend Badger Stacy.'

'There's a rare coincidence. But there's a lot of work to do before we get to the suspect stage,' Moran said. 'If we ever get to that stage.'

'Why so pessimistic?'

'Sometimes it's hard to trace who owns these old wrecks;

there are companies inside companies, many of them not even based here. Couldn't find an owner for this one yet. The company that is listed as owning it, Bremen Brothers, does not seem to exist.'

'If it's arson, that's usually for an insurance claim, isn't it, or wanting to develop the site without the heritage bodies raising a stink? Someone will show their hand.'

'We'll see. Sometimes people burn things just because it gives them pleasure. Badger Stacy used to be one of those.' John Moran turned back to his inspection. There didn't seem to be much besides rubble and charred wood at his feet. Swan shaded his eyes to try and see into the dark space on the intact side of the building. He could only make out a single tea chest on its side, empty.

The forensic investigator was raising the Dictaphone to his mouth.

'John ...'

'What?'

'Any idea what they were storing here?'

Moran indicated the gaping void above him. 'Looks like nothing at all, Swan. Nothing at all.'

Swan looked up. At what had been the very top floor, on a relatively unscathed wall, an oval of light caught his eye. It was a mirror nailed over a small fireplace, now stranded up on the cliff of brick. There must once have been someone living up there. Something fluttered on the wall near the mirror and was snatched by the wind, spiralling its way down to land not far from John Moran's feet. He picked it up and held it out for Swan to see.

'Amazing how some things escape,' he said.

It was a picture cut from a newspaper of Phil Lynott, straddling a stage with his long legs and long bass guitar; *1949–1986 RIP* was printed across the bottom. Which meant someone had pinned it up this year.

'It's recent.'

'I don't know how I manage without you, Swan.'

'Very good, John. I'll let you get on.'

Swan wanted to phone in to headquarters to see if there was any news on the boys they had under arrest. He started to root through his pockets for change. No money, but he found he still had the keys to Kieran Lynch's nearby flat.

There was a faint smell of tobacco in the stairwell, so he knocked at the door this time, in case his family or someone else was inside, and waited a moment. All remained quiet and, inside, the flat seemed just as it was the day before. He went to the phone and called the unit office. No one answered, so he asked to be put through to Islandbridge Garda station.

'Why don't I give you the number and you can dial it yourself.'

'Is that you, Arlene?' Arlene's powers as head of the telephone exchange were often wielded capriciously.

'Do you want the number or not, Detective Swan?'

'I've no pen on me.'

A click and he was in the strange purgatory of silence, not knowing if he was cut off or waiting.

'Islandbridge Garda station.' He was through.

After a tedious series of relays, he was told that the two boys they had in custody had not been interviewed yet, and that Hannigan and Barrett were due soon to conduct those interviews. Swan hoped they would manage some sleep first. The sergeant he spoke to confirmed that the boys were already known to the station.

He dialled Considine's home number. She would want to know what was going on, even if it meant waking her. She answered straight away.

'Yes, hello?'

There was something hasty and breathless about her tone, as if he had caught her in the middle of exercise, not sleep.

'I don't know where you got to this morning, but there are two boys in custody at Islandbridge for the latest killing.'

'Is that where you are?'

'Not yet. I'm in Kieran Lynch's flat.'

'Why?'

'It was on my way somewhere.'

'I'll meet you there.'

'There's no need. Hannigan and Barrett are doing the interviews.'

'Give me five minutes.'

He began to protest, but she had already hung up. Now he'd have to wait for her. He did a careful circuit of the room, looking again at the things he had looked at the day before.

He opened the doors of the built-in wardrobe. He pulled out the drawers on the chest of drawers. The top one had a stash of condoms amongst the socks. Quite a lot of them. Swan thought of the bowls of condoms he'd seen on the bar at Tabú. You did hear that gay men had a lot of sex.

He went over to the bedside table and pulled out the little drawer. A notebook and a detective novel. Wouldn't you store your condoms there if you had any kind of sex life? Or maybe Kieran's sex life had all been al fresco. There had been a condom by the body, after all.

He stood by the window and waited, looking at the sunlight play across the buildings on the other side of the river. There was a yellowish haze of smog hanging under the blue of the sky, the traffic fumes trapped on this windless day, or maybe the remains of smoke from the fire. A loud buzzer startled him and he went and fiddled with an intercom thing by the door.

'Press it again!' Considine's voice sounded small but furious. Swan managed on the second try and heard the door bang on the ground floor. He returned to the window and listened to her pound up the stairs while watching the soothing flow of the water.

'What are you doing here anyway?' she said from the doorway.

'I came to use the telephone.'

'A likely story. I was curious to see it myself. The Technical Bureau haven't been in?'

'And probably won't, unless we can find a good reason. Martin's being very mean lately with forensic resources. Without a wall of blood spatter, no one cares.'

She started to walk slowly around the small flat, taking it in. He couldn't help noticing how shattered she looked, her skin was pale and her expression, though concentrated, had a kind of stretched look to it, like it was held there by effort.

'It's smaller than I thought,' she said. 'Very monastic.'

'Except for the industrial number of condoms.'

Swan saw her flinch. He went and opened the drawer to show her what he meant, that he wasn't making some crude joke.

'When I was at the gay centre they had these very same Durex on offer, like, just sitting out in bowls on the countertop. Promoting safe sex, the barman told me. He also said that Kieran did advocacy work. What would that be?'

Considine approached the opened drawer, nodded at the pile of condoms. 'It could be what brought him to the park. Not cruising, but talking to people. Volunteers usually going out in pairs, offering condoms and talking about how to avoid AIDS.'

'What does that change?' asked Swan.

'Probably nothing. If he was targeted by gay-bashers, they wouldn't care why he was there.'

There were two high stools at the edge of the kitchen counter. Considine abandoned her tour of the flat and sat up on one.

'Tell me what I missed at the park.'

'A chase. A scuffle. I wasn't at the head of it, you won't be surprised to learn. A pack of little shitheads. Two got away, three got caught, but one of those was only thirteen and had to be let home to his mammy. But not before we got his clothes.'

'Blood?'

'Yes, visible traces on all their shoes and clothes.'

'That means it could be over. If those savages are responsible for Kieran as well as last night's victim, that might be that, and nothing we did in the last few days helped find them.'

'It doesn't matter, as long as they're caught.'

She did not look consoled. Swan thought she would be pleased. All these emotions were too hard on no sleep. He stood up to go, and a familiar cold pulse started in his right temple.

'Let's go down to Grace's and get a nice milky coffee.'

She sniffed loudly and he looked over to see that she was crying. He had never seen Considine cry before.

'No!' he said, as though he could halt whatever this was. 'You're just tired. You've been up all night.'

'I'm not tired, I'm really angry.' She drew her sleeve energetically across her mouth and nose.

'Can I make you a cup of tea?' he offered.

'Of course you can't! It's his flat. We might need a closer look at it.'

He didn't think that would happen, but it wasn't worth arguing. He had the sinking feeling that what she was upset about had something to do with him, and not merely the circumstances or the lack of sleep. In earlier times, before he'd made a fool of himself, he might have offered her a hug.

'This isn't like you,' he said softly.

She looked at the ceiling, blinked rapidly, then gave him a level look. 'Okay. Here goes.'

Far below, they heard the slam of the street door shutting. No footsteps followed.

'Maybe we should check that.' Swan started towards the door.

'Leave it!' She grabbed his arm.

He stepped away, out of her reach. 'If it's about what I said last night, I do really regret it.'

Considine sat down again, shaking her head. 'Not that. I'm in a kind of trouble. It's hard to talk about.'

Swan couldn't imagine what was so bad that she couldn't find a way to tell him. Could she be pregnant? If she was, she'd have to give up being a detective. You couldn't be a single mother in the force. Couldn't be a married one, either.

He stopped staring at her, to see if that would help. He focused on the edge of the countertop.

'Okay,' she said again and exhaled. 'Superintendent Martin called me to his office about a month ago. He said some information had come his way about what he called my lifestyle. That I lived with a woman. I think he used the word "carnally", which is one you don't meet every day.'

'You denied it.'

'I denied it. I had to.'

'You *had* to?'

She looked back at him evenly, waiting for the penny to drop. How could he have been so thick? Considine didn't look like a lesbian, Swan found himself thinking. Then he remembered the table of lesbians in The Earl. He'd thought they'd been teasing her because she was a policewoman. They were teasing Considine because they knew her.

'Martin said he couldn't just forget what he'd been told. That they would be keeping a watching eye. That's why this case has been particularly hard. You never realised, did you? I often wondered.'

'I'm sorry,' he said.

'Don't be sorry for me.'

'That's not what I meant. I'm sorry I put you in an awkward position last night. I'm sorry that Superintendent Martin has been making your life difficult.'

'Well, now you know.'

'Let's go get that coffee.'

'Give the office a call first. I want to know if there's news.'

He did as she asked, waiting to be transferred from the desk to anyone in the murder squad who was there. Eric Joyce came on the line eventually. The boys were in the process of being interviewed, with Hannigan and Barrett going between them. No report back yet.

While Joyce spoke, Swan watched Considine flipping through a copy of *Garda Review* that she had found on the bookshelves. Her brows dipped in concentration, and he found himself relieved that her mood had shifted away from upset. Other people's tears were far worse than your own.

Joyce asked him if he was at the depot, and Swan said he was 'in town' following up on the Temple Bar blaze.

'That's hardly a murder-squad priority,' said Joyce. 'There's a post-mortem at eleven-thirty you could be coming to.'

'Lovely. Grand.'

He hung up the phone. Considine replaced the magazine on the shelves and followed him towards the door. He opened it and stepped back for her to go through.

'Still treating me like a lady, I'm pleased to see.'

He smiled, appreciative of the attempt at humour. 'I'm sorry for not realising. And I'm very sorry for the misunderstanding between us.'

'Not everything is about you, Vincent.' She said it kindly, which was worse.

He was still smarting, going down the stairs. Passing one of the doors on the floor below, he noticed that the thick dust had been recently disturbed by hands or fingers around the lock. He stopped for a closer look and knocked quietly on the door, heard nothing. Tried the handle, but the door was locked.

When he got downstairs, Considine was already out on the pavement writing something in her notebook. She slipped it in her pocket as he got near.

'Someone's been in the flat below,' Swan said. He looked up. Except for Kieran's flat, all the windows were dull with grime. Between each set of windows, faded white words on the red brick marked its former life as SMYTH'S UMBRELLA MANUFACTURER, one word per floor.

'Did you see anyone?'

She shook her head.

'If Robert Lynch owns this whole building, do you think he owns others in the area?'

'I guess that's what developers do,' she said. 'Then wait for the payoff when the place gets redeveloped. Everyone knows CIE is buying.'

'When I saw the fire investigator this morning, he said it can be difficult to know who the real owners of a building are.'

'I can go to the corporation offices, I know someone who might help me dig. Won't be until Monday, though.'

'No rush. Coffee is the priority. Coffee and aspirin and perhaps a nap before the morgue.'

He smiled stubbornly as his head throbbed.

29

Grace Mangan is a decent skin. She let me leave my bags in a storeroom upstairs from the café and told me to have a wash while I was at it. A wash is as good as a rest, I told her, and she put her damp hand to my cheek. Maybe she'll take me in. She likes that I call her Mrs Mangan, with respect.

It's hard not to feel persecuted when they burn down the roof over your head or throw you out on the street. Desmond found me on his library chaise this morning and evicted me without breakfast, though I'm sure there are tens of bedrooms going spare in his Georgian wreck. Most of the doors are locked, but I don't know whether he's hiding treasure or dark perversion. Anyway I called him a capitalist pig with the emphasis on 'pig', so there's another bridge burned. I regret *rien*. Mrs Mangan gives me a strong mug of coffee and some toast for free and I tuck myself in the corner behind the coat stand.

There's a weekend paper lying on the table: 'MURDER AT GAY HAUNT'. Is that what we do in the trees – haunting? I have a *haunting* in my trousers. There's many feeling persecuted in this town today. The paper doesn't care about us, they just want to chew over our dark deeds and sexual tastes. What do these benders expect, when they live like this? My finger caresses Kieran's name in the text. He did not deserve what happened. Correction: none of us do, I forgot.

The bell goes ting and in comes an odd couple, weary to the bone. Crumpled mackintoshes all the rage this season. Well, mercy me, it's the policewoman again, who Kieran spoke to outside the pub. She looks hellish rough this morning and I am glad to see it. The man with her is pouchy and dark-circled too, filthy clothes. But there's a certain set to him, tired but not defeated, ready for another round.

She doesn't see me, scarcely sees anything at all. I'm wearing my cap, salty tweed, man of Aran, with my hair hidden, and these scholarly glasses from Desmond's desk. I have decided to travel incognito as a shy 1940s academic. I use the newspaper as a screen.

The policeman has an appetite, the woman less so. They hardly talk. He shoves in eggs and rashers and calls for another round of toast. She drinks coffee and smokes. I can't hear what they talk about when they do talk. But when the man goes to use the jacks (he has a little chat with Mrs Mangan on the way, because Grace is everyone's friend), the woman puts her face in her hands, and her shoulders seem to shudder. So much more than tired.

The paper also has a short bit on the fire – breaking news – but it mentions only the gay centre, not the warehouse that has been our home. I am mere collateral damage of this August pogrom.

Paddy B comes in wearing his civvies – he's always here in the mornings. *Bewley's has nothing on you, Grace my darling*, he'll say to Mrs Mangan. *So cheap*, he'll say to me. He stops by the police table and the man asks how Paddy's doing this morning. Ah, Dublin, no degrees of separation. Paddy starts telling them about a protest they should know about. The drag queens and the cops and the fucking arsonists and the celebrities. I want new faces, a big city of new faces, a decent anonymity. And someone to fuck who I never have to see again.

Paddy sits down at my booth and says we're on the warpath. He's been hanging on the telephone, and everyone agrees. It's time to make a stand. Some system of jungle drums has been activated. Bed sheets are being sacrificed for banners. They are trying to kill us every which way, Paddy says, by beating, by burning, by plague. You know I'm apolitical, I protest. You look like fucking Yentl, he says. How can I take you seriously?

I don't tell him I've no place to live. I don't tell him that my best friend has gone missing and my other best friend is dead.

He writes the time and place of the protest in biro on my hand.

Eleven o'clock is *obscenely* early, I say.

'Bring people,' he orders and I nod, as if I have a brigade of them.

'I have to go to a pawnshop on Capel Street first.'

'See if they have any pikes and muskets,' he says and kisses my lips as he goes, just for the cause, not because he likes me.

30

Considine's vision kept blurring on the short drive to Merrion Square. She bit the inside of her mouth hard, just to push some adrenalin into her system.

She couldn't go home again. But she needed to sleep, so she parked under the trees on the quiet north side of the square. It was early enough that the annoying parking touts, the 'lock hard' men, weren't yet out. She tumbled herself through to the back seat and shook out the rug that she used to hide packages and wrapped it around herself. The moment before she let herself slide into unconsciousness was absolutely delicious.

She woke sweating and sticky-mouthed. The sun had turned the car into an oven. Frantically she threw back the rug and scrambled out of the door, into the sweet, fresh air. A couple on the pavement looked over at her with anxiety. Considine supposed she looked drunk or mad, someone who might need to be quickly avoided. The worst of it was that, according to her watch, she had only slept for an hour.

It would have to do. She got back into the driver's seat, checked herself in the mirror and pulled a comb through her hair. There were a couple of hours spare before she had said she would be at the depot, and she had an idea of how to spend them.

The image of Terry, standing in the bedroom doorway, flashed into her mind. *We've had a good run.* It was a kick in the gut, but it wasn't quite a surprise. Why hadn't she felt surprised? Why had she just felt the weight of *here it is.* It was something to think about later.

The National Gallery stood in sunshine in its grounds beside Leinster House and the Natural History Museum. The only previous time she had been inside was on a school trip that took in both museums. Some of the tedium of that day seemed to take hold of her the moment she stepped inside, her energy draining down into the polished floors. She turned left, into a room as high as a church. The paintings here were huge, figures gesturing every which way. She didn't know much about art, but there was nothing here to make her want to fix that. It felt like the visual equivalent of some old guy boring on about his favourite subject.

The painting she had found on the shore was old, not just painted on old board, she was pretty sure of that, so she wanted to see if she could find something that looked similar – something that might give her a clue about how old it was. If she hadn't picked it up, it might be halfway to Holyhead now, or sunk in the bay for ever. She simply wanted to find out a bit more about it, and why it was there.

Up and down stairs she dragged herself. There were a lot of saints and a lot of worthies, and quite a few paintings of nice things lying on tables. And in every gallery there were people looking at them, a surprising number of people.

Some had well-behaved children with a longer attention span than she could manage herself. The middle classes were very mysterious.

In a back gallery of Italian art she finally found some paintings a little like what she had hidden at home. They were simpler, to her eye. Flat-looking madonnas mostly, one with a baby who showed a full set of teeth. A real miracle boy. One picture of the Annunciation was the same size as the one of the burning boy. It had touches of gold in the same way hers had, and the reds and pinks were bright, like some of the clothing in hers. The label said 'Fifteenth century, egg tempera on wood'. It described it as a 'predella panel', which Considine dutifully wrote down so that she could look it up later. Not in her police notebook, but in the back of her week-to-a-page diary, among the phone numbers. Her new friend, Predella Panel, followed by a made-up number. Her sister Tempera below that.

What on earth was she doing? Taking some time, that was all, Considine reassured herself, just doing her research.

As she was leaving the room, she noticed a square area of the wall that was darker than the rest. A picture that had hung there had been taken away, revealing a deeper shade of green behind it. There was a postcard in the middle of this square, an ordinary white postcard pinned by a gold drawing pin that dented the wall. She looked closer and discovered that all the walls were padded and covered with some kind of rich material, not wallpaper or paint. The thought of such elaborate softness gave her a shimmering wave of tiredness.

The postcard stated that the painting had been removed

for cleaning, and acknowledged it as a loan from 'Phillip R. Brewster III'. That name was familiar. Considine tried to think.

The answer didn't get delivered by her brain until she was already outside in the warming morning air. The Brewster robbery from last year. A dozen important paintings taken from the Connemara castle of an American oil baron. He had already loaned half of his collection to the National Gallery, fortunately, or else they would all be gone.

Considine had seen pictures of the stolen paintings; they had even been briefed by the serious crimes unit that was investigating. The assumption was that the IRA or a criminal gang had taken them for ransom. She couldn't remember any updates since then. If they had been recovered, she would surely have known.

She had never seen a photograph of the picture that was now in her hall cupboard, she was sure of that, so it probably hadn't come from there. She was aware of a certain possessiveness that seemed to have taken hold of her. She still had more than an hour's grace; the National Library was around the corner, and it had a good newspaper archive.

Walking up Kildare Street, she became aware of a crush of people outside Leinster House, chanting angrily. Banners, some with pink writing, triangles, women's symbols. *Gay Health Action*, read one. 'We're here, we're queer, get used to it!' chanted a megaphone voice. Did they not realise there would be no politicians in there on the weekend? How can people get used to queerness – she hated the word – if you pick the wrong day? Typical.

A group of three women leaned against the railings, just by the entrance to the library. She recognised one of them, a perennial student called Isabel Flynn, and ducked her eyes to the pavement. But the gate to the library was closed. It was Saturday. She'd picked the wrong day herself.

'Hey, Gina!'

Isabel was trying to get her attention. Considine pretended she had heard nothing and turned from the gate. Isabel went to step in front of her, smiling, and Considine dodged her with a frown.

'Excuse me,' she said, pretending they had never met.

31

The urgent protest has gathered. Three banners and twenty-three benders, and I know every one of them to see. My people are beautiful and heroically pathetic. That woman with the crucifixes and the nice tweed suit is there beside them, singing to God up in the sky to come down and save Ireland from these sodomites. A fat security guard stands near her, in case of trouble.

I lean against railings outside Buswells Hotel and look at people looking at the gays. I can be too alive to insult, so I try not to interpret their impassive faces as disapproval. I don't think I'll join the march. It's very earnest. Not, you know, very me. I'm looking out for Jess, she loves this kind of political shit.

I shouldn't have let her go alone to her uncle's house. I think we might be a teeny-weeny bit out of our depth. Mr Brylcreem, with his hot eyes and violent boss, is much on my mind. I do wish she would turn up, though with Jess it's always a possibility that she simply fell into a very good party.

A couple of suited civil servants scurry through the security gates looking scared, which is cheering. I wish I could import a dozen fierce drag queens on roller skates, or leather dykes on Harley-Davidsons, just to glamour this scene.

The Jess-voice in my head tells me to shut up, that San

Francisco cannot be compared to Dublin, that this is authentic and important and I'm merely surface. Jess is an activist to her fingertips and I applaud her worthy heart. I really did think she would be here, shouting loudly at the front. Not an actual lesbian, but so sympathetic to the cause that she might turn for the right woman, she says. That's commitment.

Paddy B appears at my side.

'I thought there'd be more people here.'

'Maybe they're on their way. I told you it was too early in the day. No one should march before noon.'

He shrugs.

'You should have worn your drag,' I say.

'Please. I lost everything in the fire. Practically lost my life. Got stuck up on the roof. And did you hear about the guy in the park?'

I entwine two fingers and hold them up to his face. 'Kieran and I were closer than that.'

Paddy rolls his eyes. 'Honey, we all thought that. He had such a talent for looking entranced – it was quite irresistible. But, no, I mean the new one.'

Well, that stops me.

'They killed another poor boy. It was on the radio news just now. They found him last night, up in the park, kicked and stabbed, they said. They're trying to slaughter us all.'

His eyes shine like he gets a kick out of that. Or he's glad to have it all out in the open.

'Fight back! Fight AIDS!' he yells suddenly, joining in with a new chant. I cover the ear nearest to him. I'm still taking in the news. I'm shocked, despite myself.

We should do a banshee wail. Dress in black shawls,

like famine drag. This is war all right. An anxious-looking woman in an army jacket comes up and hands me a leaflet for a meeting about socialism. I mean, what the fuck? I flick it back. This is *our* show.

'Have you seen Jess?' I ask Paddy. He screws up his face, thinking. He doesn't know who I'm talking about. He doesn't remember girls and I'm not going to say *she's the black one*.

Two student boys in fluorescent vests are moving the protest onto the street and Paddy goes to join them. He looks back and flaps his hand a little, like I'm his following doggie. There's only thirty people gathered now. They need numbers. If Jess was here, I probably would join them. The chant changes to a repeat: *Fight back! Fight back!*

One of the student boys has a transistor radio pressed to his ear. He holds up an arm to stop the march moving, though the Guards are trying to get them going. The traffic has been stopped down at Trinity, and a couple of horns start parping their protest.

The boy with the radio shouts, 'They've made some arrests!' and everybody cheers. I feel a swelling in my chest that comes from nowhere and presses tears out of my ducts. An interesting phenomenon.

'Fight back!' I cry from my pavement corner and cartwheel across the road to the front of the march. Give them a little showbiz. My awkward brothers and my strange sisters. My persecuted tribe. I strut and tumble and dance and clap, for that is what I do. I draw the eyes of the stolid pavement people. Between acrobatics, I hold my fist high and clenched, like Jess would, if she were here.

32

Swan could not rid himself of the smell of smoke. Now it was wafting over from the chair on the other side of the bedroom, where he had hung his suit and shirt. Though he had almost fallen asleep standing up in the shower, once he lay down and closed his eyes, he kept flashing back to that moment on the ladder, stepping down into nothing in the darkness. The rung slipped from his grip and he lurched awake.

He heard his mother moving about in the house below and the smell of coffee rose up the stairs in its insistent way, mingling with that of the stale smoke. There wasn't time for a decent sleep anyway.

He dressed in fresh clothes and bundled the dirty ones into the wardrobe.

'Have you been up all night? You look like hell,' his mother said when he entered the kitchen.

'Good morning, Mother.'

She was sitting at one end of the table with her cross-word and a small plate of biscuits. He went straight over to the coffee jug and gave thanks it was half full.

'It's hard to tell if you're leading the life of Riley or working too hard. Wouldn't hurt to take your shoes off in the hall, when you come in.'

'You have a talent for making me feel youthful, Ma. It's like being a teenager all over again.'

'Old habits die hard,' she said crisply and started again on her crossword as a barrier to further exchange. Swan kissed the top of her head and stole a digestive off her plate.

He picked up his briefcase in the hall and shouted his farewell. He really did need to think about getting a place of his own. It was six months he'd been staying with her now, a tipping point from temporary arrangement to something more permanent. She'd encouraged him to think he was doing her a favour when she offered to take him in. The company, the helping hand, a share of the bills. And she was great, never asked about Elizabeth, never made suggestions for what he should be doing with his life. But her complaints about the material things – all the cooking and the laundry that his presence necessitated – were becoming more frequent. It reminded Swan too much of when his father was alive, his mother martyred by dull domesticity. Cast in the role of oppressor now, he didn't much like it.

He drove into the city centre, along the quays and around the back of Busáras to the old morgue. Everyone called it the old morgue, because a new morgue had been promised for years now, but had yet to materialise. The building had a certain charnel charm, with its white glazed bricks and floor guttering, but it was hardly a credit to a twentieth-century police force. The assistant who let him in was already masked and gloved and wearing a long apron. As Swan had hoped, the pathologist was Terry O'Keefe, efficient and measured.

Detective Eric Joyce was standing against one of the walls, and Swan was surprised to see Superintendent Martin beside him. Joyce looked morose and Martin looked tense. Superintendents did not usually find it necessary to attend post-mortems, but Martin was proving to be an odd bird.

On the porcelain slab lay the body Swan had met so recently, now naked. Where the skin was unbruised it was unearthly pale, almost as pale as the porcelain beneath. The man's hair was black as a crow's feather, straight and long. Perhaps it was Swan's tiredness, or the overly bright lights of the morgue, but everything he looked at seemed harsher in contrast than usual, and the purplish tones of the bruises on the young man's torso were as florid as a rose bouquet. The short slashes where a blade had pierced him gaped crimson.

O'Keefe had not yet started his inspection. He was laying out instruments and notes on a side counter, like a priest readying a complex sacrament.

'Do you have Sergeant Considine with you?' Superintendent Martin asked.

Swan indicated she was busy elsewhere. He hoped she was busy sleeping.

'I thought she could go and talk to the mother. She phoned the emergency number early this morning to say that her son was missing and he answered the description of this victim. A nephew came to make the ID half an hour ago.'

'Bill Riordan is the deceased's name,' said Eric Joyce, and Martin gave him a scowl for butting in. The right to talk uninterrupted was an important perk of power.

'The family were in Dublin for a funeral, the mother's brother,' Martin continued. 'Staying at the Ormond Hotel on the quays. They're due to leave today, but I want them to feel we are doing everything for her son, and I want to know a bit more about the circumstances. I thought Considine would have the right touch. Why have a woman on the squad if you don't use her particular skills.'

'I don't mind going,' Swan said.

'You can go together then. And let the mother believe he was just out for a walk.'

'How do you mean?'

'She's had the loss of her brother and now her son. She doesn't need to know anything he might have been up to.'

'He may have been up to nothing.'

O'Keefe had taken up position beside the body, notes at the ready, waiting for the talk to finish. Swan half turned, to include him in the conversation. 'I don't suppose there's anything obvious to link this to Kieran Lynch's death?'

O'Keefe shrugged. 'Nothing yet to link it, nothing to exclude it. Both suffered blunt-force trauma – kicks and blows – though I would say this one was more sustained. And there's no injury to this subject's head, but there are stab wounds.'

'The boys might confess, if we're lucky,' said Swan. 'How's that going?'

Neither Joyce nor Martin answered immediately, reluctant to allow Swan to lead the conversation or determine what was happening in this room with its rituals and protocols. But O'Keefe was a friend and seemed happy to learn the answer himself, raising his eyebrows to indicate this.

Eric Joyce spoke at last. 'They say they're getting there. They have some names for the boys we didn't catch, and they're being brought in. The Tech Bureau say they've plenty of evidence to go on – the footprints, a discarded baseball cap, even a cheap signet ring that snapped under force.'

'So much more to go on than we had with Kieran Lynch,' Superintendent Martin said, and Swan noticed his eyes flick towards one of the mortuary drawers.

'He's still here?'

'Family haven't kicked up a fuss about getting him back yet,' said Joyce. 'It wouldn't be wise to release the body, now that we have another to compare.'

Terry O'Keefe had had enough chat. 'If we've satisfied your curiosity, DI Swan …'

'Appreciate your patience. I'll get myself and Considine to the Ormond Hotel. What's his mother's name?'

'May Riordan,' said Superintendent Martin. 'And remember, nothing about sex.'

Swan took a parting glance at the body, the pale young face set in rigid melancholy.

'Do we have an age?'

'Twenty-one, according to his details,' said the pathologist. 'Key of the door.'

33

Considine was putting quick distance between herself and the protest, escaping the shame of blanking Isabel Flynn, when she realised she was just outside De Courcy Fine Arts. *Sometimes a person is as good as a library*, she thought, and went in the unlocked panelled door and up to the first floor.

In a dark-green room busy with paintings and sculptures on plinths, Desmond de Courcy was rearranging things in a glass display case. His hand shook as he placed some kind of silver jug on the shelf.

'Did you have a big night, Mr de Courcy?'

'Cheeky girl,' he said, turning to regard her over his diminutive glasses. 'You're not exactly looking peachy yourself.'

She'd first met Desmond de Courcy following a stabbing incident in Henrietta Street. He'd witnessed the attack from the window of the huge shabby house that he claimed to be living in, though to her it looked like it was undergoing major works. After that, she would run into him from time to time at the Moonlit Gate. Although Terry thought him creepy, Considine enjoyed his tales of old Dublin and his encyclopaedic knowledge of practically everything. He had an Anglo-Irish accent, but once confided that he came from the

Liberties and had educated himself in libraries and through attachment to various mentors in the antiques trade.

'I'll make you some mint tea,' De Courcy said and took an ornate metal teapot from one of his desk drawers. 'Are you here to arrest me, or are you escaping the militant tendency down the road?'

'You mean the protest?'

'I thought you girls were very political these days.' He took a brown paper bag from another drawer and took out a handful of what looked like weeds.

'The police aren't allowed to be political.'

He went into a curtained alcove and filled the teapot with hot water from an electric samovar.

'I don't like protests,' he said. 'I don't think anything good comes from putting our heads above the parapet. We live our interesting lives, we are tolerated in the main, but we are not them. *Umbra Sumus* – we are shadows. I don't want to be a part of what they have, do you? The suburban dream?'

To her horror, he stuffed the bunch of leaves and stalks into the teapot and poured hot water over them.

'I don't feel like a shadow,' Considine said, 'I feel like a human.'

'If you draw too much attention to yourself, though, if you start being too strident ... well, next thing it's the boots on the stairs and a chain-link fence, isn't it? Bad enough they think we're spreading a contagion now.'

She didn't have the energy to argue. De Courcy was a man of some wealth and influence, but she'd heard this particular line of catastrophic argument from him before, and today it seemed particularly depressing. She turned away and began to inspect all the works on the walls. They were mostly landscapes: sea views and glens with towering clouds above, castles and cottages. A few were boldly abstract – great gold suns and energetic swoops of paint.

'What's the oldest painting you have here?' she asked.

'I try to stick to the twentieth century. It keeps the insurance down. I have some very inexpensive prints in the back, if you want to buy someone a gift. Here's your tea.' He sat down behind his desk with a glass of water. A steaming mug of green awaited her on one corner.

'Aren't you having any of the tea?'

He took a small tin of Andrews Liver Salts out of a desk drawer.

'Last night was gratifyingly excessive – I need something more medicinal.'

She watched him stir the powder into his glass, trying to find the right way to bring up what she wanted to talk about. But cleverness eluded her tired head and she decided to dive in.

'I was thinking the other day about the Brewster robbery. Did they ever find those pictures?'

'What brings this on?' he asked, still stirring.

'Just popped into my head. Wouldn't you be the kind of person who would be approached if somebody wanted to offload them?'

'Pah! I am a minnow, a mere sprat. Those are priceless things – practically unsellable, certainly to any legitimate dealer.' He started to open and close desk drawers, searching for something.

'So why steal them at all?'

'*I* don't know. To hold as hostages, or bargaining chips. The IRA are given to such things. Even racehorses. Poor Shergar, eating his oats in heaven, they say. I think Brewster deserved it, frankly, for not operating adequate security in his castle. His elderly housekeeper was trussed up like a turkey for two days, poor woman.'

'Do you know the case well?'

Desmond looked up from his ransacking of the desk drawers to give her a steely look. 'Is this what you're like with the criminals? Coming in like an old friend, then turning on the thumbscrews?'

She laughed. He pulled out a cardboard file, took some stapled pages from it and spun them across the desk at her. They were information sheets with a Garda shield at the top, and rough black-and-white photographs of paintings underneath.

'They paid me a visit, as they did all the dealers, with a warning to keep a lookout if these crossed my path. I think I'd notice if someone dragged in a Rubens.'

The first and largest photograph was of the Rubens; she remembered it now, some incomprehensible tussle between armoured men and an inadequately clothed woman, her flesh swelling like dough where they grasped her.

'And this is worth hundreds of thousands?'

'Not everyone can appreciate its value,' De Courcy said, annoyed.

'Indeed.' She quickly dragged her eyes down the listings and the smudgy photographs. There were only eight photographs, but the text talked about twelve paintings being stolen.

'Where are the photographs of the other ones?'

Desmond got effortfully to his feet and headed towards the back room. 'I'm sure you could afford a drawing,' he said. 'Come here and I'll show you something very special.'

Considine stayed sitting. 'Why are there only eight photographs?'

The back room had framed works stacked against the walls, and Desmond was now flipping through these. He sighed and stopped. 'Well, that's what I mean about Brewster. The art came from his mother, and it was as if he didn't understand how to look after it properly. He didn't have proper documentation, the provenances were a mess, and some weren't even photographed. She brought them from Antwerp to Texas during the war, so there will be some dodgy lineages.'

Considine looked at the last page. There was a list of four paintings there – measurements, materials, but that was all. The titles were *Flowers and Delftware*, *A View near Würzburg*, *The Martyrdom of St Lilio* and *At the House of Martha and Mary*.

She wanted to ask Desmond who St Lilio was, but sensed it would be a mistake. She dropped the pages back on the desk, as if her interest was waning, and went to join him in the back room, leaving the cup of steaming herb water where it was.

'How would a dealer know that a painting was a stolen work, if no one knows what it looks like?'

Desmond was holding a framed drawing of a man's torso. The head and everything south of the navel were missing. What seemed important was the twist of the body and the shapely muscles under the skin.

'We know what the important ones look like – they're the ones that matter. Of course they'll be in Amsterdam or Hong Kong by now.'

'Why do you say that?'

'Oh, for God's sake, Gina! Enough questions.'

She dropped the subject and pretended to admire the figure drawing, then another, and another.

'The thing you haven't discovered yet – the thing that escapes many people of your age – is the hold that a really good work of art can have. Something beautiful and immortal is worthy of the highest feeling, the greatest sacrifice.'

As he moved the simple drawings out of the way, they revealed a painting of a boyish young man, sitting naked on a floor, limbs arranged to preserve his modesty. His all-too-familiar face stared confrontationally out at the viewer, his lipsticked mouth almost smirking. As if enjoying the ways in which he could taunt her.

'This is interesting.'

'It's the same artist. Amazing lines – slightly derivative of Schiele, but that's no bad thing. I could commission him to do a female nude, especially for you. I'm sure he'd be versatile. Or *of* you! Little gift for the girlfriend.'

Considine couldn't speak for a moment. 'Do you know this model?' she managed.

'Alas, yes.'

'And would you know where I could locate him right now?'

'I imagine he's selling my gold carriage clock to one of those merchants who *do* handle stolen goods.' Desmond's

240

whole person seemed to deflate, and he put down the drawing he was holding. 'He came to the little soirée I gave last night. When he left this morning, so did the clock. People take me for a fool, but they don't take me twice, I'll tell you that much.'

One of his hands was holding the other, stroking it slightly as a little comfort. Despite all his treasures, it was not easy to be Desmond, she thought. But then he looked at her directly and there was something hard, almost calculating, in that look. Perhaps the deflation was only play-acting.

'I'll find him,' she said, 'and I'll box his ears.'

She picked up the details of the Brewster paintings from his desk and he nodded to agree that she could take them. All his flowing talk had dried up.

'One last thing. Do you know a developer called Robert Lynch?'

Desmond looked up at the ceiling, studied the plaster-work a while. 'Don't think I've heard of him. Is he rich?'

'He seems to be. I was wondering if he was the type to be interested in art.'

'I know all the sleek buckos in need of some class.' His voice rose in bravado, his chest swelling like a pigeon. 'Are you going to buy something or not, my poppet?'

'I'd love to buy a painting from you,' she said, 'and once I have somewhere to put it, I will.'

'What's your surname again?'

'Considine.'

'And your address?'

'Why?'

'I'm going to send you invitations to my openings, my dear.'

'I tend to be busy with work.'

'Oh, come on.'

She recited her address and he wrote it on a little index card for his file box. She was going to mention that she might not be at that address for long, but even the thought of saying it made her chest hurt.

All was quiet on the street; the protest had marched on. She had to jog back to her car because she was late again. Her eyes watered from the wind in her face and her tiredness, that was all.

34

It is always good to get the front seat at the top of the bus. That's a given, whatever your age. The sight of the bay and the strand from up here is enough to absolve the world of its sins. I don't come to the seashore often enough. When times are better, I will walk along Sandymount Strand or out at Sandycove or the pier at Dun Laoghaire. I will do it on a summer Sunday in the middle of a busy run of a critically acclaimed play. Wearing sunglasses, so that people won't stop me and force their praise on me. I can imagine how tiring that would get.

It's not improbable that Jess has done a runner on me. She is young, and as selfish as I am. I only hope she didn't try to sell the picture – that would bring instant trouble down. Even among the crooked dealers who'll buy a gold-plated carriage clock as hot as a hot potato, that painting will ring bells. I got thirty pounds for the clock, by the way, filling out my pocket nicely, and Desmond will forgive in time.

Jess still has some friends out here in Blackrock, and Monkstown too. Many sofas that would receive her, I imagine. What's sticking in my mind, though, is her rhapsodising about the treehouse at the back of the Smiley Home, how she stayed there sometimes when she'd nowhere to go;

and that if it wasn't in the grounds of the home she hated, she would happily live in it. That all she needed was her guitar and a doll's tea set.

I need to find her. I need to check she got the painting back to where it needs to be, and that she's safe. Then she can do what she wants. We've shared too much together lately. We've eaten out of bins and we've both waited in alleyways for the other one to finish bringing a stranger to satisfaction. Our bohemia is threadbare this summer. It is easier to preserve our fine dreams if we don't keep catching each other's eye.

I'll always love Jess, and I will always keep her secrets. Why am I thinking of her in this elegiac way, as though she's come to harm? Because of Kieran; because it feels as though every bush could hold a killer, or burst into flame.

I get off in Monkstown, find the gate of the Smiley Home and slip down the side of the driveway. A young face appears at an upper window, but stares so blankly, I know they won't give me away.

The garden behind is vast, and behind every tree the ground is strewn with cigarette butts and tissues – smoke and tears. The treehouse is well hidden, and I shin up the few bits of plank nailed into the bark with a *Ta-da!* on my lips, but Jess isn't there, and the treehouse is not the Beatrix Potter house she described. There are gaping windows and the chipboard floor is soft and bent from damp. I daren't stand on it.

I go to the front door and ring the bell, my hair tucked up in the cap, playing the normal boy. The man who opens the door – knife-crease jeans and a bad V-neck jumper – is all too eager to help me, but doesn't recognise Jess's name. I ask him to let me look around and he turns unreasonable.

What is left to me? Only the mansion that Jess claims belongs to her uncle and aunt. The den of the silver fox and the enchanted queen. *Valparaiso*. Perhaps that's a fantasy too. Jess said it was on the headland just up from the baths, where there used to be a falling-down brick cottage.

It takes me half an hour to find the gate. I know these seaside suburbs like the back of my hand, and every street assaults me with memories. Jess and I used to wonder whether we ever passed on the winding streets before we knew each other. Me a tiny punk with a safety pin through my cheek to show I wasn't a sissy, Jess a solo walker at the back of a line of paired-off white children. The unfortunate orphans who were not really orphans, just illegitimate and taken from their young mothers. *I'll wash the black off of you*, the nuns used to threaten. *There's nothing of Jesus in you, girl.*

Jess's memories of the home enrage me more than my own war stories. That's the weird thing. It might be my salvation that I found someone I can be angrier for than I am for myself.

The gate to the house is locked, of course it is, but they have a bell and a little grid to speak into beside it – *Forgive me, Father, for I have sinned*. The woman who answers doesn't sound like Kieran's mother. Her speech is flat and fast. No, there's no one called Jess or Jessie living there. When I ask to speak to Mr or Mrs Lynch, she says they're not home. I believe she lies.

I know where there's a tunnel near here, by the side of

the convent school. It ducks below ground and under the railway line. There used to be a well in a little branching passage when I was a boy. Some old bastard who lived in the convent when it was a mansion built the wall and tunnel, so he wouldn't have to see the common people come and fetch their water. Thought himself a great philanthropist for not filling in the well. We used to come down here and draw stoned pentagrams on the wall, light a bonfire on the rocks and pretend we were wild and dangerous.

It's creepy to find myself back here in the dark, so I call Jess's name ahead of me as I go. Someone has blocked up the entrance to the well, and I am relieved. Just ten feet of tunnel to go before the rocky shore. My breathing seems to echo off the damp walls and the air starts to rush and rumble. It's a train, I realise, but my pulse is galloping regardless.

My younger self – young Maurice, as I think of him – used to mitch school to hang about this shore, dreaming himself onto the ferries. Before I was Mottie the punk, I was a schoolboy angel, short blond hair and clear blue eyes. Always attracting the attention of girls and older men. *Those eyelashes are wasted on you, Maurice. And that pretty mouth*.

How could I stay home when I had so many questions? I spent my evenings down here on the rocks, while my parents wrung their hands. I would sit at the fire and watch the other kids kiss and fondle each other in the semi-dark, behind a veil of sparks.

My feet remember these boulders; I can hop across them easily, avoiding the green slicks and the crust of seaweed waiting for the touch of the tide. When we used to come here, though, there wasn't that monstrosity. Jesus Christ! Mr Lynch's mansion rises above me like something from Disneyland, walls the colour of butter. There is something rude about its newness, though the windows are as dark and glossy as ponds. You can't tell if there's anyone behind them.

They have wound barbed wire on posts hidden in the gorse bushes, but it is a trifling thing to someone like me, veteran of the revolutionary Archaos circus. Juggler of chainsaws and piranhas, trapeze tumbler in a leather catsuit. *Trained in Paris, don't you know*. I check that the windows are still blank before I clamber across. No alarms sound, nothing moves, no slavering guard dogs appear. I think he feels too confident about his own safety, does Mr Lynch.

35

When Considine finally appeared in the office at lunch-time, Swan made an effort not to show any impatience. He wasn't annoyed, just frustrated. He would have gone to talk to Bill Riordan's mother himself, only Superintendent Martin insisted that Considine be with him. At least he'd made good use of the sparc time.

She stopped beside his desk and cast an eye over the newspaper clippings he was reading. They were all to do with suspicious fires in the city centre.

'You look well,' she said, meaning the opposite.

'I didn't get much sleep in the end. You?' He wasn't going to say she looked about as fresh as a consumptive, but that was the truth of it.

'I had to forgo the pleasure of an actual bed.'

It was the kind of stuffy language he liked to use himself. He smiled.

'What?'

'You're amusing.'

'Stop it. What's the crack?'

He explained the need to go to the Ormond Hotel and talk kindly to Bill Riordan's mother.

'Isn't that place a bit of a dive?'

'It usedn't to be. They're country people, up for a

funeral. Perhaps their hotel knowledge is out of date. Actually, the Ormond Hotel features in *Ulysses*.'

'Let's see if we can manage not to mention that to a grieving mother.'

He followed her out to the car park, glad that her sarcasm had returned. But his moment-to-moment consciousness of how they were getting along was burdensome, and wanting things to be normal was a sure sign that they weren't. He was also worried for her. What would Considine do if they forced her out of her job? She was just about the smartest detective on the team. And what would he do if she left?

She had the keys to a navy Sierra, and he was happy for her to be the driver. She leaned over and unlocked the passenger door, but didn't switch on the engine, even when Swan was well settled in his seat.

'I didn't go home,' she said. 'I had a nap in my car, it seemed easier. When I woke up, I thought I would have a look at that gay-rights protest at the Dáil we heard about – I thought Mottie Deegan might have been there. Or that I might hear something useful. Don't look excited. I was wrong on both counts.'

'Worth a try.'

The traffic on the quays was heavy. They might have made it as quickly on foot. Considine rolled down her window as they inched along, letting in the sound of crying gulls and idling engines and the swampy Liffey reek.

There was no parking place outside the hotel. Considine cursed and began to make a circuit of the block.

'Just leave it on the double yellows,' said Swan.

'It's hardly an emergency,' she said. 'Why aren't they letting us take part in the interviews? Why do we keep getting shoved down to family liaison?' She beeped at a car about to reverse into a free space, then nipped in instead of them. Amazingly, the driver did not get out to shout at them, but simply drove on. A wise move.

'It's not just family liaison. We know nothing about Bill Riordan or what he was doing there.'

Considine was right, though. Superintendent Martin was sidelining her – and Swan along with her.

'So what is happening in Islandbridge?'

Swan got out of the car, and Considine followed him. As they walked round to the front of the hotel he explained that although they had picked up the two other boys who had escaped them in the park, the first ones had definite alibis for the night of Kieran Lynch's murder. 'And they've had to let another one go home on account of his age.'

'Let's not be telling the mother that. Little shits.' She was digging the car key into the palm of her hand as she spoke.

'Do you want me to go in and talk to her on my own?' Swan offered.

'Stop acting weird. I'm fine.'

'No offence, Gina. Tiredness makes us all ragged.'

'Jesus, you can see his flat from here.'

They were at the front of the Ormond Hotel now, directly across from Essex Quay, where Kieran had lived, his building immediately recognisable by the lettering painted on it. Swan tried to imagine what possible connection there might be between Kieran Lynch's flat and Bill Riordan's hotel.

'When did Bill Riordan get to Dublin?' asked Considine, obviously thinking along the same lines.

'Thursday night for a funeral yesterday morning, apparently. So Kieran was already dead. It could just be the proximity of the park they have in common. We know that advocacy or health work may have taken Kieran up to the park, but what took Bill? Would a lad from Kildare know what went on up there?'

'If he was looking for sex, there are ways to find out. Gay Switchboard, maybe. But to back up a bit – are we sure Kieran went to the park that night?'

'We're sure he ended up there.'

Traffic was stopped by the lights, and two seagulls fought over a bread wrapper on the tarmac in front of them.

'This is what I've been thinking,' said Considine, taking out a cigarette. Swan decided that if a speech was coming his way, he'd need to rest his back against the wall of the hotel.

She started to pace the pavement in front of him. 'We have hardly any evidence from the location that Kieran was found. Because they took him to hospital, there was no real effort to secure the site, and so on – it wasn't a murder investigation. But if he had been attacked somewhere else and dumped there, the result would be the same. If he was doing advocacy work he would have been talking to people, approaching people. He would have been noticed. No one has come forward to say they saw him there. The only person who saw him is the mystery jogger who found him.'

'You've said yourself that gay men don't trust us. Think of the Grierson case. That's why we're doing it low-key.'

'I don't think that's the only reason it's low-key.' Considine took a long drag of her cigarette. 'Martin and the other high-up ones seem to be determined to turn Garda Lynch into Citizen Lynch. No gays on us. And we have nothing useful, Swan. Nothing. And if the little gurriers up in Islandbridge didn't do it, we're back to square one.'

'We're not. We just can't see the picture clearly yet. No one's abandoning Kieran Lynch. Let's do this thing in front of us and keep the head. We'll both feel a whole lot more intelligent on eight hours' sleep.'

It was draining, standing on the pavement arguing over the noise of the traffic, breathing in the fumes and her smoke. Swan made a move towards the door, but Considine was still pacing, frowning. She said something and he moved back beside her to catch it.

'The empty condom,' she repeated. 'It annoys me. It was unused, so someone just unwrapped it and flung it onto him. It makes you think it's a sex thing, but it seems like contempt to me. A nasty flourish.'

The hotel receptionist directed them to a lounge at the very back of the building when they asked to see May Riordan. Stacks of chairs occupied one side of it, ready to be brought into the adjacent ballroom. In the far corner, two purple sofas faced each other, and on one sat three women in black. The two outer women leaned in to the centre one, buttresses of comfort. They were all middle-aged, fifties or early sixties, and had an old-fashioned look to them, face powder and brooches, touches of fur trim and pearls.

Swan and Considine approached respectfully and

introduced themselves. May Riordan was the centre one of the trinity, pale under her smudges of rouge, eyes slightly unfocused. A felt hat was pinned onto her grey curls with an actual hatpin, the likes of which Swan remembered his grandmother wearing. In her hand she had a lace-edged handkerchief with pink smears on it that matched her lipstick.

Swan shook the women's hands, and Considine followed, expressing sympathy for their shock and their loss. The women flanking Mrs Riordan introduced themselves as her sister, Jane Conners, and her neighbour, Mrs Owens.

'Are you comfortable to talk to us here?' asked Swan, hoping she would take the chance to lose her bodyguards and make things simpler, but her sister, with a sharp voice, cut across his attempts to set an intimate atmosphere.

'We told Bill not to go out wandering! We told him that Dublin is full of drug addicts and thieves.'

'He was a gentle boy,' added Mrs Owens. 'A beautiful young man. I would be proud to have a son like him.' A touch of bitterness in her voice.

Swan and Considine took their places on the sofa opposite. Mrs Riordan's lips moved as though she was about to say something, but nothing emerged. She was still in shock. On the coffee table in front of them were some silver teapots and a plate of dainty but dry-looking sandwiches, untouched.

Considine reached across the table and rested her hand on Mrs Riordan's knee, palm upwards. The woman grabbed it with both of hers, the handkerchief squeezed in their midst. She seemed to focus on Considine then, as if having physical contact enabled her to see better.

'The shock must be awful,' Considine said, and the woman nodded, her lower lip tremulous. 'We're doing everything we can – I swear to you – to find out what happened to your precious son. We have made arrests, and we are hopeful that we are near an answer.'

'I want to go home,' said May Riordan, squeezing harder on Considine's hand.

Swan revised his intentions for this chat. He had no appetite for pressing this woman on what time her son left the hotel or who he knew in Dublin. They already had the key pieces; they knew how he was killed, where he was killed, and the awful fact of him lying in the morgue. The boys in custody had her son's blood on them. Superintendent Martin had sent them here to impress Bill Riordan's family with the force's great efficiency, but Bill Riordan's family were in pain.

'We won't ask you questions at this point, Mrs Riordan, if you'd prefer.'

Her sister Jane answered. 'She's had enough of those.'

'How do you mean?' asked Considine, gently extracting her hand from the mother's grip.

'There was an awful, cheap man here, asking dreadful things about Bill. He didn't say he was a journalist until we'd been chatting some time,' said Mrs Owens on the right.

'You know you don't have to talk to anyone from the press,' said Swan. 'If you like, I can ask the hotel to ensure you're not bothered.'

'I want to go *home*,' said May Riordan.

While Considine went to talk to the hotel receptionist

about protecting the Riordan family from any journalists or busybodies, Swan used the payphone to call Island-bridge. He was put through to Declan Barrett.

'We got them, Swan. We fucking got them. Their confessions are being written up now.'

'Excellent, Barrett. You make sure you get some sleep now.'

'I'm buzzing.'

'Don't suppose you cracked them on Kieran Lynch at all?'

'We done our best,' Barrett said, 'but it's not tying together.' His voice cracked slightly. The whole team was exhausted.

Swan went over to the reception desk where Considine was looking through the papers laid out for guests. 'SECOND KILLING AT GAY HAUNT' was the headline in the *Evening Press*.

'Look at this trash,' she said, showing him some more articles with pictures of ominous woodland and distant, lurking men. 'This doesn't stop anyone getting bashed, it encourages it. If you're wondering how young Bill Riordan might have known that the Phoenix Park had cruising areas, all he had to do was pick up a paper.'

The fire at the gay centre was featured lower down on the front page, describing it as a place 'catering to the homosexual'. Swan had to admit to himself that he wouldn't have noticed the bias in the past.

He ordered some coffee from the receptionist and encouraged Considine to sit with him on a strange striped sofa behind a pillar in the foyer – quiet enough to talk about what they should do next.

'While I was waiting for you earlier, I called up a few clippings from the library.'

She nodded, only half engaged with what he was saying.

'Remember we were talking about Kieran Lynch's father earlier, and whether we could find out if he owned other buildings or could even find out what he owned? Well, there were three articles that mentioned him. One about him purchasing some land from Dublin Corporation in Irishtown, then another about the architecture award for the housing that he built on it.'

'So he's not just in it for the profit?'

'I'm sure there was plenty of profit. They may have won an award for their "post-modern sensibility", but they still look like egg boxes to me. Anyway, there was some puff-stuff about his career, and they described Lynch as the owner of multiple city-centre properties. The key cabinet in his big house was rather well stocked.'

'Interesting.' She poured out coffee for both of them, with more of a light in her eye.

'That's not the best bit,' he said. 'They said Lynch started in business with a coal yard in Irishtown. Who else used to have a coal yard in Irishtown?'

'Dan Barry! I think he still has it. After every raid or robbery we go and search it and there's never anything to be found. It's the kind of game that Barry finds massively amusing. Bremen Road, I think it's on.'

'Irishtown is a small place … I couldn't find a trace of any other coal yard past or present, so I'm guessing there's some connection between Barry and Lynch.'

'Wait. The man in the picture with baby Kieran – what did they say his name was?'

'I don't think they did. Just said he was Kieran's godfather.'

She huffed a quick laugh. 'Godfather! There's an irony.' Considine dived into her satchel and found the photograph of the picture in Kieran's wallet. They bent their heads together to look at it. It might be Dan Barry all right, younger, thinner and hairier.

'The slightly flashy style is the same, and he still has the sideburns and the Crombie coat.'

'But where does it get us?' asked Considine.

'I don't know. Either Lynch is still an associate, which makes him even dodgier than most developers, or he's managed to shake off a youthful alliance. Why was Kieran carrying Barry's photo around in his wallet as if Dublin's most wanted was his childhood sweetheart?'

'Could Kieran have been placed on the force to look out for Barry's interests?'

'That's what I was wondering, but his record's as clean as a whistle.'

'Well, it would be, if he was any good at it.'

They ground to a halt. It seemed a real stretch to Swan. The idea that this paragon of the gay community was a Garda was difficult enough to swallow. That he could also be a plant for Dan Barry the gangster was bizarre.

'Anyway,' he said, 'the last article I read was all about Lynch's new house contravening planning laws, ruining people's views of the sea, closing public access to a bathing area. His neighbours accused him of getting special treatment or bribing someone. Planning permission had been refused on that site for decades. There were scuffles, vandalism, all sorts.'

'So he's not as respectable as he looks.'

'Don't all the biggest criminals wear suits?'

Considine took a few coins from her pocket. 'Drink up that coffee there, I'm off to make a call.'

While she went to the phone, Swan noticed the Riordan sisters and a young man, who must be the nephew who had identified Bill, checking out of the hotel. It was a sad, quiet sight, the little old-fashioned suitcases they held and the lost looks they gave each other. They negotiated themselves out of the big front door and into a waiting taxi with no words exchanged, merely small hand gestures of 'after you' and 'here you go'. Returning home with only a spare train ticket to mark their enormous loss.

Considine arrived back as the taxi pulled away, landing on the sofa with such vigour that she bounced Swan to attention.

'I called the station in Blackrock. I have a friend who's a sergeant there. Just to check if Robert Lynch had been a good neighbour since the monstrosity was built. He said there'd been no real trouble, but that the burglar alarm kept being tripped. It's a silent one that goes straight to the station. He said they're going to withdraw that privilege to the Lynchs, on account that it keeps going off. It went off today as well.'

'Faulty?'

'Or set up wrong. He said they have a kind of cable along the fence by the seashore – he thought it was foxes to blame.'

'You think we should pay the Lynchs a visit to advise on adequate security?'

'You read my mind.'

36

They decided to leave the car on Frascati Terrace. Considine didn't feel up to tackling the Lynchs' precipitous driveway on four wheels and justified it to Swan as a chance to look more closely at the grounds. She pressed the buzzer under the little metal grid and waited. There was music coming from somewhere, drifts of it on the sea breeze. After the third long ring, the voice of the housekeeper issued from the intercom, aggrieved.

'You don't have to lean on it! No visitors, no deliveries.'

'Is everything okay, Mrs Duggan?'

'Who's that?' she shot back.

Considine received a little nod of admiration from Swan for conjuring the housekeeper's name. Oh, she might be tired, but something in her head was functioning. She reintroduced herself and told Mrs Duggan they needed to check the security on their perimeter. That it was essential.

A crackly mutter and the gate release buzzed. They walked across the little bridge over the railway, stopping briefly in the middle to marvel at the straight vista of tracks either way. The flat green nose of a DART train was heading straight at them from the direction of Blackrock station. The wall on the bridge was so low you would almost be tempted to jump over it onto the back of the moving train, like they would do in a film. Considine almost said that to Swan before realising how odd it would sound.

They started walking down the steep drive and the music grew louder. It was coming from an open bay window high on the front of the house. It was something from the past that she had heard before but didn't know well.

'The Doors,' Swan said, and it took her a moment to realise he was identifying the music, not talking about the house. She laughed, swallowing it down as Mrs Duggan appeared on the driveway below them in her housecoat and a pair of men's slippers, fists on hips, looking mightily displeased.

'Are you going to fix it, so?' she asked.

'Fix it?' said Considine.

'The alarm system!' She was practically yelling at them. Mrs Duggan jerked her head round and up to glare at the window the music was emanating from.

'We'll certainly take a look at it,' said Swan soothingly. 'Is Mr Lynch about?'

'No, he is not,' she declared and stomped softly back to the house.

Considine shrugged at Swan.

'Let's look around,' he said.

There was no car parked outside the house, and the double garage with the fancy cottage roof was empty except for gardening equipment. Considine stared back at the house from further away. She couldn't see what was happening behind that intriguing bay window, but she thought she heard the sound of someone laughing along with the swirls of hippy music. Mrs Duggan suddenly appeared behind the glass of the front door, shooing them away from the house with flapping hands, down towards the sea.

The path curved between two high boulders, then turned into steps, twisting down between rocks and wind-dwarfed furze bushes with desiccated golden petals. Suddenly the sea was beneath them, on the other side of a waist-high wire fence, the kind you might find in a field: alternating rows of plain wire and barbed wire, with what looked like an electric cord at the top. The tide was at its highest mark, churning and sucking between the rocks and throwing up erratic splashes. There was no jetty or secret bay, just rocks and water, but the rough stone steps continued their descent under the fence and down to the water's edge and beyond. A stairway into the sea.

As Swan started to inspect the state of the fence, Considine couldn't resist glancing down the coast a bit, to the place near the sea wall where she'd found the bag with the painting in it. The waves were crashing right up onto the wall and the changing shelter. If she hadn't taken it, it would have been destroyed. The thought of the picture wrapped snugly between blankets in her house warmed her heart as much as it pricked her guilt. She would surrender it, but she also longed to see it again, that little face shining in the midst of turmoil.

'It's not exactly Fort Knox,' Swan commented, returning to her side. He pointed down the coast to the place where the little tunnel emerged onto the shore, near where she had been gazing a moment before. 'It would be easy enough, if you were a spry thing, to scramble along the rocks from there to here. And this fence is hardly high enough.' Swan flicked the topmost wire, the one with the rubber casing, which was likely to be the alarm trigger.

'That'll be Blackrock station alerted again,' said Considine.

'I think your friend there is mistaken about foxes. They can easily pass in and out through the lower wires.' He pointed to a gap where the grass seemed flattened on either side. 'They wouldn't have to jump it.'

'So it's faulty, or there are comings and goings.'

'Let's look around a bit more.'

But the area enclosed by the wire fence was actually quite small. The grounds only seemed large at first glance because of the wide sea views and the borrowed landscape of what was probably railway land on either side. They climbed onto a mound to the side of a stone wall to get a better view. They could see Blackrock's narrow beach to the north, where a few distant dogs and children were running about, having a lovely time.

Considine noticed there was something oddly squared off about the little hill they stood on, and when they came down to look at it closer, they found an old metal door set into a wall on its far side. It had a rusted and heavy padlock preventing them from looking inside.

'It might be an old icehouse or something,' suggested Swan.

'Or a military store.'

The Dublin coast, like any populous coast, was studded with fortifications, from the elegant, stubby Martello towers of the Napoleonic era to twentieth-century lookouts and boltholes. This lock-up seemed a part of whatever was here before Robert Lynch built his grand folly.

'Let's go see if we can talk to Charmaine Lynch,' said Swan. 'Her husband being out might be to our advantage.'

'You said you were here to look at the alarm system. Do it and go,' said the fearsome Mrs Duggan at the front door.

'Kitty!' Charmaine Lynch called melodiously from upstairs.

'Ki-tty!' echoed a younger female voice. 'Can you bring some tea?'

Mrs Duggan pressed her lips together in annoyance. 'This close,' she said, 'I swear I'm this close to handing in my notice.'

'Is everything okay with Mrs Lynch?' asked Swan.

'She's grieving. Apparently. It takes many forms, isn't that what they say?'

'At least she has people with her,' said Considine.

Mrs Duggan gave her a withering look, but suddenly stepped aside, drew the door wider open and said, 'Tell you what. Why don't you just go on up? I'm sure she won't mind a few more visitors.'

Considine led the way up the curved stairs. She had been to Mrs Lynch's bedroom previously to collect the photograph of Kieran, and that seemed to be where the music was coming from now. It had changed from The Doors to something else – a gravelly woman's voice singing insistently.

She gave a gentle knock as she opened the door and stepped into the room, Swan close at her shoulder.

Charmaine Lynch was swaying in the middle of her bedroom, singing along to the record, dressed in a floor-length orange kaftan with a cigarette in one hand and a glass of wine in the other. Trails of tears ran down her face, but she was smiling through it, lost in the sentiment of the lyrics, about someone called Lucy Jordan and the things she hadn't done. She didn't seem to notice that they had come in; all her attention was on her two companions, who sang the song back to her. Considine could hardly believe what she was seeing.

The girl, Jess, was sitting cross-legged at the foot of the bed in a towelling dressing gown, and behind her, sprawled elegantly against a mound of cushions and pillows, was Mottie Deegan. He wore a voluminous cream-coloured jumper and leopard-print trousers. A long diamond earring trailed from one earlobe. The wardrobe doors on either side of the bed were open and garments spilled from a mirrored chest of drawers. There were plates and teacups and wine bottles dotted throughout the room. Whatever this party was, it had been going on for some time.

Jess threw them an amused smile and Mottie Deegan raised an eyebrow. Gradually Charmaine Lynch became aware of their presence, shaking off the trance of the song. As she recognised them, she clutched her heart and her wistful expression turned to pain.

'We're sorry to trouble you. It was Mr Lynch we were looking for,' said Considine.

'Is there news?'

'Nothing significant, I'm afraid to say.' She cut a glance at Mottie Deegan. 'We didn't realise you were with guests …'

'I see you and I feel dread,' said Charmaine, 'but I have to remind myself that the worst has happened already.'

She seemed a lot more lucid than earlier in the week, Considine thought. Swan had stepped back into the doorway, prepared to physically block Mottie and Jess from leaving, if it came to that.

'And that other poor boy at the park ...' Charmaine shook her head slowly.

Considine took a stride towards the bed. 'I'm Gina Considine, this is Vincent Swan.'

'Just a couple of ordinary people passing by,' said Mottie Deegan.

'Don't be rude, Maurice,' said Charmaine, then, confidingly to Considine, 'I let them run all over me – I know I shouldn't. This is my niece Jess, my beautiful girl, and her friend, Maurice, who is such a talented artiste.'

'We're having a wake,' said Jess.

'Kitty!' Mrs Lynch shouted at the ceiling with sudden gusto.

A faint 'Yes, ma'am' came from below.

'There'll be more of us for lunch!'

Considine muttered that there was no need to include her or Swan in the arrangements, but Mrs Lynch had started to whirl around the room, kaftan sleeves waving in the breeze, picking up cups and saucers, clattering everything onto a tray. Swan stepped aside to let her pass, then quickly closed the door in her wake.

'Well, this is convenient,' he said. 'You don't mind if we chat?'

Mottie Deegan affected to look bored, half closing his

eyelids and turning towards the window. Jess crawled up the bed to sit close beside him.

'Go on then,' she said.

'It's Mottie we want to talk to really. But if you can help us in any way, do pitch in.'

'Don't you want to read me my rights?' asked Mottie. He had a strange, almost American drawl.

Swan gave Considine a quick look, a signal for her to take over the conversation if she wanted, but she nodded at him to continue. She didn't trust Mottie not to mention seeing her outside the Moonlit Gate, and she preferred to keep him looking at Swan.

'This is just a friendly chat,' said Swan, and proceeded to give Mottie the rundown of what they knew – that he had been seen with Kieran on Tuesday night, the night before he was found. 'Can you run us through what you remember of that evening?'

Considine noticed Jess give Mottie's hand a little squeeze, though whether it was of solidarity or of warning, she couldn't tell.

'We-ell,' said Mottie expansively, as if there was nothing he'd like more, 'I bumped into Kieran at the Moonlit Gate, it's sort of a gay hangout. I don't know if you're familiar with the gay bars of Dublin?' and he shot Considine a glance as he said it, sharp as a pin. A sweat broke out at her temples.

'I prefer The Earl, on balance,' said Swan, and Mottie granted him a smile.

'We had a drink together, we parted. I wish we hadn't. No big story.'

'Where did you part?' asked Swan.

'Temple Bar. Near the gay centre. I think Kieran was heading for his flat.'

'What time was that?'

'Don't remember.'

'And where were you headed?'

'Don't remember.'

'Maybe you'd remember if you thought about it a bit more.'

'Where's my friendly chat gone, Officer?'

A gong sounded in the hall downstairs, startling them all. A shriek of 'Lunch!' followed. Considine checked her watch. It was nearly four o'clock.

'Better wash my hands,' said Mottie, springing to his feet and heading for the en suite.

Jess stood up too, revealing a frilled pink nightgown under her bathrobe. She must have somehow gained access to the house late last night, after Considine had seen her. Maybe that's what she was doing in the phone box, arranging her visit.

Swan moved towards the girl saying, 'Let me walk down with you.'

Considine stayed put, listening to Swan pick up a conversation with Jess about her relationship to Kieran. She waited until their voices had faded and went straight into the en suite. Mottie Deegan was struggling with the side zip of his fancy trousers.

'My kingdom for a fly,' he said, completely unembarrassed. She was glad to see he was moving the zip up, not down. He went to the basin, whistling.

'What's going on here?' she asked.

His reflection in the mirror looked blankly back at her.

'Okay, forget that, just talk to me about when I saw you with Kieran that night. What were you going to show him?'

Mottie soaped his hands and shook his head. 'Nothing.'

'Kieran asked me to come with him to see something. You had a torch in your hand. What were you going to look at?'

'Honestly, lady, this is nothing to do with him getting attacked.'

'He *wanted* me to see whatever it was. For his sake, you should tell me.'

'I guess you missed your chance.'

'Were you going to show him some paintings maybe?'

Mottie dried his hands slowly on a huge white towel. His silence was different from his backchat.

'Okay, how do you know that what you showed him had nothing to do with him being attacked?'

'I think he got unlucky,' said Mottie, looking at her properly now. 'I think he was in the park and he got unlucky. It happens.'

'Who would he have told about the things you showed him? Who else knew?'

He held her eye for a minute, a slight wavering.

A shout from below. 'If you don't get down here, Maurice Deegan, and bring that Ban Garda with you, you'll know about it.'

'Coming!' yelled Mottie. Then, to Considine, 'She's famously unhinged, our Charmaine. Better not keep her waiting.'

*

270

Lunch consisted of oxtail soup and sliced white bread, served with dramatic resentment at the big farmhouse table by Mrs Deegan. Jess appeared with another bottle of wine. Mrs Lynch talked expansively while Mottie, Swan and Considine eyed each other suspiciously and Jess drank and heckled her aunt.

Considine and Swan both refused the wine. She felt disembodied enough as it was, as though they had lost all volition since entering the house – exhaustion and politeness keeping them captive at this bizarre meal. They needed to get Mottie and Jess to a station for questioning and statements, no matter the consequences for herself.

Charmaine Lynch was in the mood to tell anecdotes about her happy family, about Kieran – *my shining boy* – about the mews house near Baggot Street where they lived in the seventies, the parties they would have there, and how Kieran could make a perfect gin and tonic by the age of eleven. *You remember?* she kept prompting Jess.

Jess would reply that she never got invited to most of the parties, or that her aunt was too ashamed of her, or that they wouldn't let her out of the home in the evenings, but the sparring was oddly playful for the situation they were describing. Jess's mother, Charmaine's sister, was not 'responsible' enough to look after a child, was the story, and so Jess had mostly lived in a children's home.

'Just down the road from here, funnily enough,' said Jess.

'I would have taken you in, my darling, but the mews was so small. And my sister would have been jealous. I mean she was jealous already, of my husband, my house—'

'Your lover.'

Charmaine Lynch didn't even notice Jess's interjection. 'But it's all water under the bridge now. Isn't it?'

'I'm sure you can make it up to me.' Jess raised her glass to Mottie with an odd smirk.

Considine had given up eating her soup. She was hungry, but it was as salty as brine.

'I don't even like this house,' said Charmaine, her cheeks ruddy with emotion. 'Too many rooms, not enough people. It has a cold feeling – very much an expression of my husband. I mean, I don't even drive. I'm basically a prisoner.' Two fat tears ran down her face.

'We won't leave you lonely, Charmaine,' said Mottie.

Swan caught Considine's eye. It felt like they were right in the middle of a grift.

Charmaine brought her hands up in front of her face. 'I miss my boy.' Her shoulders began to heave.

'A song!' said Jess. 'You need a song. How about "Danny Boy"?'

'Too sad,' said Charmaine from behind her hands.

Jess clambered up to stand on her chair. 'I've got it!' She began to sing 'La Cucaracha', holding her hands up by her head and miming invisible castanets. The frills on the hem of her nightdress bounced. Mottie started to guffaw. Charmaine Lynch uncovered her face and looked at her niece in sozzled wonderment.

'Dear God,' said Swan.

Considine looked at her watch.

37

The aunt has taken to her bed. Jess calls her a lush, but a proper alcoholic could handle a bit of daytime drinking. I think she's just sad. Sad for her lost boy, but sad for longer than that. You can tell by the lines that her mouth falls into. Jess went upstairs with her, the police went to make some phone calls and I'm left alone in the kitchen, under the gimlet eye of the housekeeper, Kitty. Hellcat, more like. She is our biggest threat – I told Jess that. Never underestimate the feudal loyalty of the domestic servant.

This house is incredible. Jess says she didn't even know it was this big. I've done a whirl around its every room. Half of them are empty. I think I would take the little room at the top of the tower for my bedroom. Grow my hair long, specially for visiting suitors to climb up. *If* we're let stay. There's even a swimming pool in the basement. Not a big one, and a bit basementy, but still.

I thought I was going to have to rescue Jess from her evil family, and here I am already half in love with her wacky aunt and her entire hostessy wardrobe.

'Why,' I asked Jess, 'have we been sleeping in an attic with a hole in the roof when your family owns a fucking mansion?'

'We've had our ups and downs,' she said, 'and I was waiting to get invited.'

Kitty is giving me a headache, the way she clatters those dishes. And that soup was unforgivable. If I could cook, I could replace her in a hot minute. I wander upstairs and hover outside the room where the police are using the phone. It's supposed to be Jess's uncle's library, but there's only a desk and a phone in there and a leather sofa wrapped in the plastic it came in. The detectives seem to be arguing, but I can't make out about what. One of them wants to do one thing, the other something else.

The woman, Considine, was trying to make me feel guilty. I won't do guilt. But I should never have shown Kieran the stolen stuff. I think the excitement got the better of me. He was always too moral. Is she right: did Kieran tell someone about it before he died? That would be just like him, the handsome fool. I didn't know his father owned the building. I didn't ask where Kieran got the keys, I merely said *thank you*.

The police stop talking and I sneak off up to Charmaine's boudoir in case they emerge.

The curtains are closed, the room in half-light, but I can see them both on the bed: Charmaine asleep, her face slack, Jess curled into her aunt's back, thumb in her mouth. Her head bobs up when she senses me there and she quickly rolls off the bed and comes with me.

Down at the bottom of the garden I make Jess show me exactly where she left the painting, and we climb over the fence and down to the shore and she points to a spot close to where I walked this morning. There was no bag there then, and there is none now. The tide has taken it away. Or someone found it.

'I hid it here,' Jess says again. 'I hid it when I realised you were right that we should have dumped it. If my uncle has the other paintings, he's not going to be thrilled that we know about it. Anyway I planned to come back and get it. I didn't know how high the water came.'

'Maybe it will float back to us,' I say. 'Wood floats.'

We wander about on the rocks for a while, looking into the water, searching for a particular shade of green. It makes my heart hurt to think of that little martyr. He could survive the burning, but not the drowning.

'So how did your uncle take it when you turned up out of the blue?'

'I phoned ahead, and my aunt answered. I said I wanted to come because of Kieran – I wanted to give my sympathies. Uncle Robert was outside. Rushing around the place. He sent me inside to see my aunt and said that she'd be glad to see me. No one seemed to notice it was the middle of the night. Auntie Charmaine was playing records. I think they really need me now.'

Jess is forever optimistic.

We climb up on a mound to get a wider view. There is a man on the shore towards Blackrock, he's holding two heavy buckets and a long net. He seems to be looking at us, but maybe he's just waiting for the tide to go out. You can't get cockles when the tide is this far in.

'See, Jess, there's all kinds of people along this shore. Anyone could have found that bag.'

'I hid it,' she insists.

There is the sound of an engine close by and a flash of car coming down the drive.

'My uncle's back,' says Jess. 'Let's see how your charm works on him.'

'Let's see if he gets rid of those police first.'

We chase each other around the rocks for a while, waiting for the grown-ups to sort themselves out. But suddenly there's a man standing between us, beautiful as an ad for expensive cigarettes, silver-fox hair, light suit, a dangle of keys in his hand. Weirdly, he has an old rolled rug in the crook of his arm, like he's about to do some yoga or magic flying.

'What do you think you're *doing*, Jessica?'

He speaks quietly, but waves of irritation come off him.

'Just showing my friend around.'

'On what basis?'

'What?'

'Don't say "what", say "pardon". You are supposed to be supporting your aunt, not pleasing yourself.'

He's not even looking at me, he's so intent on making Jess submit. And you just know he's done this many times before. All his attractiveness vanishes. Jess has her chin down and looks about twelve. I think we might be here for some time. But then something seems to switch off in him; whatever engine was fuelling his ire has faltered.

'Go inside,' he says, and we run.

38

Swan was irritated that Mrs Duggan kept bringing pots of tea to the room – they'd told her not to, but the door opened again while he was on the phone to Eric Joyce and there was another tray, another slopping teapot. Considine thanked the woman and reiterated that they needed nothing, showing her out of the door once she had swapped tray for tray. The housekeeper was obviously spying, trying to get a sense of what was under discussion.

He hung up the phone and waited for a moment, moving as far away from the door as the room allowed.

'What did Joyce say?' asked Considine.

'He says they're wrapping up there, and there's a case meeting in a couple of hours at the depot. He's not particularly interested in our questioning Mottie Deegan at this stage, he says, though we're free to take informal statements here.'

'It feels like we're getting shut out.'

'Nonsense, we're being given a choice of how we spend our time.'

'And we're spending it extravagantly, hanging around here.' She picked distractedly at the wrapping on the sofa.

'We'll have a proper talk with that Mottie boy,' he said.

'He's a trickster.'

'Maybe we should sweat him a bit.'

'*Sweat* him? You've been watching those old gangster movies again, haven't you?'

'Mottie was the last one to see Kieran. It's all we've got,' Swan said, trying to be equitable in the face of her irritation, which he put down to tiredness. He poured himself another cup of tea and settled into the comfort of Robert Lynch's office chair.

'It's not all we've got,' said Considine.

'It's the only solid thing,' he said. The chair was far too comfortable. If he stayed there, he'd lose consciousness. He stood back up and took his cup on a circuit of the room. 'All the rest is fragments – a possible connection to Dan Barry, an arson attempt on a warehouse near Kieran's favourite nightspot, Badger Stacy hanging around the place.'

'What if there was something in the warehouse that Kieran found out about. Something illegal.' She wasn't looking directly at him, she was staring down at her entwined fingers in her lap. Her voice was tense.

'What kind of thing?'

'I don't know. Drugs, maybe.'

'So Kieran was going to grass up his father?'

'Or his godfather,' said Considine, suddenly more animated. 'Maybe that's why he had the photograph in his wallet. He wasn't going to grass up Dan Barry, he was going to appeal to the old bastard's soft side. Try to get him to do the right thing, or something.'

'That would never work.'

'But that's what everyone says about Kieran: that he had a kind of zeal, that he was too sure of himself.'

Swan returned to the tray to put his cup down. 'We just need one more thing – a proper crime scene, a witness, a suspect even.'

Considine sighed. 'Okay, we'll talk to Mottie Deegan again.'

'Good girl.'

'Don't call me that,' she snapped.

He turned quickly to the window, exasperated with himself and with everything. Something moved in the garden, a person. It was Robert Lynch, appearing magically from behind a boulder, coming up the path from the shore with a rolled rug under his arm.

'The fecker!' Swan shouted and ran for the stairs. Out of a side window he caught sight of the parked Mercedes. That's why the housekeeper had been so solicitous; it had given her a chance to check that her master's arrival hadn't been noticed.

Robert Lynch already had the driver's door open when Swan got to him, grabbing his elbow and hauling him away from the car.

'Don't you lay a hand on me!' Lynch pulled his arm from Swan's grasp, and Swan noticed that some of the knuckles on his hand were skinned.

'I'd prefer not to physically detain you, but we've had a long wait for the chance to talk to you.'

Considine emerged from the house and stood waiting by the door.

'I don't have time for this. I have a meeting.'

'You work too hard, Mr Lynch. We won't keep you long.'

'Just a brief chat,' said Considine, pointing the way in.

He glared but obeyed. They followed him into the high circular hall. Mrs Duggan was at the bottom of the stairs, stiff-backed as a soldier, and when Swan glanced up, he could see the heads of Mottie and Jess looking down from the highest level, backlit by a round skylight, so that it wasn't possible to read their expressions. When Robert Lynch followed his gaze, they ducked their heads out of sight.

'What is going on?' he asked Mrs Duggan.

'You'll have to ask the missus.' She rolled her eyes piously, an innocent, sorely tried.

Robert Lynch addressed Swan and Considine. 'I will give you five minutes, no more.'

He opened a nearby door into a new room, a dark one. He flicked on some Art Deco wall lights, and it appeared they were in a small, well-appointed bar. Velvet seats were stacked up in the corner beside a shrouded pool table. He didn't offer them a seat, just stood with one hand dug into his trouser pocket, the other – the uninjured one, Swan noted – flicking the car key impatiently.

'This is pretty deluxe,' said Considine. 'How long is it you've lived here?'

Mr Lynch sighed. 'Two years. It takes time to get things exactly as you want them.'

'Grand place for parties, I imagine,' said Swan.

'That's the theory,' answered Lynch. 'What was it that was so pressing?'

Swan thought the room looked as if it had never contained a good time. The pristine bar and the immaculate velvet had never encountered a scuff or a spill.

'We're looking into various properties in Temple Bar – in connection with your son's death – and hoped you could clarify how many properties you own in the area.'

'I don't have those details to hand.'

'Roughly.'

'I'll get my assistant to send you a full list, how about that?'

'What about numbers twenty-four to thirty Temple Lane?' asked Considine, consulting her notebook for the correct address.

'What about it?' snapped Robert Lynch. 'How can any of this be about Kieran?' He was breathing heavily.

Swan took a step nearer, hands tilted in a conciliatory manner. 'We're not here to upset you. It would be quicker for all of us if you could just confirm what's what, then we'll get out of your hair. Do you know that warehouse?'

Robert Lynch looked at the ground, said nothing. Swan noticed that the seam along the right shoulder of his jacket had a tear in it.

'It burned down last night,' said Considine.

'I have many interests in property in the area. I'll have to talk to my office to get you the details. I don't see how this could be relevant, and I have a suspicion that you're exploiting the death of my son to conduct intrusive enquiries into me. Why are you even in my house?'

'We need your help,' said Considine plainly. 'When did you last talk to Kieran – was it on the phone?'

Robert Lynch lifted his clenched hands towards his head and made an exasperated growl. 'I need to be somewhere else.'

'We can look up the call logs if you don't want—'

But he was already heading for the door, flinging it open to reveal both Mrs Duggan and Charmaine Lynch standing outside.

'For Christ's sake!' he shouted, pushing past them. His wife caught onto his shoulder and tried to turn him towards her.

'What's happening, Robert? I saw a man in the garden—' Her eyes were wide with dread. Swan approached them, noticing that Mottie and Jess were down on the lower steps now, closer to the action. He hoped somehow to persuade Robert Lynch to stay, but the man was in a rage, swiping away his wife's hands, complaining about her letting *all sorts* into their home, saying she wasn't right in the head.

Jess ran over to take her aunt's side, calling her uncle some choice names in the process. Their voices echoed on the hard polished surfaces of the hall. Mrs Duggan wrung the hem of her housecoat. But Robert Lynch was making for the door, hunched with the effort of escape.

Considine went over to the women. Swan followed Lynch outside and watched him disappear around the corner to his car. It wouldn't be useful to drag him out of it again, but he could at least try to calm things.

He heard a car door bang. An engine roar and the scrabble of gravel followed. The shining Mercedes roared up the drive dangerously fast and braked just before it crossed the bridge.

It was hard to make sense of what happened next. There was a flash of orange up on the railway bridge and a burst of black smoke. Swan thought the car had crashed, but then came the noise, a sound as big as the sky. It ripped the air and shook the ground. Bits of metal started to rain down from the smoke cloud into the garden of Valparaiso.

39

Considine found herself crouched on the marble floor with her ears ringing. The bomb had not blown her there; the sound was so immense, so wrathful, that she had instinctively dived for the ground. She lifted her head and looked about. Mottie, Jess and Charmaine were in a scrambled, embracing heap by the far wall. Only Mrs Duggan was standing, looking up at the circular skylight and the white spider of cracks that now stretched across it.

'Christ! Everyone move – into the kitchen, now!' Considine's voice sounded muffled in her ears, but it must have carried because they obeyed immediately.

She grabbed her coat, thinking of it as extra protection, and looked out of the window beside the front door to see if it was safe to go out. All was sunny and still. She ran out and around the side of the building and the prospect changed. Smoke was rising from the railway bridge. As she started to run up the driveway, she noticed the gravel was studded with crumbs of glass and shards of shining metal, some of them smoking. Her heart thumped painfully in her chest. *Where is Swan?* It was hard to make sense of what was in front of her – branches and bushes had been ripped apart and scattered on the drive. A car bumper was planted where a tree might be, bundles of detritus bloomed in the flowerbeds. Then she saw movement on the bridge and a figure standing beside some twisted metal. It was Swan. He was alive, thank God.

'Swan!' she shouted, running towards him, passing a lumpy piece of car seat on the side of the drive.

'Stay back!' he called. She paused to catch a breath, remembering suddenly that a key part of their training was to look out for a second explosion – an explosion that would come once the security services had closed in on the wreck of the first.

'Look out for booby traps or wires!' she shouted.

Swan raised his head – the bridge wall masked most of what he was examining – and looked in her direction. There was something horribly blank in his expression.

'Is he there?' she called.

'I just can't tell.'

He was moving in an odd way, slow and stunned. She would have to go and get him to come away, but she also needed to go back to the house to raise the alarm. She was wavering between these options when she noticed that the car seat she had passed was moving.

It was lying on the edge of the drive, under a rhododendron bush. It was made of dark-grey material, and it was no longer a car seat. It was a curled back, and beyond the shoulders of that curled back she could make out Robert Lynch's silver hair blowing in the light breeze. The shape squirmed. He was trying to straighten himself out.

She must have made some kind of noise, because Swan was running towards her now, pushing past her to squat down beside Robert Lynch. Considine had not managed to move one step.

Swan was leaning over him, whispering to him, and she could see Lynch's profile, just make out his lips moving in response. Swan was pulling off his necktie, calling her forward.

'Help me roll him,' he said.

She knew you shouldn't roll injured people, but it wasn't possible to leave him crammed around the trunk of a rhododendron bush, either. She decided to trust Swan's judgement and went to squat down near the man's hips.

With a lurch, she saw that his legs were gone. That's how he fitted into this small space.

'Give us your belt there,' said Swan.

As best they could, they tied Swan's necktie and her mackintosh belt as tourniquets around what remained of his thighs. She was not convinced it would help.

Robert Lynch's eyes were open. He was looking up at the blue sky and the trail of smoke across it.

'Another fire,' he mumbled.

Swan manoeuvred himself so that he was sitting on the side of the driveway and Lynch's head and shoulders were across his lap. He held the man firmly in his arms. Lynch looked relatively unhurt above his lost legs, though his face was dotted with little slashes, some of which seemed to hold fragments of glass.

Considine shook out her coat and placed it over the wreck of Lynch's lower body. Mottie Deegan was approaching up the hill, his eyes wide, looking ready to turn back in an instant. She ran down to him.

'Call nine-nine-nine. Get an ambulance – maybe a helicopter, tell them. Do it now. Wait! The train line. Go! Tell them to stop the trains!'

She gave him a little shove to set him moving and headed back up the steep driveway, passing the pietà of Swan and Robert Lynch on the way, blood now seeping onto the granite cobbles from under her best coat. *Don't get distracted*, she told herself. She had to check the railway track to see how bad it was.

By the time she reached the bridge she was gasping for air. The wreck of the car was an amazing thing – the roof was gone, but some of the gold and silver metal that had formed it twisted outwards from the centre, as if some huge supernatural thing had escaped from it. The flayed cream-leather seats looked like pieces of slack skin, and where there should be a floor and a handbrake there was a hole. The hole was full of light because it went through the car and through the bridge, offering a queasy glimpse of the tracks below.

She wrenched her eyes away to look up towards Blackrock station and down towards Seapoint. Nothing was coming. A train stood in Blackrock station, but the tiny dots of people on the platform were standing still, not boarding or disembarking. There was also a man on the track, heading towards Blackrock and carrying a net and a bucket, it looked like. Blocks of the bridge wall had fallen down onto the rails. She realised that everyone would have seen the bomb go off, including whatever train drivers were heading their way. She had a sudden memory of the film *The Railway Children*, of red petticoats being waved and brave girls on the track. There would be no need for that.

Considine looked down at her fingers as they clutched the edge of the stone wall. She realised she was gripping it to stop them trembling. That her knees were trembling too. She had to move, to get off the bridge and back to Swan. She half turned and noticed something flapping on the ground near her foot. It appeared to be a small waving hand and she could make no sense of it at first, but anything was possible now, even a hand waving from the solid ground. She managed to keep looking at it until it resolved. It was not a real hand, but the image of a hand, painted onto some kind of cloth, and it was the wind that was giving it a freakish life.

She pulled at it, and it tore away from the shard of metal that had pinned it there. The back of it was a dull kind of canvas, the front stiff with paint. There was something familiar about this hand. She had to stop looking at it, she told herself, and ran back down to where Swan was. A distant siren threaded the air.

Swan was still holding Robert Lynch in his arms, talking to him with fierce encouragement. But the man's face was clammy and pale. She threw herself down beside Swan and felt for Lynch's pulse. Swan's monologue, she suddenly realised, was not the comforting kind.

'Tell me,' he was saying, 'tell me while there's time. Who did this? Was it Dan Barry? What have you been up to, Robert? Has this to do with Kieran?'

Lynch was trying to look away from Swan, to keep his eyes on the sky. Considine put a restraining hand on Swan's sleeve. 'The ambulances are coming,' she said.

Several deep thumps shook the ground, and a horrible scrape of metal followed as the bridge collapsed behind them, dragging the wrecked Mercedes down with it.

She felt a cold touch on her hand. Lynch was looking straight at her and trying to grasp her fingers with his. She moved the scrap of painted canvas to her other hand so that she could oblige.

'Is there anything you want to tell us, Robert?'

He mumbled a word. It sounded like *Kieran*.

'What about Kieran?'

'My boy,' he said, his face creasing in pain and upset.

She looked at Swan. He shook his head as if to say, *It's hopeless*.

'Do you want me to get your wife? Do you want me to fetch Charmaine?'

He stared at her, then nodded once.

'You hang on,' she said and loosed his grip.

'What have you got there?' asked Swan, looking at the canvas scrap in her other hand.

'I think it's a bit of a painting.' She held it up for Swan to see and noticed Lynch's eyes moving to it. 'Can you tell us what this is, Robert? It must have been in your car.'

He shut his eyes against her and turned his head away.

A whoop of siren came from up near the bridge. Then a battering on the big wooden gate. Considine ran up towards the bridge again. The gate swung open as she got within sight of it, and she had to spend some minutes shouting across the void at the two ambulance men, telling them what had happened and how to get round by the shore. While she was doing that, a police car appeared behind them, and the ambulance men started to relay the story to them.

'There's a man very badly wounded here!' she shouted,

and started to jog down the driveway once more in search of Charmaine Lynch. She felt that this precipitous, exhausting driveway would feature in nightmares for the rest of her life. She didn't even look at Swan and Lynch this time. Mottie and Jess were standing together by the side of the house, arms around each other. They told her Charmaine was in the kitchen. She instructed them to look out for the ambulance men or the police and get them to where Lynch was lying. They nodded, full of solemnity.

She skirted the edge of the circular hallway, wary of the cracked skylight. Mrs Duggan was nowhere to be seen. Charmaine Lynch was at the kitchen table, her face in her hands and a steaming mug of tea in front of her. Considine called her name, but she didn't look up.

She went to her side. 'Mrs Lynch, could you come and be with your husband?'

'I'm scared,' she said, fanning her hands in front of her wet eyes. 'I don't think I can.'

'He's badly injured. DI Swan is with him, but he really needs you, I think.'

'Is he going to die?'

'There's every reason to hope he won't.'

'I've lost my son, you see. It's too much.'

Considine felt a flare of anger. She wanted to grab her by her stupid kaftan and march her outside. But she took a deep breath and allowed the anger to fade. Maybe Charmaine was right. It was all too much.

Above the house she heard the judder of helicopter blades and was relieved, before wondering where they would find to land on this outcrop of towers and rocks.

The helicopter circled and came in closer to the house, searching. Considine realised what was going to happen just before it did. She ran to slam the kitchen door as the helicopter passed close over the house, but the deafening rotors were not loud enough to mask the sharp cracking as the skylight gave way under the helicopter's downdraught. The sound of an avalanche of glass filled the marble atrium, shards bouncing off the other side of the closed door like vicious hail. Charmaine Lynch put her head back and began to scream.

By the time Considine got back to Swan, it was too late for anyone to hold Lynch's hand. One of the ambulance men had made it to his side; the other was still tangling with the barbed-wire fence. She felt very little, as though all her feelings had been used up. The light was turning the mansion walls golden. After all the noise, the quiet was unreal, almost holy.

Robert Lynch's face looked peaceful now, even with its multiple cuts. Swan was slowly working his way out from under the body, a defeated set to his face. She thought of Lynch's pristine private bar, where no friends had ever laughed or enjoyed his company, and of his wife who wouldn't come and hold his hand. Reminded of hands, Considine took the scrap of painting out of her pocket and turned it this way and that. She realised where she had seen it before.

40

Jess and I were discussing how Valparaiso has been improved by the accident. Fresh air and sea breezes right in the heart of the house. Our last home had a hole in the roof too – *it's kismet, baby*. Yes, the marble stairs are slippery when it rains, but that's more than compensated for by the visual effects. There was a really heavy shower last night and it made a rippling waterfall all the way down the stairs. I told Jess it reminded me of the cascade at Parc de Saint-Cloud.

'You should come to Paris with me next time.'

'Let's not kid ourselves,' says Jess.

'About what? About getting away?'

'About us, Mottie. Let's just enjoy the end of the summer.'

Jess thinks one of us will meet a boy and run away with them. I'm not romantic like she is. I'm not a fool. I tell her it's better to have a friend, someone who sees you clearly.

After the bomb, Charmaine and Mrs Duggan moved out. Robert had already departed, in both senses. We told Charmaine we'd stay and mind the house. She was very grateful. She promised she would send us the keys and make things official, but the postman can't get near here any more.

Official-looking men crawled over the grounds for days. They searched the house from top to bottom and finally found the other paintings in a rough old store down near the shore, beside where I met Robert Lynch the day he died. We heard them shouting; that's how excited they were. Jess and I went down to watch them walk along the stony shore, with rolled-up canvases and two wrapped panels. No sign of our painting yet, though we check along the shore every day. Jess is convinced he will come back to us. As I say, romantic.

What I don't tell her is that the sea will swell that old board and the paint will crack and flake off it. Or that sea snails and barnacles will eat trails across the soldiers and the flames, and whatever remains of the beautiful boy. It's better not to get it back at all than have to set eyes on that kind of disaster.

Speaking of disaster, there were all kinds of cranes and lorries and even more men in white jumpsuits up on the railway tracks today, clearing away the final remains of the car and the bridge. I asked when they would replace it, and they said it was a private bridge and the owners would have to arrange for that. Valparaiso has become a tidal island. Keeps away the riff-raff, but makes a walk to the shops quite tedious.

There's enough food in the fridge and the chest freezer to keep us going luckily, though most of it was created by Mrs Duggan's salty hand. We already knew where the wine cellar was. Jess thinks we should have a big party here, a session with musician friends that would last for days. I'm managing to talk her out of it. We'd have to clean up all the broken glass in the hall, and people would only rob things and leave a mess. I know they would. I've checked through most of the ornaments myself, though, and there's little worth selling. It's all brand new, *tant pis*, apart from a few pieces of Georgian silver that I have my eye on. I would punt them to Desmond de Courcy, but he's probably still not speaking to me.

We couldn't find Charmaine for days, then Jess managed to locate her at her ancient mother's house in Irishtown. It's hard to imagine her there in one of those poky little cottages. She's convalescing, she says, as if she's on the mend from the flu. I don't know how a person gets over a double loss like that. Some of us know how to shut down the old heart, but apparently Charmaine was always on the verge of sentimental tears, even before Kieran was killed. Jess's mother is in the little house too, which means Jess refuses to visit. Her mother is a *legendary bitch and dipso*, she says.

Everyone is a dipso, in Jess's book. I think that's because Jess is also overly fond of her wine, but mostly we have a grand time, with singing and dancing and wafting around our new home. I did try sleeping up in the turret, but the wind was bothersome. We spend nearly all our time now in Charmaine's boudoir or down in the kitchen. Jess has filled the place with vases and jugs of montbretia – it's blooming all over the grounds and on the banks of the railway line. Orange sprays and sharp green blades on every surface of the kitchen.

'We're like millionaires now,' I tell her, stroking one of Robert's cashmere jumpers that suits me particularly well.

It is so very relaxing, so *healing*, to have a sufficiency, to stop hustling for a week, a month or however long it lasts.

We did have one big night in Robert's home bar, the two of us, music on the jukebox, playing pool and drinking his fizz, but there are no windows there, and it made me nervous not to know if anyone was creeping up on us. That's why I prefer to leave all the glass lying at the bottom of the staircase – it's our burglar alarm.

Sometimes Jess falls into a sulk with me and with the world. I'll find her leafing through the family photo albums on the big bed: summer holidays, Christmases, people laughing over the remains of boozy lunches, with bottles on the table, red cheeks and red eyes. But Jess can't find herself anywhere.

'Photo albums are never the truth.'

'I know that. But I thought I'd be in there somewhere. I was there. I felt like I was part of their family, despite everything. I was very cute when I was little.'

'You're still very cute, my darling. And more than that, you're clever and you're alive.'

'Are you saying that Kieran and Uncle Robert weren't clever?'

I sit down at Charmaine's dressing table and start looking through all her make-up. Jess is watching my reflection in the mirror.

'What did you talk to that policewoman about when she chased you into the bathroom?'

'I told her the truth. I said the last time I saw Kieran was on a street in Temple Bar, and I thought he was heading to his flat.'

I start to put on mascara, leaning in close to the mirror so that Jess can't catch my eye.

'Isn't it funny how no one wants to ask me anything?' she says. 'It must be my innocent face. Or they think I'm dumb as a plank. I was there too, Mottie, I met Kieran the night he died – must have been after he left you. He was at that phone box in East Essex Street, and I was coming home from the restaurant. He said he was waiting for a friend and I asked: didn't he have a phone of his own and a flat to wait in?'

I fiddle around with a mascara wand, pretending to be absorbed in getting the brush covered with just the right amount of black stuff. Finally I look at her.

'Kieran was all out of sorts. Jumpy. He started talking about finding us somewhere else to stay, somewhere safer. You showed him all the goodies, Mottie, didn't you?'

I lift one shoulder slowly and pout, trying to be cute.

'Well, that was fucking stupid.'

I put away the mascara. Jess is never angry with me.

'Remember Mr Brylcreem?' she asks. 'We always thought he was trying to pluck up courage to go into the gay centre. Always hanging about. Always watching. Well, he was parked there, sitting in his little Renault van. Pointed towards the phone box, engine running.'

'Was he the friend?'

'No, Kieran wasn't looking at him, he was looking out for someone else.'

'I think Mr Brylcreem's name is Badger,' I say, because I have just figured out that his boss, his very scary boss, was calling his name at the warehouse.

'Badger Brylcreem?'

And all at once we're laughing, tears streaming down our faces, Jess drumming her heels on the mattress, she's so hysterical. I'm wiping mascara all over my cheeks. We laugh until we can laugh no more. In the fresh silence I can hear the waves below.

'I'm sorry, Jess, I'm sorry I showed Kieran the stuff.'

'We can't bring him back now.'

'I wish we could.'

'It's not your fault, Mottie.'

'We don't know that.'

41

The glass ashtrays in the commissioners' meeting room were as big as dog bowls, but were filling up rapidly by the time the halfway point in the meeting was reached. Swan took the chance to go and open one of the windows wider, taking a gulp of fresh city air as he did so. Superintendent Martin had the big seat at the head of the oval table, everyone else crammed in as best they could: all of the murder squad, some of the anti-terrorism unit, the serious-crime squad who were dealing with the art theft and with Dan Barry's activities, and an unnecessarily large delegation from Islandbridge station. Some people love a meeting. Not just for the free sandwiches, but for the attractive mix of importance and inactivity.

Superintendent Martin had already established himself at HQ as a meeting-loving man. He'd even got someone to do fancy acetate photographs of the victims, to be projected on the big screen. Everyone already knew who the victims were and their permanent status, so Swan considered this a bit of a gimmick.

They had spent two hours on all the known facts of Kieran Lynch and Bill Riordan's murders, so the refreshment trolley arriving was a joyous event. Swan returned to his seat with a tea and a chocolate biscuit – no plain Mari-ettas in this section of the building – noticing Considine embroiled in an intense-looking exchange with Declan Barrett on the far side of the room.

'What was that about?' he asked when she returned, looking tight with aggravation.

'You remember that address book from Kieran Lynch's flat? You found it under the phone.'

Swan remembered.

'I gave it to Barrett to put with the rest of the case evidence, but it's not there, and he says he doesn't remember me giving it to him.'

'It was a rushed time. It'll turn up.'

'It'd better,' she spat.

Considine's mood had not improved in the fortnight since that sleepless weekend. He would have liked to ask her if everything was okay at home, with her girlfriend, thereby demonstrating his own insouciance and recovery from a dented heart, but she was managing to project such a force-field of annoyance lately that he didn't dare.

Superintendent Martin coughed drily and the room fell gradually silent. Aidan Balfe from anti-terrorism got up to speak about the investigation into the car bomb that killed Robert Lynch.

'It was a relatively simple incendiary device. They used materials packed into a large hairspray can, which could have been an amateur effort, but it was almost definitely radio-detonated, which suggests a link to paramilitaries, and also that someone had eyes on the car as it crossed the bridge. Maximum chaos. We believe it was attached to his car at his house. His wife told us of seeing a stranger in the garden before the explosion.'

There was general talk about the slim likelihood that Robert Lynch had dealings with the IRA, which led nowhere useful, until one bright spark brought up an incident the previous year against a security van – a robbery connected to Dan Barry and to a renegade INLA man, who had helped set up the explosive device. If Barry was motivated to attack Lynch, he had the means.

What no one dwelt on was the finding that if Robert Lynch had been blown in the opposite direction, near the public road and adequate emergency intervention, he would still be alive. The flashback of embracing the man while his life flowed from him came back to Swan in dreams, but he trusted that would fade in time.

Goretti Flynn, one of the best scientists from the Technical Bureau, stood up to give an update – more acetate photographs – on what Robert Lynch had been transporting in his car.

'The fragments we have recovered correspond with the Rubens *Triumph of Mars over Venus* from the Brewster robbery. We only have a few scraps of any size.' She put an acetate on the projector of three painted shreds, including the one of a hand, none more than six inches large, by the ruler photographed alongside them.

'Chances of restoration are minimal, as you'll understand. The other paintings found in the earthen store on Robert Lynch's property were more lightly damaged, mostly from being cut from their frames during the robbery and carelessly rolled. There is one painting unaccounted for, a very small wooden panel depicting the martyrdom of St Lilio. We can't discount the possibility that it was also in the car and was destroyed by proximity to the explosive device. We haven't found any wood fragments, but it is possible they burned completely.'

Considine interrupted Dr Flynn with a sudden hand-gesture. 'I just wanted to say here that the phone logs from Robert Lynch's house show that he called an art dealer called Desmond de Courcy on Saturday morning. We believe he was taking the Rubens to prove to de Courcy that he had the Brewster paintings. De Courcy is claiming he never got that call.'

A detective from the serious-crime squad then took them through the evidence they had to indicate that it was Dan Barry who had arranged the Brewster robbery. There were so many links and connections going on that Swan wondered if they might suddenly happen upon a unified theory of recent crime in Ireland.

Dan Barry and Robert Lynch had been close friends, business partners in the early days, but no longer associated. Lynch was making a play for respectability and property riches, yet for some reason was storing stolen goods – not only the paintings, but a large quantity of drugs and jewellery in a store in his garden, presumably for Barry. Yet Barry and Lynch had been seen scuffling in the street outside Barry's home on the morning that Lynch died, like two young scrappers.

'Swan,' said Superintendent Martin, 'I believe you have some theories on the whys of this.'

Having no photographic aids, Swan sat where he was to answer.

'It's not watertight at this stage,' he started, 'but we have been focusing on the warehouse that was burned down. It is owned by a company called Bremen Brothers, registered in England, but with no real entity beyond a name. Bremen Road was where Robert Lynch built his first houses, near a coal yard owned by Barry. At this stage they were very close, so we think Bremen Brothers is a reference to that friendship – that both Barry and Lynch had a stake in the warehouse, and access to it. Forensics concluded that the warehouse was not storing anything when the fire occurred, but we talked to Bert Christie, the manager of the gay centre next door.

'Former gay centre,' said Considine.

'Yes, former, because it was destroyed too. Detective Sergeant Considine has put all this together with me, by the way.'

'This isn't the Oscars,' said Eric Joyce, 'we need to finish by lunch.'

'Okay, in brief: Bert Christie saw men loading up a hire van with boxes from the warehouse the day before the explosion. He remembers because they were blocking his deliveries, and a man fitting the description of Robert Lynch got shirty with him. Dan Barry would never use a hire van, too traceable.

'We think it's a story of rising tit-for-tat. Barry stored the stolen goods in the warehouse without Lynch's knowledge. Lynch found out and kidnapped them, so to speak. Barry throws a fit and burns down the warehouse – or Badger Stacy burns it down for him – and in response Robert Lynch goes to Barry's house and starts a fist-fight out in the street.'

'We'd all like to do that,' commented the officer from the serious-crime squad.

'Anyway, Barry loses face, in front of his own men and your plain-clothes officers who shadow him everywhere. He's fit to be tied and orders the bomb attack. That's the theory. But we all need to do more work to make it stand up.'

'We brought in Dan Barry, with his solicitor,' said Eric Joyce, 'but it was the usual round of "No comment". The only thing that roused him was mention of Kieran Lynch, which triggered a lot of abuse about how we hadn't found his killer, how we were a bunch of dumbfucks, et cetera.'

'No need for language,' said Martin. 'But how does Kieran Lynch fit in?'

Considine got to her feet, holding some printed pages. 'I've been tracking the various telephone logs. We know that Kieran Lynch rang his parents' home on the night of his death, but there were no corresponding calls on his home phone. One of the numbers that called the Lynchs' house that night came from a phone box on East Essex Street, at the time and just near where Kieran was last seen by his friend Maurice Deegan, in front of the warehouse in question. It seems fair to conclude that Kieran saw something, or something happened there, that caused him to phone his father without waiting to get home to his nearby flat. After that, we know nothing of his movements until he was found in the Phoenix Park.'

She sat down amid silence. There were too many gaps, and the forensics search that Martin finally conceded for Kieran Lynch's flat had turned up absolutely nothing of use. As blank as the flat itself.

'And Badger Stacy?' Martin barked at the table.

'Gone to ground,' said Ownie Hannigan. 'No trace. But Swan saw him, with his own eyes, looking at the fire that night.'

'Outside the gay disco, wasn't it?' clarified Eric Joyce, the trace of a smirk on his usually miserable face.

Swan was about to protest his professional reasons for being there, when he realised it would be playing Joyce's game. 'That's right,' he said simply, and waited a second before speaking again. 'In any case, Dan Barry seems to be grieving his godson and the loss of his paintings in murderous fashion. It doesn't feel like we're at the end yet.'

Muttering broke out among the detectives at the table. Finding something that they could jail Dan Barry for was the holy grail. Barry knew they were mobilised against him. Guns, usually available for risky short-term operations, had been signed out to all the detectives on the Lynch cases, along with mirrors on sticks to check the underside of their cars each time they parked. The thought of Barry's psychopathic impulses combined with the skills of some mad Provo made everyone jumpy.

DI Joyce brought the conference back to where they had started, with the two deaths in the Phoenix Park. 'I think we are at the stage,' he said, pushing back his chair, 'where we can say that Bill Riordan's death was the exception in whatever this emerging picture is. His cousin came to us to say that Riordan had confessed to homosexual interests that the rest of the family didn't know about. It was simply a case of him being in the wrong place at the wrong time, and some young thugs taking the law into their own hands. We've charges pending for all the boys, and the DPP is bringing them forward for trial.'

Satisfied murmurings filled the room.

'What law?' Considine asked, her voice cutting through the midday torpor.

'How's that?' asked Joyce, sitting up.

'You said they were taking the law into their own hands. What law says that a gay man walking in a park should be stabbed to death?'

'Gina …' Swan muttered, but she didn't even notice.

'Just a figure of speech,' said Joyce. 'I mean their sexual acts are illegal, not that the boys … Don't misinterpret me.'

'All the same, a person might get the impression that Bill Riordan was somehow in the wrong, from what you said. Maybe you'd like to rephrase that.'

'Sergeant Considine!' said Superintendent Martin.

'It's a fair point,' said Swan. He could not bear to see her alone against the lot of them.

'No fool like an old fool,' muttered Hannigan at his elbow.

Martin quickly called the meeting to an end, saying they were in danger of going into overtime, but then elaborately thanking everyone who had spoken and summarising their contributions. Swan tried to catch Considine's eye, but she was pretending to be absorbed in the documents in front of her.

At last Martin stood and they all pushed their chairs back, some making a break for it, others hanging around to chat. Considine was one of the bolters, but Superintendent Martin was waiting by the door to catch her. Swan did not like the way his hand lay on her sleeve, or the way he talked so close to the side of her head. It reminded him too much of the Brothers in his school, a kind of intimate terrorism, very controlled. Martin would not have liked Considine challenging Eric Joyce, especially on that particular prejudice.

But she'd hate it more if Swan tried to intervene, to be her rescuer. He saw Martin pinch the material of Considine's sleeve and twist it surreptitiously as they walked out together. But what could he do?

42

The night had a cool touch of the autumn to come, but Considine was well wrapped up in a scarf and warm jacket. The beech tree she had stationed herself against had become a familiar. Leaning into the bark, she dozed on and off, her jacket open at the front so that she could reach the gun on her hip with speed, if necessary.

The air was soft and dry, the sky purple, brightening where it touched the lights of the city. She could see the big-hitter stars, the Plough constellation and a small rind of moon. The comforting smell of roasted barley from the Guinness brewery came and went. It was nice being out at night, alone. Men came and went too, but less so towards morning. She suspected the one she was waiting for wouldn't come until dawn.

She had never stayed out all night before. There were tons of things she had never done, never felt. She had never before listened to two men having sex, ardent and absorbed. It made her feel simultaneously aroused and terribly innocent. In the middle of the night she lay down in the long grass for a nap and experienced a kind of floating feeling, as if the ground was moving under her.

She remembered a night when she had gone swimming with a girl from her Gaeltacht house. Some kind of bet that the whole house of girls had made at teatime, but at midnight it had been only herself and Mary Ryan naked in the silky waters of the lough. The brave ones. The physical freedom she felt that night, and all the things that might have happened, but did not.

Joining the Guards hadn't been a brave decision, it just appeared so from the outside. The violence and chaos that she dealt with every day distracted her from the chaos within. Living with Terry, the first woman she had slept with, had not been brave either, nor was lying about it to everyone she knew. What might she have done, if she hadn't been so scared? What should she do now?

She got up then and took the gun from her holster and aimed it across the meadow, squinted down the barrel. There was a herd of deer nearby; she wasn't aiming it near them, but one lifted its head and looked directly at her. She slowly lowered the pistol. It wasn't that she wanted to hurt anyone – that wasn't it.

Dawn was glowing on the horizon when he appeared, lolloping along one of the curved paths. Green shorts and yellow T-shirt, a small rucksack on his back. The mystery jogger. His work clothes would still be in the locker at the depot. Considine stepped into the spot where Kieran Lynch had been found, trusting that he would instinctively look towards it.

He glanced, he stumbled. He stopped and stared at her.

'Declan!' She beckoned.

He looked all around, to check if there were others with her. Seeing no one, he ambled across the grass to her, slowing as he got near.

'What the fuck are you doing out here?' he asked.

'Thinking.'

'You should watch yourself. It's not safe.' He kicked a toe of his running shoe into the rough ground. Jogged a little on the spot. 'Did you want something?'

'Yeah, I wanted to see you run into work. The path you took.'

'Me?'

'You, Declan. You were with me that time in Kerry when Kieran Lynch was part of our course.'

'I never said I didn't know him.'

'You never said you did. He kept a copy of *Garda Review* in his flat. There's a picture of the two of you rowing on the Liffey in some regatta. It's not a great shot, but I recognised you, which means others would too.'

'I didn't know him well.'

'And yet you took him to Kinsale.'

Declan shook his head and looked away.

'It's the only thing I know about Kinsale. When Martin made us get that nice photo of Kieran being a civilian, so that we could play down the fact he was a Guard, Swan said it was taken in Kinsale, and you flashed in and out of my mind. Because your family has a holiday home there and, to be honest, it stuck in my head because I was envious of the very idea of it. A home that was there just for holidays.'

'You're mad, you are.'

'I wouldn't have thought much about it, only you took Kieran's address book and lied about it, straight to my face. Even though I put it in your hand. Why would a person hide an address book, Declan?'

'I handed it in to Evidence. They lose things.'

'Remember I was in charge of the telephone logs, Declan? Kieran rang his parents' house from a phone booth. I looked at the phone-booth records and the next call from that box was to you. To your house.'

He took a step back from her. 'You didn't report that. Are you trying to blackmail me?'

'Don't be stupid. I'm trying to give you a chance.' She took a step towards him and the front flap of her jacket moved.

'Is that a fucking gun?' Declan tightened up, as if he was deciding to physically tackle her, so Considine had to pull it out, had to point it at him. It was crazy, but that's where they suddenly were.

Barrett began to sink to his knees, like he was submitting, like his life was all over or something. The gun shook in her hand. Anyone could come along and see them like this. She took a deep breath, put the gun back in her holster and made her voice soft.

'Declan, I just wanted to know what happened. I wanted to know why you left him here.'

Barrett sank further, sitting on his heels and rocking his head back and forth like a sad animal in the zoo. She had to squat down, to try and get eye-to-eye with him.

'Kieran asked me to pick him up, then bring him here. He liked the park.'

For a moment they both gazed into the trees, the insects rising from the grass as the light grew strong.

'There was something he wanted to tell me, but he was taking his time. I thought he wanted something else, you know – I wasn't into that ...'

'I don't want to hear about you.'

Declan's hands started to shake.

'Then this crazy fucker comes out of the dark, swinging a baseball bat and I ran. I thought Kieran did too. I thought he was going to be all right.'

'Did you see the man with the bat?'

'Not well. Heavyset, not young, wheezy. He had a moustache.'

'We can find him, Declan. We have to tell.'

'It wasn't my fault! Kieran could easily have got away. I came back in the morning and he was lying here.'

'Why didn't you come back to him when you phoned it in? Why did you pretend to be a passer-by? At the very least, he was your friend.'

'I'm not gay, you know.'

Considine got to her feet. 'I believe you. You don't love a man if you leave him dying in the dark.'

43

Swan went downstairs to fetch another box from the car and realised he was whistling. Maybe his subconscious was trying to cheer him up, as there were at least six more boxes to go and his new flat was on the top floor of the building. Just like Kieran Lynch's.

It was when he'd been walking back from Lynch's flat to his mother's that he spied the *To rent* sign high up in a window on Arran Quay. The north quays were the only quays worth living on. He could never be a southsider; for one thing, that's not who he was, but more practically, the buildings on the north quays got the sun all the livelong day. And if the sun shone brightly enough, you wouldn't even see the ugly corporation buildings at Wood Quay, for squinting. He had three rooms and a working fireplace. He could walk easily from Arran Quay to his mother's, or to the depot, or across to the Graceland Café for food.

Oh yes, it would do nicely, he told himself. There was even a wide stretch of pavement where the buildings took a step back and you could park your car to unload it. He unlocked the boot of his car and pulled out a box. He had the river to look at – *lock the car again* – and you would never get tired of that – *swop car key for door key*

– because the waters of Anna Livia were both eternal and ever-changing.

Just who was he making up this cheery shite for?

He realised he was rehearsing a speech for Considine again, with the vague anticipation that she'd come and visit for coffee or a drink soon. He would welcome her critical once-over, for she was always powerfully interested in properties and the homes that people made in them. The warm glow of Considine's regard could transform what – in darker moments – Swan feared would be a shabby little life into something more exalted.

She'd been off sick for the past fortnight, and he didn't know if it was 'flu' or actual flu. Every morning he went into the office and looked at her empty desk. He missed talking to her. There were things he wanted to sound her out on. About how he suspected that the murder of Kieran Lynch had nothing to do with him being gay, and how the fire at the gay centre wasn't prejudice, but accident. He wanted to emphasise these things to make her believe that the world was fairer than she thought it to be.

But he knew how she would answer back. She would look at him and say, *Bill Riordan.*

He had almost called her house to tell her about Kieran and Robert Lynch's odd double funeral, how Dan Barry had turned up at it and went to lay a hand on the chestnut veneer of Kieran's casket. How Charmaine Lynch had screamed at him not to touch her son, until the priest and congregation shook with fear.

And then there was yesterday's news. Badger Stacy's body emerged, bloated in the scum and flotsam of Grand

Canal Dock with a bullet in his head. Declan Barrett had been sent to attend the recovery and had some kind of nervous collapse, they said. Swan wanted to know what Considine would say to that. It seemed that loyal Badger had made a mistake somewhere along the line. Swan wondered if the mistake was to get rid of a nosy policeman who he had no idea was the boss's godson.

Proving that would be hard. Swan felt determined to keep working the case, but hadn't he been just as determined about Sonny Grierson's killer at the time? He imagined a vast purgatory holding all the unavenged souls, the ones waiting for late confessions or overlooked evidence turned up by careful work.

So often you had to settle for less than fairness.

Swan put down the box on the floorboards of his new front room, turned round and went downstairs again. He unlocked the boot and took out his stereo stack system, wondering if it would be foolish to balance the speakers on top.

There was a sudden skirmish in the corner of his vision. Further down the pavement, a teenage boy was pulling a headscarf from an elderly lady and she was twisting to and fro, trying to simultaneously hold on to it and see who was behind her. Another boy darted up to pull at her handbag.

Swan screamed a loud 'Hoy!' and put his sound equipment down on top of the closed boot. The woman fell to her knees but would not give up her bag, though the youth was still hauling on it. Swan ran towards them and the boy looked him full in the face before giving up and belting off, his pal careening after him, throwing a quick arm round his neck in solidarity. Both of them vanished around a corner.

'You're a fierce fighter!' he said to the woman, assessing the damage and helping her to her feet. Her knees were badly scraped, blood oozing through her beige nylons, but she was making great protestations about how she was *grand, just grand*. Someone brought a chair from the solicitor's office next door for her to sit on.

The boys were long gone. Swan had recognised the one pulling at the handbag strap as part of the gang who had kicked and stabbed Bill Riordan to death. They'd been let out on remand by a judge who had a worrying tolerance of youthful violence. Only the boy with the knife was still in custody.

Swan returned to his car. The music centre had slid off his boot and lay on the pavement, surrounded by broken bits of its black plastic casing.

So often you had to settle for less than fairness.

44

A big suitcase, a small suitcase and a rucksack. Considine wondered if this was what they meant by taking your life in your hands. She lifted her luggage and set off up the gangway.

The ferry left at eight-thirty, but she found herself in Dun Laoghaire well before that, eager to be on board and past the point where anyone could call her back. Terry wouldn't, she was certain of that. Terry was all too eager to move her new girlfriend into the space Considine had vacated. It was like when they changed the actor in a long-running television series. The new girl would sleep on Considine's pillow, drink from Considine's favourite mug, use all those props she had decided to leave behind. She was sure that there would be pillows and mugs in Scotland.

She stowed two pieces of luggage in a wire locker and went up on deck, found a bench to sit on and started to smoke. The filter stuck to her chapped lips. She was having awful trouble with her lips these days and suspected that she had been licking them nervously, like a dog. Everything seemed hilarious and tragic all at once. Someone at the rail was waving a handkerchief to someone on the shore and crying. Men in donkey jackets stood stoically facing the lowering sun as it headed on its way to a west-of-Ireland sunset.

Noises started up: steel plates clanging and chains being reeled in. The boat gave a deep hoot that started below decks and burst forth from the funnel above her head. She went to the rail then, to see the moment when water ran between herself and the country she had never stepped off of in her life. It was impossible not to think of the others – the hundreds of thousands – who had sailed from here before. The ferry company should hire an on-deck ballad singer to channel this overwhelming feeling, ridiculous and heartbreaking.

She spotted a man standing on his own on the pier in a slightly rumpled suit, his tie blowing sideways. She lifted a hand to wave, but it wasn't him, it wasn't Swan. How could it be, when she had done everything to prevent him finding out that she was leaving?

He was the one with the tentacles, the only one who might have stopped her going. She would write to him when she got to Glasgow; she would explain that Superintendent Martin had offered her a shining reference for the Strathclyde Police, who were looking to recruit female detectives. He wanted her out of the murder squad or he wanted her very close. Breathing down her neck, day in, day out – the old goat. She knew his type, obsessed with sex and deviance to a suspicious degree.

All the street lights were coming on around Dublin Bay. An embrace of lights. A lit train slid its way silently along the coast into town, and as she followed it, Considine picked out Lynch's yellow mansion on its rocky outcrop. The lights were on there too. She had heard that Mottie and Jess were still in residence. Well, good luck to them, the reckless dreamers.

She knew very little about Glasgow: Billy Connolly, street gangs and rain. Humour and violence. She had met Scottish people and liked the way they talked. She expected it would be easier to settle there than in England. There was a friend of Fintan's who was a stage manager in a theatre called the Tron. She could stay with her for the first week. The diaspora provided.

They were slipping out of the bay now and still she looked back, Howth Head on the right and Killiney hill on the left. The arms of Dublin slipping from her. *Ah, stop trying to make yourself miserable.* The little red lights on top of the Poolbeg chimneys twinkled on.

There was a chill wind out in the channel. She looked down at the water, at how it kept folding back from the ferry's hull, giving way. She imagined, as she had a hundred times, Kieran Lynch in his final moments, standing in front of his death, believing goodness would prevail. The bat swinging through the dark towards his smile.

She waited for the other passengers to give up and go inside. She had one more thing to do. She unzipped the little tartan case that she held between her feet. Perhaps she could just slip the painting between the lower rungs of the rail while the others were fixed on the last sight of home.

The picture was a liability, and she needed a clean slate. Taking it was almost the worst thing she had ever done, the most unprofessional. It was handling stolen goods. The American oilman playing the squire in Connemara had probably claimed the insurance on it already. The little saint had not only survived his original bonfire, but had been rescued from the waves once already and had not been blown to smithereens in the car bomb, despite the official version.

Was she really going to be his final executioner?

A man in a dark coat was moving about on the deck. He went up to talk to a young man with a beard and rough trousers, who looked like a labourer.

'How are you, Son?' said the man in the coat.

'All right, Father,' replied the bearded man in a resentful tone.

The priest turned in her direction then, his collar a bright badge of office. He looked to be some kind of ferry chaplain.

Considine picked up her little case and re-zipped it as she made for the doors into the lounge. There was the smell of chips and spilt beer. A hundred chatting voices. There were lively tables of people playing cards or arguing, and there were sleepers stretched out everywhere on the floor and in the reclining chairs. After the chill of the deck, the animal warmth and clatter of the lounge were irresistible.

She was only going away for a time, having an adventure. There was no need to make it into a drama, and maybe no need to abandon the little fella yet when he'd already been through so much.

ACKNOWLEDGEMENTS

Setting out on the writing of this book in March 2020, I never imagined that it would not be possible to visit Dublin during the time of its making. Special thanks therefore go to my Irish friends who talked with me about those times or corrected my mis-rememberings, especially my brother Jonathan White, Jane Daly, John Comiskey and Robert O'Byrne. Credit too to *The Irish Times*'s online archive, various anonymous posters of 1980s Dublin video footage on YouTube, Donal Fallon's wonderful history podcast *Three Castles Burning* and the music of the mighty Lankum for keeping me in a virtual Dublin in my Scottish room. Varuna Writers' House in Australia and Cove Park in Argyll were joint hosts of a virtual 'residency' in July 2020 that helped me keep the momentum going. My thanks to the other writers for feedback, and especially Carol Major.

The inhabitants of my adopted town of Cromarty have been a wonderful support in these dicey times, with special thanks to Estelle Quick at the post office and to Gail Stuart-Martin at Cromarty Arts Trust, who provided an attic retreat when I badly needed one.

My best and biggest gratitude goes to the unbeatable team at Viper, especially the brilliant Miranda Jewess,

Drew Jerrison, Graeme Hall, Lottie Fyfe, Alia McKellar, Mandy Greenfield and Samantha Johnson. I raise a glass in thanks to my agent Jenny Brown and hope to clink a real one with her before long.

The Martyrdom of St Lilio is a purely fictional painting, but owes much to Fra Angelico's *The Attempted Martyrdom of Sts Cosmas and Damian with their Brothers*, which hangs in the National Gallery of Ireland, and which I have known all my life.

ABOUT THE AUTHOR

Nicola White is a writer, former curator and documentary maker, who grew up in Dublin and New York and now lives in the Scottish Highlands. She won the Scottish Book Trust New Writer Award in 2008, and in 2012 was Leverhulme Writer in Residence at Edinburgh University. *The Rosary Garden* won the Dundee International Book Prize, was shortlisted for the McIlvanney Prize and was selected as one of the four best crime debuts of the year at Harrogate Festival. Find her on Twitter @whiteheadednic.